# THE
# FANGS
## OF THE
# HOODED
# DEMON

Also by Geoffrey Marsh
published by Tor Books

The Tail of the Arabian, Knight
The Patch of the Odin Soldier

# Geoffrey Marsh
# THE FANGS OF THE HOODED DEMON

## A Lincoln Blackthorne Adventure

**TOR**

A TOM DOHERTY ASSOCIATES BOOK
NEW YORK

THE FANGS OF THE HOODED DEMON

A TOR BOOK
Published by Tom Doherty Associates, Inc.
49 West 24 Street
New York, N.Y. 10010

Library of Congress Cataloging-in-Publication Data
Marsh, Geoffrey, 1912–
The fangs of the hooded demon : a Lincoln Blackthorne adventure by Geoffrey Marsh.
p.   cm.
"A Tom Doherty Associates book."
ISBN 0-312-93100-X : $17.95
I. Title.
PS3563.A7145F36 1988
813'.54—dc 19          88-19718
CIP

First edition: October 1988
0  9  8  7  6  5  4  3  2  1

## AUTHOR'S DEDICATION

I am advised by all concerned that it is bad form to dedicate one's work to oneself.

What the hell.

I'm an old man.

This one's for me.

# One

The low rolling hills of northwestern New Jersey had been topped with nearly a foot of new snow in less than twenty-four hours. Deer were driven out of the forests to forage and flounder in backyards and fields; farmers dumped truckloads of hay for those portions of their herds still trapped in pastures; and state police helicopters buzzed constantly overhead, desperately searching for stranded motorists and lost skiers.

By dawn of the second day the snow had stopped falling, and though the sky still held clouds boiling ominously out of Pennsylvania, the latest weather report swore that the unusual December storm was over and part of history.

The people of Inverness, however, had learned from experience not to believe everything they heard.

So when they looked up, and when they felt the bite and snap of the slow wind, the moisture still heavy in the air, they knew that the season's first blizzard was only taking a breather; it was, they decided, like the eye of a hurricane—the lull was pleasant enough, but the worst was yet to come.

The streets, then, were cleared as quickly as possible by bright yellow snowplows that hadn't stopped working since midnight, sidewalks and steps were shoveled and the ice beneath coated with layers of rock salt, and automobiles which had either been abandoned on the country roads outside of town, or buried in snowbanks when the plows went by, were dug out and warmed up. The three supermarkets were crowded, the three schools remained closed, and those who had put off buying their new snow tires until after the first of the year were stoically waiting in lines at the garages.

Firewood was hauled in, oil deliveries were made; jagged icicles were knocked down to be sucked on or used for swords; colored lights were rehung on the bushes in front of porches.

The temperature, which had dropped near to zero just after midnight, hadn't quite reached twenty by the time the lunch hour had passed.

By midafternoon, when the storm hadn't yet returned, Creek Road, the main street of the little hillside town, was filled with the lighthearted noise and good-natured shove of heavy pedestrian traffic—last-minute Christmas shoppers forced by perilous road conditions to forsake trips to the shopping mall twenty miles away and patronize the local stores along the three-block business district. The bargains were incredible, the price-gouging respectable, and the tinny sound of joyful carols wafting over the street mixed naturally with the almost bell-like rattle of tire chains, the laughter that rose from battlefields of snowballs, the shrieks of children on fast-moving sleds.

And above it all the quiet, the unique silence that only falls when there's snow on the ground.

2

Despite the blizzard, then, and the hazards, everyone in town was feeling the pleasant effects of the season.

Everyone, that is, except Lincoln Bartholomew Blackthorne.

Without the protection of either coat or hat, Lincoln stood grimly in front of his narrow-fronted, unobtrusive tailor shop on the west side of the street, trying to thread a needle and, at the same time, keep watch on the entrance of the Inverness Tape and Record Shoppe across the way. The skill with which he handled both tasks was a significant indication of his current state of mind: on the one hand, he had a silk-and-worsted suit to finish for the mayor's third cousin's New Year's Eve wedding; on the other, he didn't want Carmel Estanza to leave her family's store before he had a chance to talk with her about her own wedding plans.

The wind settled to a breeze that drifted powdered snow over the brick sidewalk and reddened the cheeks of those who lingered too long outside.

The sunlight was little more than a feeble grey glow.

Linc shivered in his shirtsleeves.

He supposed he could have stayed inside where it was warmer, thus sparing him the stares of passers-by and the chattering of his teeth; he supposed he could have ducked into the relative peace of Ginny's Olde Time Tavern to his right and watched for her from the small window, most of which was covered by a neon Miller sign and sprayed-on snow; he supposed as well he could walk over and confront Carmel on her own turf—though that would be tantamount to proposing to her himself, a position he had managed to avoid for some time now, not because he didn't have affection for her, and not because he didn't want to be part of a large and boisterous family.

He hadn't proposed because he didn't want to place

3

her life in danger, in jeopardy, and in conjunction with his own, which, as far as she knew, was concerned mainly with getting the mayor's third cousin's suit ready in time for the nuptials.

A pair of fur-coated elderly women passed him, looked at him, looked at each other, and sighed, remembering the days of Valentino and the stir he'd caused in their mink-snuggled breasts.

A trio of sweatered and ski-capped college women home for the holidays passed him, looked at him, looked at each other, and shivered, remembering how he looked in summer, with that shock of gentle brown hair, those not always gentle eyes, and the smile that made them want to set their boyfriends in concrete.

Linc ignored them.

He wasn't handsome, nor was he large or impressively muscled; but he had a way about him that gave others pause, gave a few others pleasant dreams, and a few more some nightmares they could just as soon do without.

A young man and his wife, both laden with gaily-wrapped bundles, stared at him in amazement, shook their heads and moved on. Paused. Glanced over their shoulders, and as they moved on again collided with the backs of the pair and the trio, who had stopped in front of the aluminum-fronted drugstore to peer in the window, and to look back at him. The resulting confusion made Linc aware that he was probably making a fool of himself. He grinned and waved to them all, backed into the shop and stood at the closed door. The needle in his left hand was forgotten. The thread in his right floated to the floor, was caught by a draught slipping under the door and was feathered around his right ankle.

He looked down after a moment and wondered if it was a sign he ought to consider.

He opened the door again and stepped out, gasped at the cold that settled like knives in his lungs, and returned inside with a shiver. It was the fourth time he'd done so in less than fifteen minutes.

"You know," a voice said behind him, "if you keep this up, they're going to think you're some kind of new weather predicting machine."

The tailor shop's interior was narrow. Forming a center aisle immediately inside the door were two display cases under whose glass one could see a carefully-arranged display of handmade ties and shirts, which took nothing away from the shelves on the walls that held equally-careful displays of hats and bolts of cloth. In back there was a raised platform that supported the oldest operating foot-pedal sewing machine on the East Coast, and an array of mirrors which permitted his customers to view themselves from angles they'd never believed possible outside a certain famous house on the back streets of New Orleans.

A comfortable wooden chair had been placed in front of the scarred table that held the sewing machine. In the chair was a portly, white-bearded man in a three-piece black suit; on the floor beside him was a green Tyrolean hat with the feather half chewed off.

Lincoln stuck the needle into his shirt collar and walked back slowly.

"I'm worried, that's all," he said.

"You're too young to worry about someone your age getting married," said Macon Crowley.

"She's not marrying me."

"So? Christmas does have its blessings."

"But she's not marrying me because I'm not marrying her."

"Spite," said Macon, "is a horrible thing."

Linc stepped onto the platform and dropped into

the ladder-back chair behind the table. "Jesus. I mean, really, Macon—Ellshampton Yark?"

Macon shrugged. "It could be worse."

"You don't seem very concerned."

"The girl's a teacher. She's too smart to go on with it."

"Her aunt's already bought the wedding gown."

"Cut it down, use it in the spring."

"Her father's rented the VFW Hall for the reception."

Macon shifted.

"And her mother's made her aunt take down all the posters of Fernando Lamas in the apartment."

"Jesus," Macon whispered.

Linc set his elbows on the table, set his cheeks in his palms, and stared at his reflection across the room. It wasn't the way he had hoped to spend the holidays; he had hoped to finish the suit, take Carmel out to dinner, read a little, relax, go through his photograph album, and maybe take in a movie in the theater down the street.

Quiet.

Peaceful.

Macon scratched his beard and shifted again. "Perhaps," he said, "we ought to ask Alice to have a word with the lass. She does have a way, you know."

Linc groaned.

The door opened and an old woman entered.

"Speak of the devil," Macon said, and rose graciously to give Old Alice his seat.

She was, in human terms, much too old to be walking around in little more than a red tartan poncho, a Gucci sombrero with plastic fruit around the brim, and wooden Greek sandals; her only concession to the weather was a pair of purple kneesocks with white hearts scattered through the weave, and a set of silver fox earmuffs she used to protect her Cartier watch.

"She's getting married," Old Alice said, adjusting the poncho around her turkey-thin legs.

"He knows," Macon reminded her.

"Does he know she's going to Puerto Rico on her honeymoon?"

Linc turned away from his reflection, only to see another one staring back at him.

"Nice place," Macon said.

"Hot."

"Not in winter."

"Warm."

"Probably."

"It shouldn't be warm in winter. It ain't natural. Winter should be as cold as a . . . winter. Otherwise, you get ideas." She pulled an engraved gold cigarette case from her oversize purse, extracted a lavender cigarette, and struck a wooden match with her thumbnail. "You have any ideas, Blackie?"

"Don't," Lincoln said.

Old Alice grimaced at her unconscious use of the nickname he abhorred, and asked him again.

"Ideas about what?" he said.

"About saving that girl from that idiot, Yark."

"He's a banker, he's rich," Macon observed as he wandered up and down the aisle between the display cases.

"All right, a rich idiot. So what are you going to do about it?"

"Nothing," Macon said.

"I don't know," Linc told her. "If I go over there and tell her she's making a mistake, she'll either split a chair over my head or think I want to marry her myself. Either way, I don't win."

"One way, you don't get a headache."

He looked at her, and she stared back through a cloud of smoke almost as tinted as the cigarette wrapping.

Macon, who had stopped his pacing long enough to stand at the righthand display window and was watching the shoppers from around the elbow of a male mannequin dressed in a tuxedo that hadn't been dusted in eight years, whistled softly. He shifted to the door, then to the lefthand window, where he leaned over to see around the hips of a tilted female mannequin dressed in a white silk ball gown.

"What?" said Old Alice.

"That woman."

She squinted down the length of the shop. "What woman?"

"The one that just passed."

"He's randy again," she told Linc. "He gets this way in December. Feels it's his duty to perpetuate his line before he croaks. He's lost count of the bastards scattered from here to Scranton and it worries him." Another puff of smoke, and she looked back at Crowley. "She's too young for you."

Macon looked over his shoulder. "So am I."

Old Alice nodded. "Profound. Very profound."

"And she's coming back."

Lincoln turned slowly in his chair.

"Third time she's walked by."

"Damn," Old Alice muttered. "Y'know, it's days like this that make me wonder about a Divine Creator."

Macon whistled again, and grabbed a comb from his jacket pocket which he then proceeded to run through his white hair and beard.

"I mean," Alice explained, "that every time we sit down to have a nice conversation, someone comes along and drags Blackie off to one of those exotic places that we never get to see because we have to stay here and mind the store. I mean, it happens every damned time!"

"You went to New Mexico," Macon said without looking back. "There she goes again."

8

Lincoln rose and stepped off the platform.

"You went to England and Scotland."

"I'm allowed to leave the country."

Old Alice, without an ounce of wasted motion, pulled a plastic grape from her sombrero and caught Macon directly in the middle of his rump. Which assault wouldn't have moved a mouse if it hadn't been for the refinement she'd developed after the last time she'd seen a James Bond film. Macon yelped and pulled the grape from his cheek, stared at it and crushed it beneath his heel.

"I shall probably require medical attention," he complained as he massaged the wounded area while he watched the outside.

"Who is she?" Linc asked as he moved toward the doorway behind the platform.

"Can't get a good look at her face," Macon said.

Old Alice snorted, stood, stomped down the aisle, and flung open the door. "Goddamnit," she said when the woman passed by again, "will you come in here, for god's sake? You've already ruined our afternoon tea."

The woman stopped.

She turned.

She pushed back her sable hat.

"Hell," said Old Alice, and reached for her gun.

# Two

The room behind the shop was small, overly warm, and contained only enough furniture to make it look as if it were used for no more than a room that held furniture no one ever used. The Thrift Shop table in the center of the floor wobbled, the aged armchair near the doorway had long since lost much of its stuffing, and the poster of Clint Eastwood on the righthand wall was scarred at the bottom, as if visitors felt it necessary to kick at the Nameless Cowboy's boots in either envy or Liberal disgust. A small refrigerator on the lefthand wall seldom held more than a liter or two of Dr Pepper in cans. And the walls themselves were virtually obscured with chrome-framed prints of movie posters proclaiming their owner's love for musical biographies and Japanese monsters; it had been quite a while since any of them had been dusted.

I am, Lincoln thought, asking for trouble.

He perched on the edge of the table, one foot on the

worn carpet, the other swinging nervously back and forth while he tried to keep his balance.

A few minutes before, Old Alice and Macon had decided it would probably be a good idea to bring some Christmas cheer into their lives by heading next door to the tavern, after Alice had been persuaded to put away the revolver since it was hardly the season to be taking potshots at richly dressed women in the middle of town.

And in the chair sat the woman.

Her floor-length sable coat was open, her sable hat settled on one knee, and her green silk dress was so snugly bound to her figure that more than one man who had the good fortune to visit her place of employment was compelled to admire the way modern paint had acquired such a lifelike gloss.

Linc smiled. "I'm not going to do it."

Clarise Mayhew smiled back without a trace of mirth. "It isn't for George."

"I'm still not going to do it."

Clarise worked as a private secretary and estate manager for George Vilcroft, a respected and wealthy collector of antiques, oddities, and assorted baubles, most of which were safely and prominently displayed in his Victorian home on the Knob, that portion of Inverness which topped the hill whose western slope held the rest of the community.

Lincoln had also worked for him on occasion, which was why Vilcroft had so many antiques, oddities, and baubles in his collection.

"It's a present," she said, as if she were giving him a weather report.

"For George?"

She shook her head.

He raised a friendly, albeit skeptical eyebrow. "Clarise, don't tell me you have someone special in your life after all this time?"

Her hand touched at a rich fall of brunette hair, settling it into place with a flick of her finger. "Everyone in my life is special, Lincoln." She reached into her purse and pulled out a slip of green paper. Held it. Waited. Looked at it and sighed. "I would consider it a favor."

"That means you won't pay me."

Her eyes narrowed. "I always pay my debts, Lincoln. Always. And if you'll tell me your usual fee, I'm sure I can more than satisfy you."

He looked to the beaded curtain that separated the room from the shop, and he rubbed the side of his neck. "I don't know, Clarise. I was hoping to get through the holidays without getting shot at."

When she laughed, he hugged himself against the cold.

"Lincoln, you are very amusing."

"I am filled," he said truthfully, "with the spirit of self-preservation."

"Nothing will happen. It's a straightforward matter of going into the city, picking up the item, and bringing it back to me. I will then pay you, wrap the present, and put it under the tree on Christmas Eve."

Linc looked at her, looked away, and looked back because he wanted to be sure she was still breathing. That she sat so motionlessly, so emotionlessly, bothered him; for all the money she would have to pay to get him out of the shop, she might as well be purchasing a side of pasture-fed beef for the local kennels. It wasn't right. He knew it wasn't right, and he knew he'd hate himself for accepting the job. Which, he reminded himself, could just as easily be done by a messenger service.

"No, it can't," she said with patently false regret when he explained his misgivings.

"Why not?"

She crossed her legs. He shivered at the husk of nylon over knee.

"Why not?" he asked again.

"Because it requires a certain amount of tact and diplomatic élan, which George tells me you have plenty of in your better moments."

Thank you, George, he thought, though he wasn't sure just how far that dubious recommendation would take him.

"Clarise, is this legal?"

She nodded.

"Are you telling me the truth?"

She nodded.

Through your teeth, he said to her silently, and was relieved when she rewarded his perception with a brief, genuine smile. At least now he knew where he stood, which was in the middle of his back room with a beautiful woman who was trying to get him to go into New York City to pick up an ostensible present for a nonexistent special person in her life.

It made sense.

About as much sense as Carmel marrying that jackass banker, Yark.

"No," he said regretfully. "I have too much work, and I can't take the time."

She frowned, then plucked the hat from her knee, pushed herself to her feet, put the hat on the chair, and walked over to him. When there was less than a hands-breadth between them, she took a slow deep breath. By virtue of Lincoln's position on the table, and her height, he was unable to meet her gaze squarely and stand his ground. A clever maneuver, he admitted, and one which she probably had to practice in front of a mirror before she got it right.

He grinned, took light hold of her arms and gently eased her away as he rose. "Clarise, my love, go home.

This stinks, you know it and I know it, and besides, I have other things to take care of."

"You've already said that," she said, shifting her hips, her torso, her hands to pull the sable coat cloaklike over her shoulders. "I'm asking you as a friend."

He looked at her sideways. "A friend?"

"Lincoln, this is important."

"A friend?"

She placed her palms warmly on his chest, moistened her lips, and allowed a hint of a tear to appear in the corner of her left eye. "If I don't get this present . . . I can't tell you what will happen."

Insane, he thought.

"No," he said again, though more gently this time. She moved another inch closer.

"Then will you do it for George?"

He couldn't move back; the table was in his way.

"Does George know about it?"

"No."

"But it isn't his present."

Another inch.

"Right."

"Then how can I do it for him if he doesn't know about it, and it isn't for him?"

She said nothing.

He looked into her eyes, at the smooth lines of her face, the delicate waves of her hair, and didn't much care for the feeling he felt stirring in his stomach.

"Am I to assume," he said at last, and with no little trepidation, "that by doing this for George, you mean that he will continue to be able to employ you as his private secretary? That not doing this for George will mean that, one way or another, you will be forced to leave his employ and vanish from his life as if you never existed?"

She was flush against him now, her cheek on his

shoulder. "Yes," she said, in a whisper so soft he barely heard it.

He embraced her then, friend to friend, and was about to ask her what kind of trouble she could possibly get into in a town like this, when the beaded curtain parted and Carmel stomped into the room.

Clarise didn't move.

Lincoln smiled.

Carmel slammed her hands on her hips and glared. "What the hell are you doing?"

"Helping a friend," he said weakly.

"Right," she said.

He dropped his arms.

Carmel was a head shorter than he, with long, gleaming black hair that matched wide black eyes she couldn't have made look innocent if she had been raised in a convent, which she hadn't been though her mother was beginning to regret it. Her figure was not nearly as pronounced or potentially sinful as Clarise's, but none of the adolescent males in her high school Spanish classes ever confused her with the retired Marine gym teacher. At the moment she was wearing a bulky white Irish sweater, faded jeans, and a pair of white snowboots with black leather fringe; in her left hand she held a packet of envelopes she tapped against her hip.

"Do you know what these are?" she demanded, holding the packet out and shaking it in the air.

He looked. "No."

Clarise pushed away and resettled herself in the chair, adjusting her skirt slowly, breathing deeply, ignoring Carmel completely.

"They are the best wedding invitations my poverty-stricken family can afford," Carmel told him, her voice dangerously low. "At this very moment, I am on my way to the post office to mail them."

"Carmel—"

"Momma says I have to do it now or no one will come to the wedding."

"Carmel, look—"

"Ellsie thinks we ought to elope and save everyone a lot of money."

Lincoln blinked. "Ellsie?"

"Do you know what I've been doing today, Linc?"

He covered his brow with a palm, hoping he had the healing touch so that the sudden headache he felt would vanish before he screamed.

"I'll tell you what I've been doing," she said, slapping the packet against her thigh. "I've been standing in the goddamn window waiting for you to come over and try to talk me out of it." Her lips quivered. "Momma says that if you were a real gentleman, you'd do that. She doesn't want me to marry Ellsie. She thinks he's a jerk."

"Carmel, listen, if you'll just give me a chance to say something here about—"

"Do you have any idea how cold it is in that window? Do you know what it's like having every goddamn shopper in the universe stare at you like you're some kind of promotional gimmick for a record company?"

"If you were there," he snapped, "you saw me, too."

Her mouth opened, closed, and she looked down at Clarise. "Hi," she said. "How's George?"

"Very well, thank you."

"Good." She took a step toward the chair, changed her mind and stepped toward Lincoln. "Yes, I saw you, since you're so interested. Out there like a jerk without a coat on. Poppa says you should have come over and beaten some sense into me." One eyebrow arched. "I wouldn't have minded. You should see what I have in my closet."

16

"Carmel," he said patiently, "it's your life. If you want to marry Ellshampton, that's all right with me and I wish you all the happiness you deserve. But if you don't really want to marry him, what the hell are you doing with all those stupid wedding invitations?"

Carmel shrieked.

Lincoln blinked, and didn't understand when suddenly she threw her arms around his neck and kissed him, hard; he didn't understand when she handed an envelope to Clarise and told her that white wasn't going to be the operative color at this affair; and he didn't understand when she tossed an envelope at him and ran out of the shop, laughing as if she'd won the largest lottery in the history of the Union.

Women, he was the first to admit, were not his strong suit, and he was about to toss it aside when Clarise cleared her throat and said sweetly, "Lincoln, you are an idiot."

She held up her invitation. He didn't have to squint; he could see Carmel's name, in silver, from where he stood. He could also see his name, right under hers, and knew without reading the rest that he wasn't slated to be the best man.

"But I didn't propose," he protested plaintively.

She stood, closed her coat, put on her hat, and said, "She is of Spanish descent. Her father is very old-fashioned. If you don't show up at the church, he's probably going to blow your head off."

He couldn't move.

As she walked by, she patted his cheek and shook her head.

And it was several seconds before he was able to groan loudly and start for the door, his temper sending a flush to his face and rigidity to his limbs. He wanted to know what the hell had happened to Ellshampton Yark; he wanted to know where she got off putting his name on the invitations without even bothering to ask him if he wanted to get married.

And he wanted to know why, as he reached the door, Clarise abruptly threw up her hands and ran across the street, her hat flying into the gutter, her purse falling to the sidewalk. He called out to her, bent down to retrieve the purse, and froze when someone said in his ear, "Touch it, pardner, and I'll cut your throat where you stand."

# Three

Lincoln, knowing a declaration of intent when he heard one, instantly discarded the fleeting possibility that it was a joke when he felt something press into his back, a long way from his throat but ominous nonetheless. It was sharp, and sharper in the cold that made his shirt feel thinly coated with ice; and he did not look over his shoulder when the point of whatever weapon it was nudged him as soon as his neck twitched with temptation.

A casual glance side to side showed him pedestrians passing without interest, so the weapon wasn't obvious and neither was his predicament.

Slowly then, and with absolutely no intention of antagonizing whoever it was standing behind him, he waggled his fingers over the purse as if trying to shoo it over the snowbank and into the gutter. Then he straightened, set his hands on his hips, and looked across the street without seeing a thing.

"Fine," the voice said. A soft voice. A man's voice. "That's pretty good, Mr. Blackthorne. Now go back inside and sew something."

He considered whirling around and surprising the man, grabbing the weapon deftly, and beating the hell out of him with it; he considered the distance between them and knew he wouldn't be able to move more than an inch before that weapon did whatever it was supposed to do and left him looking like a jerk in the morgue; he looked down the street and saw the three ski-capped college women walking toward him, just ahead of the two elderly mink-wrapped matrons, and knew that a fuss would only invite casualties of which he might not be the only one.

"Move," the voice said again. "Please."

He moved.

And as he did he caught a glimpse of a reflection in the lefthand display window—a man reaching down quickly, picking up the purse, and stuffing it into the pocket of a solid black overcoat too large for the wearer. The reflection then moved on, a black-gloved hand pulling a wide-brimmed hat low over its face.

He frowned as he closed the door behind him and without pause continued through the beaded curtain into the back room; he frowned as he stood in front of Clint Eastwood and pressed the bullets in the bandolier in complicated sequence; and he frowned as the poster, and the door hidden behind it, swung open sharply, nearly slammed him against the wall, and permitted him to race up the stairs to the apartment above the shop, then to the window overlooking Creek Road, where he raised the sash and poked his head out. Futile, because he knew the reflection in black would be gone; hopeful, because there was always that one small chance that luck had stuck around.

It hadn't.

Damn; and he dropped onto a well-used couch and picked up the receiver of a telephone fashioned in the shape of an Arabian stallion—a well-meant gift from a friend who thought Lincoln needed a bit of class in a room otherwise furnished in the manner of it looks comfortable so who cares if it matches.

He dialed George Vilcroft's number.

When George answered, he hung up.

Fifteen minutes later he tried again.

When George answered, he hung up.

He speculated on the possibilities: that Clarise had gotten herself into something which now endangered her life, which was why she needed his help; that Clarise had located a truly valuable antique, oddity, or extraordinary bauble, which was highly prized by other parties, and those other parties were actively attempting to discourage and otherwise prevent her from continuing her pursuit of said object in a manner peculiar only to true fanatics and collectors; that Clarise had stumbled accidentally into something over which she had no control through her pursuit of that object, which was about to cost her her life; that Clarise had set the whole thing up in order to make him speculate on things designed to elicit his sympathy and thus his services, even though she could probably do it herself, despite the fact she had never in her life done anything herself she could avoid. Vilcroft typed his own letters.

None of it explained why the reflection had been so interested in her purse.

He dialed Vilcroft's number, and when George answered, Linc asked to speak to Clarise.

"Lincoln, my boy!" Vilcroft said happily. "Lord, it's been a long time since we've gotten together."

"It has," he said, standing and walking to the window. "Too long. I love it. Where's Clarise?"

"I understand you're finally getting married, you old devil you."

He gaped at the receiver. "How'd you know that?"

"Then it's true?"

"No."

There was a pause. "But I got the invitation just a few minutes ago."

He scowled. Wonderful. Carmel must have decided to deliver a few in person, not trusting the post office to assist her in entrapping him.

"I'm not getting married. Where's Clarise?"

"Odd," Vilcroft said. "It has your name on it."

"A printer's error, that's all. It's supposed to be Ellshampton Yark."

"Hell of an error. That's not even close."

"George," he said, "I'll discuss my future with you some other time, if you don't mind. Right now, I need to talk to Clarise."

"Carmel isn't going to like that, not so soon before the wedding. Have you no pride?"

"George," he said, his voice flat.

"Certainly. Well, I can't help you, Linc. I haven't seen her in a couple of hours. But hang on a minute, and I'll see if she's back."

The line went flat as he was put on hold, and he passed the time watching the flow of pedestrians, frowning at each dark coat he saw, frowning deeper at each hat that obscured the wearer's face.

"Lincoln."

"George."

"She's not here."

"Tell her I called."

"What about Carmel?"

"I don't think she'll call."

He rang off and pulled a thickly upholstered arm-chair closer to the window, sat, and stared down at the street. Clarise should have gotten back to the house by now, even if she had walked, which she wasn't doing when he'd last seen her. The reflection in black had gone in the opposite direction, but that didn't mean he didn't have companions who might have been waiting for her somewhere else along the way. On the other hand, it may all be perfectly innocent and he was concerned about nothing, and what he ought to do is get hold of Carmel before she gives an invitation to the goddamned mayor.

When the telephone rang, he grabbed the receiver, listened for a moment, and assured the mayor that the suit would be finished in time and the husband-to-be would never look better, which in this case he suspected was nothing less than the truth.

When the telephone rang a second time, he was more casual, and assured the editor of the local newspaper that he was not getting married and therefore did not have a photograph of himself and his intended which could be run in the next weekly edition.

When the telephone rang a third time, he glared across the street to Carmel's family's shop and growled his greeting like an animal trapped in a corner and with no compunctions about tearing out the throat of whoever came after him first.

He apologized at once when Dennis Atwaver asked him what the hell had happened to his voice, and maybe he ought to have a look at Linc's throat when he dropped by.

"Drop by where?" Linc said.

"The hospital."

He stood. "What's wrong, Den?"

"It seems I have a woman here who insists on talking to you. She refuses treatment until she does." The doctor coughed, evidently muffled by a hand. "You'd better get down here, Linc. Now."

23

*   *   *

It took him less than five minutes to pull on a worn brown overcoat and equally worn brown gloves and get himself down into the tavern next door, where he found Old Alice and Macon sitting in a back booth, Palmer Crowley sound asleep between them. When they looked up, surprised, he told them get sober and be ready, he might need them right away.

Old Alice sighed; Macon rolled his eyes; neither of them argued when he was in a mood like this.

Palmer snored.

Then he was outside again and running, to the bookshop two stores down which had, in the rear, a counter for Dick Pell's Country Taxi and Limousine Service. Pell, a former bus driver married to one of the nieces of the man who'd given Lincoln the horse phone, leapt up as soon as he saw the tailor rush in. He grabbed a set of keys from a pegboard behind him and pushed Linc back to the street and across it, to a deep red limousine whose engine was already running by the time he'd gotten settled in the front seat.

"Where?" Pell asked as he pulled away from the curb.

"Hospital."

The young man nodded, though he was clearly disappointed. The last time he'd seen Linc in such a hurry, while he was still with the bus company, the tailor had commandeered his vehicle and they had ended up at Newark Airport, thirty miles off his route and with no fares to bring back.

Nevertheless, he asked no questions, moving swiftly and expertly through the traffic until he was able to head up the hill to the Knob, through that exclusive neighborhood and into the countryside beyond. The hospital stood on a hill of its own, new and low and surrounded by fir trees that made it look more like a

24

small, single-story hotel than a place Linc hated to visit almost as much as he hated flying.

"Wait here," he ordered.

He forced himself not to run, straightening his shoulders as he passed through the electronically-opened front doors. The silence hit him immediately. There were a number of people in the tinsel-decorated waiting area to his right, two receptionists behind a high and long counter, and a doorway to a combination gift shop and snack bar to his left; yet despite the chatter, the ringing of telephones, the muted messages over the public address system, there was that silence, a quiet less of peace than a holding of one's breath. Expectation. Apprehension.

He nodded in the direction of the receptionists and hurried past them into another waiting room where he swung to his right and stepped into yet another hall. Small rooms opened onto it, all their doors open, and on his left was another counter, this one manned by a nurse who, at his question, directed him to the fourth room on the right.

Inside was a bed, life support systems, and a huge bright light hanging from the ceiling. Clarise was lying on her back, eyes closed, hair perfectly arranged around her shoulders. An IV was set up beside her, the tube trailing from a clear plastic bag under the sheet and into her arm.

"Not bad," said Dennis Atwaver, coming up behind Linc to lay a hand on his shoulder. "I could die and do worse in heaven."

"What happened?" Linc said, moving slowly to her side. He could see no bruises, but the sheet that covered her was lightly speckled with blood.

"Hit-and-run," the doctor answered grimly, and stepped aside when two white-coated men rushed in and began the patient's careful transfer from the bed to a gurney. "When the police brought her in, she was yelling for you," Atwaver continued as the men worked, and a nurse came in to help them. "She lost consciousness about a minute ago."

Lincoln pressed against the wall and watched them without thinking, taking shallow breaths to minimize the smell of blood and antiseptic. Clarise's face was pale, too pale, and he left the room hurriedly.

Atwaver followed, a small, stocky man with dark hair and a round wrinkled face. "She'll be all right, Linc," he said.

"Okay." He inhaled deeply several times, and leaned against the wall when she was wheeled out and the interns rushed her toward the operating rooms at the rear of the building. When she was gone, he relaxed a bit and allowed his friend a smile. "I hate this place, you know," he said.

"No kidding."

"Everybody's sick here. It's unhealthy."

Atwaver shrugged, coughed into his fist, then reached into his trouser pocket and pulled out a folded sheet of green paper. "She ordered me to give this to you if she wasn't awake when you got here."

Linc took it. "Den, no doubletalk—is she really going to be all right?"

"Sure. The cops don't know who did it, naturally, and all the witnesses were too busy keeping warm to get a description of the car. She'll be fine, though. A stitch here, a set bone there, she'll be just great. And congratulations."

He looked at him. "Oh?"

"Hear you're getting married."

"I'm not," he said, walking toward the front of the building. "I am not getting married."

"A good thing," Atwaver told him as he followed. "She might not understand a dying woman asking you to rush to her bedside."

He turned and grabbed the doctor's arm. "You just said she was all right."

"She is, she is. But you can't say you rushed to a bruised woman's side, now can you. It sounds lousy."

A gnarled old woman pushed by them, muttering to herself as she yanked a large paisley scarf over her head. A young man in black walked nervously at her side, whispering to her anxiously about the laws they have in this country concerning the practice of medicine and its use of pigs' feet. A woman sat alone in a corner, weeping.

There was a Christmas tree in the window, and muted carols over the public address system.

Linc looked at the paper he'd been given and frowned—it was an address in New York City, just about midtown. "Are you positive," he said as he stuffed the paper into his pocket, "that's she's going to be all right?"

"For god's sake, don't worry about it," Atwaver assured him. "She'll be taken care of."

He nodded and hurried outside, glad to be back in the fresh air, gladder when Dick jumped out of the limousine and opened the back door for him. It was a silly extravagance, but he enjoyed it, and would have enjoyed it more if someone else hadn't been in the spacious rear compartment, holding a sword whose point just managed not to run through his throat.

# Four

"I n," the man ordered.

Lincoln understood the value of discretion versus losing a lot of blood, and did as he was told; he jumped a bit when the door was slammed behind him, but he didn't look up when Pell scurried into the front seat, raised the smoked-glass partition between them, and drove off; not, he noticed ruefully, in the direction of town.

"Well," Linc said softly, slapping a hand on his thigh.

The man on the far side of the vehicle, even sitting down, was tall, thin to the point of emaciation, and extraordinarily pale. His long face was all sharp angles, his eyes heavily lidded, his mouth thick-lipped and grotesquely large for the rest of his features. His shoes were black and pointed, his dark clothes were tailored, yet just old-fashioned enough to make them noticeable. And if no one paid any attention to them,

28

they certainly would have commented on the black opera cape with the red lining and the high, stiff collar.

The weapon, which hadn't yet left Linc's throat, was the inner part of a sword-cane, the elaborate handle of which was silver sculpted into the head of a jackal who obviously hadn't been fed in several long months.

"Good afternoon, Mr. Blackthorne," the man said in a voice hoarse and low that carried with it a touch of Tennessee honey.

"You have the advantage," he replied, trying to squirm unobtrusively away from the blade as Pell swerved around a curve that pushed him ever so slightly closer to penetration.

"I know."

The interior of the limousine was cold, and when he placed a palm over the nearest heating vent, he frowned. He could definitely feel a flow of warm air but it wasn't raising the temperature a bit. A look at the intruder gave him no clue, though he looked away again when those eyes wouldn't stop staring, and didn't blink once.

He rubbed his hands together; they wouldn't warm up either.

He prayed then for sudden intervention, for the timely arrival of a policeman needing one more speeding ticket to make his quota and eager to stop such a rich-looking car; but through the tinted glass he saw only the white-shrouded, rolling fields, the trees whose branches held nothing but snow, a few crows gossiping along the telephone wires. They were alone on the road, and when Pell soon turned into what was little more than a cow path, he knew instructions had already been given, and the police weren't going to come.

29

At least, not in time.

The man rearranged his cape with his free hand, pulling it close over his chest, though not enough to hinder the hand with the sword. "I understand, sir," he said, "that you are a tailor of some repute."

He nodded.

"I understand as well that you are also a procurer for that swine, Vilcroft."

"George gets his own women," he said with a smile.

"Indeed. I suppose he does." The blade pressed into the hollow of Linc's throat, painfully. "And since time is a question here, Mr. Blackthorne, may I suggest we set aside the banter for the moment?"

Considering the protection his skin was offering several veins and a major artery or two, Linc nodded agreeably.

"Fine. Then I shall ask you once, and only once, if you will undertake to procure for me a certain item for which I shall pay you a handsome fee. Far more than that toad would have given you, I assure you."

"I don't know," he answered. "I have a lot of work to do before the holidays."

"Double your usual fee."

"Usually," he said, "people come to me with less . . . shall we say, less unpleasant means of persuasion?"

The man glanced along the length of the blade, obviously pleased with its performance thus far. "I have your word there'll be no trouble?"

"It's my car, my driver, your sword. Absolutely."

After a moment's consideration the man nodded and slipped the blade soundlessly into its ebony sheath. Which he placed between his knees in such a manner as to make it clear that it wouldn't take more than a second to get it back out in order to slice open a few limbs.

Linc sagged into the corner and stretched out his

legs, which weren't quite long enough to reach the opposite seat. To his left was a polished mahogany unit containing a bar, a radio, and a television set. Though the light was diffused through the dark windows, he used the screen to watch the man's reflection. To watch the hands cupped over the jackal's head, and to avoid having to look directly into those eyes again.

There was something about them that whispered to him from some far and desolate part of his mind, and for the moment he had no intention of going there to get a better look—he knew he wouldn't like it, knew too that not liking it was a disturbingly vast understatement.

The man fussed again with his cape. "Mr. Blackthorne, do you know who I am?"

There had been too many men, too many of what Vilcroft laughingly called adventures, for him to keep track of every face. Some he would never forget; some he hoped he would never see again. This one, however, rang only the most distant of bells, funereal bells that cautioned him to keep his mouth shut and pretend he was on a scavenger hunt.

"No," he admitted carefully.

"Ah."

"Should I?"

"If you had met me before, Mr. Blackthorne, you'd remember."

Those eyes, he thought; what the hell is it about those goddamn eyes?

"Jannor," the man said. And waited. And frowned as his left hand absently rubbed the jackal's head. "Pars Jannor."

Distant bells; faraway eyes.

"I'm sorry," he said truthfully.

Pars Jannor exhaled in what might have been a sigh

had it not been so theatrical. He placed a hand to his brow in conspicuous contemplation and peered at Linc from under it. "You are not a student of the cinema?"

"Jesus Christ," he muttered.

"Not one of my better roles."

"You're an actor!"

Jannor scowled, and toyed with the ouie, pulling the blade out a bit, sliding it back in. "You say that with a certain measure of disdain, Mr. Blackthorne. You disapprove of the theatrical arts?"

"I disapprove of actors hijacking my limousine and making threats, yes."

"I do not make threats, sir. I make proposals. And I have made one to you."

"And as I told you, I'm busy."

"Too busy to help a lady in distress?"

He stiffened and tried not to show it. "What I do with ladies in what may or may not be distress is my business."

"Not yours alone, Mr. Blackthorne. Not yours alone."

The reflection in the television screen shimmered as the limousine thumped over a pothole.

The temperature lowered enough for him to be able to see his breath.

Damnit, he realized—the eyes!

"Pars Jannor," he said, snapping his fingers and shifting to get a better look. "Damn, but I thought you were dead. A long time ago."

Jannor raised an eyebrow. "There are those who will believe that, yes. And there are those who know better, Mr. Blackthorne. There are indeed those who know better."

Linc closed his eyes for a moment and brought to mind a flickering image on a television screen—a PBS

32

station, because no network or local station would, in its right mind, broadcast the sumptuous turkeys Jannor had starred in. He recalled Macon complaining bitterly about it once, wishing they would quit interrupting the twenty-five-part series on fifteenth-century Angola every time another one of this man's films was discovered in someone's vault.

Old Alice had told him to go suck a grape.

He had watched one once; it was godawful.

"I'm glad you're alive," he said, for lack of anything else to say that wouldn't end his life in a red limousine on a country road only a few days shy of Christmas, making Carmel a widow before she had a chance to be a bride.

"Thank you." Jannor bowed slightly. "Now, about that little matter we were discussing."

"Sorry, I can't help you."

The actor sighed loudly, shook his head, and spent several minutes staring out his window, muttering to himself as he tapped his chin with a finger. Another sigh. Another shift of the cape.

At the same time, Linc tried to get Pell to look at him through the rear view mirror by sending him hundreds of useless mental commands, most of which were laced with obscenities because the former bus driver was paying far more attention to his work than to his employer. He didn't want to know what Jannor had said to make the young man behave this way, though he supposed it would probably be helpful if he was going to get out of this in one, reasonably blood-nourished piece.

"Mr. Blackthorne," Jannor said at last, without looking away from the scenery he didn't seem to be seeing at all, "you are a most difficult person to deal with."

Linc only grunted.

"I know—and we shall have no coy denials about this—I know that you have been retained to perform a certain task for that vile man. I know that you have been instructed that the performance of this task must be completed before dawn on Christmas Day, a mere six days from now. And I know that you will not do this thing for anyone but your humble servant here present because you wish to live long enough to see the next sunrise."

He turned around and smiled without mirth.

And it was obvious, when the smile widened, that he hadn't a tooth in his head.

Lincoln didn't like nasty promises any more than he liked threats in the same vein; he especially didn't like threats when they were made in the comfort of his own rented automobile, the bill for which Pell was clearly going to pad to include some sort of combat pay; and he most especially didn't like threats when he himself was weaponless and the one who was doing the threatening had, in one blurred motion, taken the sword out again and had, again, pressed it none too lightly against his throat.

Still, he remained slumped in his seat and wished to hell Dick would stop being so damned rigid about not looking around to see what was going on. It probably stemmed from that first time in the bus, when Linc was on his way to New Mexico to help save Pell's future sister-in-law. The man had never recovered, claiming he'd never seen a bus do what Linc had it do, and the limousine was the closest he could come to such a vehicle without reliving old nightmares.

"You know where to find it," Jannor said as though stating fact.

"I don't even know what it is," Linc told him blandly. "How can I find it if I don't know what I'm looking for?"

The actor snorted.

Linc shrugged. "Suit yourself."

"You were given an address."

"I don't know. Was I?"

"My man knows this to be true," Jannor insisted, his voice even more hoarse and ominous, the sword bouncing along Lincoln's throat as the limousine took the narrow curves more rapidly.

Linc nodded. So it wasn't this guy who had accosted him outside the shop; so there were two of them, perhaps more, and they had run down Clarise in a vain attempt to prevent her from giving him the address.

But how did Jannor—an actor, for god's sake!— know about the paper?

Someone in the hospital signaling through a window, he answered, disgusted with himself for not being more cautious; and he tried to bring to mind all those he'd seen while entering and leaving, and while he'd spoken with Atwaver. There were too many. Nurses, interns, patients, patients' relatives—impossible to know which one had seen the doctor hand him the note.

The sword steadied.

"Now what?" Linc said, trying to ignore the ache in his lower back.

"You will go to that address," he was told, "and you will bring the object back to me."

"On a cold day in—"

Suddenly Pell threw up one hand in alarm and swerved sharply left to avoid a lone black cow wandering across the lane. The sword was momentarily swung in the wrong direction, to Linc's way of thinking—he just managed to find a bit more give in the leather back of the seat to prevent the blade from performing an unnecessary and unsanitary tracheotomy.

Jannor, with a growl of disgust, took the cane-sheath and rapped it repeatedly against the bar, angrily signaling the driver to slow down before they were all killed. Linc knew it was a waste of time but said nothing; once Dick got on a tear, his foot behaved as if it were grafted to the accelerator, and nothing short of a determined cop or a blatant red light was going to stop him.

Yet, unless the lane continued to swing left, following the cow paths that had been here before it, there was always the chance It would swing right for a change and give him the slack in which he could maneuver.

Jannor fussed with his cape as he waited for Linc's response.

Pell seemed determined to challenge every cow and barbed wire fence on the road.

Linc found himself slumping down even more in order to brace his feet against the opposite seat. It was uncomfortable, and even the actor appeared to be growing annoyed, and somewhat concerned.

Linc's eyes crossed slightly as he stared down at the blade, vigorously praying that he wouldn't have to sneeze.

The limousine's engine rumbled and whined.

"Good man," Linc muttered, with a nod to the front.

"Madman," Jannor spat, and thumped the bar again. "I cannot discuss business like this."

"There's no business to discuss," he reminded the actor, feeling his chin begin to wrap around the blade as he sank even lower.

"You *will* do it!"

"Nope."

"I will not have no for an answer!"

"You just did."

Pell found an intersection and swung left, just hard enough for Linc to hold his breath and be glad that the point had slipped from the hollow to his sternum; improvements where you can get them, he thought, grateful for the thickness of his coat and the fact that Jannor didn't seem to notice, torn as he was between leaning over to keep the blade on course while still banging away at the top of the bar.

"No one," the man spat, "says no to me!"

And the limousine swung right, onto a county highway and directly into the path of an oncoming truck.

# Five

D ick Pell attacked brakes, steering wheel, and accelerator with equal fervor and evidently in no particular order, which desperation resulted in the limousine's futile but valiant attempt to simultaneously bend in the middle, fly, and dig a tunnel under the speeding truck, whose panicked air horn blast was loud enough to knock the snow from several nearby trees. The maneuvers, accompanied by noises no automobile had ever been called on to make, sent Linc sliding to the floor, up against the facing seat and back again, thus denying him any one of several opportunities to defend himself against Jannor's enraged lunges with the sword.

Luckily the actor had his own problems, not the least of which was the abrupt opening of the lefthand door which prevented him from remaining inside when he was thrown sharply to the left. He departed with cape flying and sword flashing, and when Linc was able to regain his seat and look dazedly through the rear window, the only thing he saw was the empty highway and a few fleeing crows.

The limousine came to a quivering stop on the shoulder.

Linc's breathing resumed with a shudder, and he slid out shakily and leaned against the rear fender until he was positive the truck had truly missed them.

"You all right, Mr. Blackthorne?" Pell asked anxiously from behind him.

He managed a nod just this side of doubtful, a swallow to keep bile from rising into his throat, and a turn to look at the young man's face.

"Why," he asked, "aren't you pale with fear?"

Pell adjusted his chauffeur's cap. "What for?"

"We nearly died."

"No way, boss. All I had to do was use an evasion thing Old Alice taught me last month. No sweat."

He nodded, licked his lips to be sure he still had spit, and wandered down the road, searching for the place where Jannor had landed. Along the way, and between an explanation of the Old Alice Vehicular Survival Maneuver, Dick told him that the actor had threatened him with great loss of life if he wasn't permitted use of the red limo. Pell, being a newly married man, submitted. And no, he added to a question, he didn't see how the man had arrived at the hospital.

"A mystery, I guess, huh?"

"I have a bigger one," Lincoln told him, stopping and staring at the twin stretches of rubber the truck had laid down.

"What?"

He pointed to the snow that rose gently toward a heavy stand of young pine, turned and pointed to the snow banked on the other side of the road. Then he pointed along the road in both directions.

"I don't see him."

Pell took off his cap and scratched his head. "Maybe he's gone."

"Right. Where? The snow is unbroken. Any place he could have landed, we would see it."

"Yeah, but . . ." Pell turned in a puzzled circle, frowning, grunting to himself. "Wow."

As good a word as any, Linc thought as they headed back to the car; but it doesn't answer my question.

"The truck," Pell said then.

"A large one."

"Maybe the guy . . . y'know." And the driver clapped his hands emphatically.

Linc shrugged without conviction. It would be nice to think so. In fact, he urged himself to think so all the way back to Inverness, but it didn't do any good. They had already sped past the other vehicle when the door flew open and the actor flew out; and unless some freak of physics had sucked the old man into the truck's tailwind and subsequently glued him to the back, what had happened was impossible.

Pell parked the limousine with a flourish, opened the door the same way, and Linc couldn't help checking the roof before he crossed the street and walked down to the shop. A pause in the doorway. A glance over his shoulder to the Estanza establishment. And he had, quite suddenly, a compelling urge to visit New York City in the aftermath of a blizzard and at the height of the retail selling season.

He turned and walked into the tavern where the Crowleys and Old Alice were still in their booth. Palmer was snoring, and Old Alice was trying to balance little pink umbrellas on the heavy man's forehead.

Linc slid into the facing seat and folded his hands on the table. "Pars Jannor," he said.

Macon looked at him oddly, shrugged, and stroked

his beard. "A self-proclaimed Southern gentleman who thought Shakespeare was something a native did when the lions got too close."

Old Alice glared at him. "What do you know about acting, you old fart? The man was a genius."

"True. No ordinary idiot could screw a script up like him."

She reached for a grape.

Linc cleared his throat.

"I take it there's a reason for bringing up that person's name during my relaxation hour?" Macon asked stiffly.

"I've just met him."

"You haven't!" Old Alice gasped.

"I have."

"He's dead!"

"He was in my limo."

She flipped up the sombrero's brim and squinted at him.

"It's true," he said. "Ask Pell."

She lowered the brim and shook her head slowly. "Impossible. Still alive. Impossible."

"He never was," Macon said. "I've seen his movies."

"He wants me to get something for him," Linc said before she could reach for her grapes again.

"What?" Macon asked. "Acting lessons?"

"It was beautiful," sighed Old Alice, a grotesquely dreamy expression developing between her wrinkles.

"I don't know what it is," he said. "But Clarise wants it too."

Macon's eyebrows lifted.

Palmer's snoring shorted out.

"All those flowers," Old Alice crooned. "Every kind you could think of."

"Where do you have to go?" Macon asked.

"New York."

"Now?"

"I guess."

"But there's people there."

"I know."

"Millions of them! And Santa Clauses with silly little bells and pillows under their belts."

"I know."

"I cried," said Old Alice.

"Jesus, Lincoln, you'll be trampled to death."

"It was so sad," Old Alice said with a catch in her voice, taking out a lace-edged handkerchief from her purse and daubing at her eyes.

"I'm not dead yet," Linc told her.

"Not you. Him."

Macon looked affronted.

"Who?" Linc said.

"Jannor. Pars Jannor. The greatest thing to hit the silver screen since popcorn."

Linc, who was feeling bad enough about having to go to the city, scowled at her. "He," he said sternly, "stinks."

"So would you if you were dead."

"But he isn't!"

"Jesus, Blackie, weren't you listening to me? I was describing the man's funeral, for god's sake. I was there, for god's sake, at Darkriver, his ancestral manse. They gave Chattanooga the day off, for crying out loud. I touched his beautiful slender hand while he lay in sweet repose, there in his ebony coffin, on ruffled black satin, his cape on, those gorgeous eyes closed— why, he looked just like he was sleeping."

"Well, damnit," he snapped, "he must have been because he tried to kill me today."

"He," said Old Alice, "was cremated."

The apartment was comfortably warm despite the open window, and Lincoln looked down at Creek

Road. The sun was gone, the Christmas lights strung across the road and in the shop windows were lit and cheerful, carols played softly, and a light snowfall had covered the slush piled in the gutters. Pedestrians moved slowly, as if the cold didn't bother them. Traffic was so light a number of people actually walked in the street. A laughing snowball fight in front of Twainbow's Travel Agency a few doors down. The blare of rock music each time someone opened the door to the tavern.

He sighed and turned away, slumped onto the couch, and put his feet up on the cobbler's bench.

The room was dark.

He didn't much like Christmas; it made him feel like a statistic: this many people falling into depressions, that many people contemplating or committing suicide, another group spending the holidays alone, yet another group wondering what the hell had happened to the lives they had planned when they'd been dreaming in their twenties.

In the street a woman laughed gaily, a dog barked for the sheer joy of it, a child whined.

On the other hand, he thought, it's not everyone at Christmas who has a good friend put in the hospital by a hit-and-run driver and is himself nearly skewered by an actor who should have been buried six years ago.

He didn't know if that was a plus or not, but he supposed that as long as he wasn't bored he wouldn't think about being alone.

You're feeling sorry for yourself, he chided silently; you could always go to your wedding, you know.

He smiled.

He sat up, stretched, and looked over to the Estanza apartment above the record shop and tried to imagine what was going on behind the drawn shades. The store below was crowded, and he guessed that Poppa was doing a fine business as always, while his wife and sister were trying to decide if Carmel was really, this time, going to marry the odd little tailor across the street.

His smile faded.

Some days it just didn't pay; and he decided to take a walk. The cold air would refresh his mind, the sights and sounds of the holiday would revive him, and if he were lucky he'd be back just in time for Clarise to call and tell him she was fine, just fine, and not to worry about whatever it was she wanted him to get, because she had decided to get something else for whoever it was she was going to get whatever it was she had previously wanted him to get.

After all, Christmas was supposed to be the time for miracles, he reminded himself as he slipped back into his topcoat and made his way down to the street; and if one didn't happen damned soon, he was going to have to go into the city tomorrow because he didn't much like people threatening him, or his friends, during the season when threats were reserved for parents against their ill-behaved children.

A deep breath.

The snow.

A one-sided grin because he felt like it.

And when he saw the man in the black coat and black hat across the street, it took several seconds before recognition made him leap over the snowbank.

At the same time, the man saw him and ran.

Linc stayed outside the parked cars to be free of pedestrians, not trying to catch up with him, just keeping pace until there was room to close in safely.

No one noticed.

And no one even blinked when the man suddenly darted off the pavement and raced in front of an oncoming automobile, causing it to slam on its brakes and become the first in a six-vehicle chain-reaction collision.

Linc instantly veered left and reached the sidewalk

on the run, increasing his speed as the black-coated man reached the far corner at the downtown's only traffic light and vaulted a low iron railing, dropping into a parking lot set just below the level of the street.

He followed, using the narrow stone steps opposite the movie theater, and paused at the bottom. A dim streetlamp near the entrance at the back, and the running lights of the marquee, did little to relieve the darkness. Windshields glistened with frost. Newly-parked cars creaked and pinged as the engines released their heat.

Slowly he moved forward, shading his eyes against the streetlamp so as not to lose his night vision.

Cautious footsteps crackled on the frozen ground to his left, where the last store on the block rose above the lot, its back corner ending at a high chain link fence separating the lot from the backyards of the houses facing the next street and the sidestreet that sloped downward beside it.

He angled to the right, holding his pace when he saw a shadow glide furtively from behind a van two rows ahead.

The dark man tried the van's back doors, then moved on, bending over every car he passed, trying the handle, moving on, trying the next one.

By the time Linc reached the exit and stood to one side of it, the dark man was frantic, angrily kicking at tires now, and slamming a frustrated fist on a roof. Linc frowned his puzzlement—it didn't make sense. He could have tried scaling the fence, he could easily have reached the exit long before Lincoln, he could have used whatever weapon it was he carried. It didn't make sense.

Suddenly the man straightened, turned, and looked at him.

Linc nodded and slipped his hands into his pockets.

The man's shoulders slumped in defeat and he stepped into the wide aisle that ran toward the exit, shaking his head slowly.

Linc waited.

And a voice called his name.

He looked, knowing it was the wrong thing to do, and saw at the Creek Road railing the two matrons he'd seen earlier that day. They were waving to him.

He looked at the dark man.

He looked back just as the woman on the right threw something toward him.

In and out of shadow.

Spiraling.

Until it landed on the roof of the car just to his left, bounced, and rolled into the aisle.

The dark man bolted.

Damn, Linc thought, just as the grenade exploded.

# Six

Surprise and a mild concussion slammed him into the fence just as he spun away from the explosion and curled into a protective ball. Gravel pelted his spine and he cursed when he felt a cut open along the back of his skull. But he was on his feet almost at once, not bothering to look for the dark man because he knew he'd be gone. Instead he charged through the exit and headed up the street as fast as his uncooperative legs would take him.

A noisy, alarmed crowd had formed on Creek Road, and the single harried policeman who'd been trying to sort out the cause of the traffic accident was now standing at the railing with gun drawn, shouting for those making for the steps to stay back, there could be more bombs.

Someone claimed it was terrorists.

A woman screamed, and several people started running away.

Lincoln said nothing; his ears were buzzing, his head hurt, and as he scanned the crowd he could see no sign of the matrons.

He was angry.

A gloved hand gingerly touched the back of his scalp and came away stained with blood.

A second patrol car pulled up, and several policemen leapt out with riot guns and helmets.

He was angry because too many people in this town were people he didn't know, and the people he didn't know were doing their best to kill him.

He was angry because he knew they weren't trying to kill him, just scare him. Jannor could easily have used that sword any time. The dark man could have used his weapon while Linc was bent over Clarise's purse. And the grenade—it was like none he'd ever known, because there had been little more than a lot of noxious smoke and hellish noise when it should have either blown off his head or shredded him with shrapnel.

It didn't make sense.

And that made him angry as well.

He stomped into the shop, slammed the door, stomped up to his apartment, and threw his coat and gloves onto the couch. Then he stood over the telephone, trying to decide who to call to get some answers. The trouble was, there was only one person who knew what was going on, and she was in the hospital.

He called.

He was told that Miss Mayhew was still in Recovery, was doing well, and was under doctor's orders not to see anyone until she was transferred to her room which would be in a short while, but after visiting hours.

He slammed the receiver into its cradle and glared out the window.

48

He had a headache.

He felt a trickle of blood run to his neck and he stomped into the bathroom, nearly threw out his back trying to see how bad the damage was, and finally dosed a washcloth with merthiolate and held his hissing to a minimum as he swabbed the cut and slapped an undersized bandage on it.

Then he returned to the front room and glared out the window again.

He made another call.

Old Alice and Macon sat on the couch, hands in their laps, pointedly not complaining about being called away from the office party at Twainbow's.

Linc sat in the chair opposite, ignoring their silent rebukes, and strapped a Palmer Crowley knife-and-sheath onto his right forearm, a wad of Old Alice's money into his pocket, and a loaded revolver into a holster under his left arm beneath a worn tweed jacket whose elbows demanded patches. Then he shifted uncomfortably—guns he hated, the spring in the sheath hardly ever worked, and he couldn't help wondering what had happened to good old-fashioned fists, knees, and a strong word or two. Still, he wasn't stupid. He just hoped he'd only have to use the money.

Macon was somewhat miffed that there'd be no need for his huge collection of identification papers, but was assured that his memory, this time, would be more important.

Old Alice rolled her eyes.

Macon preened, and allowed as how he would, this time, be magnanimous.

"So," Linc said, "what do we know?"

His head still hurt, even though Alice had redone the dressing; his ears were still buzzing; and the noise

49

on the street had increased tenfold because of the sirens, the patrol cars, the ambulances, and the crowd.

He hated Christmas.

"He's dead," said Old Alice.

He glowered at her.

"But for the sake of argument," she added, and spread her hands sweetly.

"Thank you."

"I don't know," Macon said, scratching his beard. "You haven't given us much."

"Well, I didn't see them all that closely except for this afternoon, and I wasn't exactly paying attention."

"Pre-nuptial jitters," Old Alice told Macon.

"But if Jannor is around," Linc said, "maybe the others are connected with him."

Macon frowned.

"Think old."

Old Alice glared.

Linc stared out the window, something he felt he'd been doing a lot of lately and didn't know how to stop it unless he pulled the shade, which only came halfway down anyway so that wouldn't help much.

"Iddle," Macon said then, and Linc tilted his head slightly, an unspoken question.

"She's dead," Old Alice sneered.

Linc leaned forward.

"Marjorie Iddle. Stout, two good-sized chins, lots of delicate pink eyeshadow, genteel blue hair, one eye exotically half-closed?"

Linc nodded.

"She's dead," Old Alice said to Lincoln. "I was at the funeral."

Macon leaned back, gazed at the ceiling, and folded his hands over his paunch. His cheeks puffed in thought. "The other one is also stout, three medium chins, lots of heavy black eyeliner and silky lashes out to here, tasteful blue hair, a beauty mark in the middle of her chin?"

Linc nodded again.

"Yoman?" Alice said incredulously. "Are you talking about Irene Yoman with the hairy mole on her face? She's dead, for god's sake, Macon. It was a double service. They were buried in Omaha next to the zoo."

"One does not bury greatness, old woman," he said haughtily. "One consigns it to the ages."

"Combined, about four hundred and eighty," she said.

"They were stunning."

"Fat."

"Rubenesque."

"That's what I said—fat."

They turned their backs on each other.

"And the man?" Linc asked, feeling as if he were chairing a meeting of preschoolers trying to decide which flavor ice cream was the best in the world.

Macon looked over his shoulder and *tsk*ed. "My boy, I am not a magician. I can't tell a person's identity just from his coat and hat."

"You'd have to be a magician to raise those old farts from the dead," said Old Alice.

"Alice," Lincoln said calmly.

She looked at him from under the sombrero.

"For the sake of argument," he reminded her.

She groaned, reached for a grape, and thought better of it. "Okay. So we have one old-time genius of an actor, and two actresses from the Stone Age who couldn't emote their way out of the ladies' room."

Macon snorted his disgust.

"Coincidence, huh?" Alice said.

Linc shrugged.

"Especially since they're dead."

\*     \*     \*

Lincoln made a third call.

"Lincoln, I'm glad to hear your voice. I just got back from the hospital and they won't let me see her."

"George, I need to know if you know what Clarise is up to."

"Forty bucks an hour, and worth every penny."

He waited.

"That was a joke, son."

He waited.

"Well, you have to joke at a time like this, don't you, or you'll go crazy."

He waited.

"Linc, I haven't the slightest idea what that woman is up to. If I can't figure out her filing system, how am I supposed to be able to figure out her mind?"

"She's your executive, private secretary."

"Right. That just means she's the boss; it doesn't mean I know what's going on."

"George," he said calmly.

"I swear it, Linc. I don't know. Do you?"

"Would I talk to you if I did?"

George waited.

"That's a joke, son."

George hung up.

Lincoln made yet another telephone call, then borrowed one of Pell's cars, a bright yellow convertible whose roof was held together with green tartan patches, and drove to the hospital. Clarise was in a private room in the west wing, and when, after nervously wiping his hands on his coat, he stepped in and closed the door, she was staring at the ceiling.

Her eyes widened when she saw him.

He stood at the foot of the bed and wondered why his sheets never looked that good on him.

52

Her eyelids fluttered.

He swallowed and told himself nothing good would ever come of a hospital romance.

"Hi," she said softly.

He smiled. "Dr. Atwaver has graciously given me ten minutes to speak with the patient after hours. The patient will graciously fill those ten minutes with explanations because I am tired of being killed."

Her eyes widened farther, and he could see they were glazed, as if she were still drugged.

He sighed.

She shifted slightly and put a bandaged hand to her bandaged head. "I should have done it myself, you know," she whispered hoarsely.

It was then that he realized that there were tubes running out of her arms, out from under the sheets, and into clear sacks on IVs and monitors ranged along the wall beside her.

"Jesus," he said.

She smiled wanly.

"Clarise, give me a hint."

"I don't want to die."

"That's not a hint."

A tear slipped from each eye.

He moved to the side of the bed and put a hand gently on her arm. "You won't, you know," he said, wishing to hell people would just leave his friends alone. "George would have a fit."

Her smile was better.

"So would I. Who else would I dream about on sultry summer nights—Old Alice?"

She giggled, and coughed, and he held a glass to her lips as she took a drink through a straw.

"Clarise, what does Pars Jannor have to do with this?"

She frowned. "I thought he was dead."

He waited.

The frown faded and her eyes closed.

"Clarise?" He looked anxiously at the monitors, not knowing what he was seeing, but having seen enough television to know that those wavy green lines had better stay wavy. "Clarise?"

Her lips moved.

He leaned over.

"Are you really getting married?"

"Clarise," he cautioned, the smile on his lips never reaching his eyes.

Her lips moved again.

He listened.

And ten minutes later kissed her cheek, patted her hand, and stepped thoughtfully into the silent hall. A weary hand scrubbed his face as he leaned against the tiled wall and puffed his cheeks with a sigh. Nurses passed him, puzzled; an intern paused as if to question his right to be here so late; an orderly pushed a gurney by and waited in front of the elevator bank that led down to the basement, watching him sideways.

Linc was used to dealing with curious things, odd things, strange and sometimes exotic things, whenever he left Inverness to collect something for someone as long as the price was right and he was reasonably sure he wasn't going to get himself killed doing it. He was also used to nearly getting killed doing it because nearly everyone who sent him out to collect something usually forgot to tell him about someone else who wanted everyone else involved dead.

But he didn't have to like it.

And he didn't.

His nightmares were filled with images that normal, sane people relegated to late-night movies and the effects of bad food; his nightmares were never fantasy because none of them dealt with anything he hadn't seen before.

The elevator doors opened.

The orderly pushed the gurney in.

Linc pushed away from the wall and looked at Clarise's door. He didn't disbelieve what he'd just heard, but he refused to act on the assumption that every word she'd said was true. Too often he had seen desperate people grab at anything that would ensure them their wealth, their lives, or simply the status quo. They were the prey of the con man, and the victims of dreams.

And nine times out of ten they were bitterly disappointed.

But it was always the tenth time that Lincoln feared.

The tenth time, when all was true, and the nightmares came prowling in the middle of the day.

Damn, Clarise, he thought sadly as he shook his head; damn you, don't you die on me.

Then he turned toward the front of the building, just as the orderly popped back out of the elevator, lifted the guns in his hands, and fired.

# Seven

The first barrage shattered the tiles over his head, and the second gouged the tiled floor where he'd been standing before he threw himself back into Clarise's room. He rolled over, grabbed the room's only chair and shoved it against the door. Then he sprinted over to the window, yanked up the venetian blinds, and cursed when he made to raise the sash and found it permanently sealed.

He spun around when the thin door was punctured with several more shots, this time accompanied by the hysterical screaming of a woman and the panicked yelling of several men. A glance at Clarise, serenely smiling in her drugged sleep, and he returned to the door, pressed against the wall, and pulled the chair to him.

He had, he supposed, a number of choices.

He could throw the chair through the window and climb out, but that would only serve to alert the gunman to his destination and, probably, have him waiting

56

outside by the time Lincoln crawled through; he could also throw the chair through the window, alert the gunman to his destination, and then fool him by running back into the hall and safely out the front. Assuming the man was fooled and didn't have any ammunition left.

Assuming, as well, that the gunman was working alone.

Another round of gunfire.

The woman screamed even louder.

The men shouted again, though from a somewhat more distant position.

The guy's an idiot, Linc thought; he must think he can shoot through walls or something.

Another shot; another scream.

A swift calculation, and he sighed in resignation. There was no way, what with all the confusion and the noise, he could tell how many shots the man had fired. A lot was a good estimate, and too damned much for his peace of mind. So he pulled his revolver from its holster and listened.

To a resounding slap that stopped the woman's screaming; to the panicked men who weren't shouting anymore; and to a slow-growing murmur of uncertain voices that had him puzzled until, as he slipped the gun back into place and glad he was for it because he hated the damned thing, he opened the door and poked out his head, one hand braced against the jamb in case he had to jerk himself back.

The floor was littered with shards of tile, and the orderly was gone, the elevator doors closed.

He stepped out.

Patients were filing apprehensively out of their rooms up and down the hall, a few complaining loudly, a few weeping in fear, others wide-eyed with morbid curiosity and loud with a hundred questions. A nurse bulled past him into Clarise's room, quickly followed by an intern, and he decided this would be a good time to move on. Answering queries now would do nothing for his temper, and most likely ruffle a few medicinal feathers.

And the one thing he did not want was detainment; he knew he wouldn't be able to find the man who'd shot at him, or rather, in his general direction considering the man's aim, but he also knew that returning to his apartment was out of the question—the way things were going, some crazed World War I pilot was probably flying a bomber overhead right now, just waiting for him to return Pell's car.

In the main lobby, amid a swirl of pale-faced nurses and bemused security men, he met Atwaver just running in, still pulling on an overcoat.

"What the hell?" the doctor demanded.

"Call the cops if no one else has," Lincoln ordered tersely. "Make sure one of them stays with Clarise until I get back. All night. All day, Den. Sit on them if you have to, but I don't want her alone."

"Where are you going this time of night?"

"New York."

"New York? Are you crazy? There're shoppers there!"

Linc gave him a brave smile and left, slipping cautiously around the perimeter of the parking lot until he was positive no one lay in ambush. Then he ran for the safety of the yellow car, locked all the doors, and told himself that bomber pilot or no bomber pilot, he ought to go home.

An image of silver-embossed invitations and Poppa Estanza's no-doubt-loaded shotgun.

"Shit," he said to the steering wheel.

He sat with the engine running until the police arrived, then pulled out and drove as fast as he dared to the interstate that plowed across New Jersey from the Delaware River.

Once there, he floored the accelerator and braced himself for the rush of speed.

The yellow car jumped, shuddered, and subsequently refused all commands to exceed the legal speed limit, which forced him to remain in the right-hand lane, the scourge of those drivers charging head-long toward the city that held their evening's destiny—overpriced theaters and underdone meals. He sighed. He leaned back. He touched his coat pocket where the address lay, and he wondered what in hell Clarise and all the others wanted with a set of false teeth.

The parking lot atop the newly refurbished Port Authority Bus Terminal on Eighth Avenue was nearly full by the time he arrived, shortly after eight and in foul humor. He wasn't surprised. After twenty minutes' driving through the mazes of the three crowded levels, determined not to go out onto the streets where he would have to turn into a cab driver in order to survive, he found an empty space on the highest floor, near the glass doors that led to the elevators.

He switched off the engine, closed his eyes, rubbed the back of his neck to rid it of stiffness, and climbed out.

It was cold.

There was a wind.

Dry snow blew in his face from the piles the plows had rammed against the low walls.

The lights of the office and apartment buildings towering above him offered no feeling of contentment, no awe, no sensation that he was about to plunge into one of the most exciting cities in the world. What they did give him was an attack of sneezing, which he struggled against as he stumbled inside, leaned against the wall, and waited another ten minutes for an express elevator to arrive.

On the ground floor he braced himself.

The lobby was packed with people heading for the bus lines; the streets were still packed with snow, with automobiles and trucks that thought they could move over it; and the pavement was packed with pedestrians who seemingly decided on the spot where the right-of-way lay.

He wasted no time—with collar up and hands shoved in his pockets, he made his way through the crowds to Forty-second Street, waited for the second red light, then started across town, grateful for the bright marquees and shop windows that lined the block to Times Square. They provided an illusion of warmth, spotlights for those hundreds of wanderers who used the theaters to break the wind, and places where he could look around without being noticed, because he had the feeling, no more, that he was being followed.

Of course you are, he told himself as he left Times Square behind him and headed toward Fifth Avenue. There are a zillion-and-one people out here, and half of them are going the same way you are.

Nevertheless, the feeling wouldn't be banished.

He stopped to look into a record store window.

He stopped at the phone company building to admire the new rates and telephones being offered that week.

Five minutes taken when he stopped at a vendor to buy a hot pretzel he shoved into his pocket.

He glanced into the strobic shadows of Bryant Park behind the library, and nodded to the cheerfully whistling drug dealers who huddled around blazing trash cans to keep their wares from freezing.

But he saw no one he could tag as being out of place.

Pre-nuptial jitters, he decided with a bitter smile; Jesus H. Christ.

Then, at the corner, he swerved right and stopped in front of the first, snow-covered lion in front of the public library. Leaning against the cold concrete pedestal, he listened to a courageous Salvation Army band do its best to keep its lips from freezing to its horns, to a gangly streetcorner evangelist exhort laughing pedestrians to a religion that seemed devoted to keeping Cadillacs out of the hands of the masses, to a couple argue heatedly about being late for the opening curtain, and to a policeman tell a red-cheeked, thin-coated young girl where the nearest Y was.

He hated Christmas.

He hated New York even more.

But he looked across the broad avenue to the buildings facing him, especially the corner one, the address he wanted.

There were a number of stores on the ground floor, all of them still open for business, and a narrow entrance just to his right, where a sweatered security man stood warmly behind the glass door. When he glanced up at the offices above the facade, he could see no lights burning. When he moved back to the corner and looked down toward Grand Central Station, all he could see were more lights from more shops. There was no other entrance save the one in front.

Damn, he thought.

With shoulders hunched and eyes squinting against the wind, he walked down to the next traffic light, crossed over, and ambled back toward the office building. He took out the pretzel and nibbled on it while he checked the sour-faced guard and realized charm wasn't going to work, and a bribe probably would get him more trouble than he wanted.

Which meant that he was going to have to find a room for the night. Which meant spending Old Alice's money, a decision not made lightly considering the way she checked the receipts.

Snow began to fall—not as heavily as before, but increasingly steady, driven sideways by the spinning wind and directly into his eyes.

He felt his hair turn to ice and wished he'd worn a hat; he felt his cheeks dry and threaten to crack and wished he'd worn a muffler; he felt his toes and his earlobes fade from stinging to numb and wished he'd stayed home.

Five blocks later he finished the pretzel and turned down to Park Avenue, brightly lit and deserted save for the occasional taxi and foolhardy private car.

He decided to stay at the Waldorf, if they had a room on a night like this. Then he would take a long, obscenely warm shower, call the hospital to see what Atwaver and the police had discovered, call Old Alice to give her a heart attack, and sleep until noon.

On the other hand, heading straight for the Waldorf would give the person walking behind him a fairly clear indication of where he would be staying.

On the third hand, he wasn't about to roam around the city on a night like this just to satisfy the rules of shaking an admirably dogged tail. Let the guy get his own room, he decided, and we'll have breakfast in the morning.

He gave himself credit for stopping once before entering the hotel, just to see who it was back there.

No one.

Just the snow.

And the wind.

He frowned and shook his shoulders; the storm was getting to him. Imagination and a maniac gunman were making him see specters in every doorway, on every curb of every street. And he did not believe for a minute that any of the geriatric assassins who'd been at him that day were going to risk double pneumonia just to play at being spies.

62

A second look, a smile for the doorman who had more braid than a Russian general, and he hurried in, breathed the warm air as if it were champagne, and thanked the stars on the lobby's dome for the available room on the ninth floor.

Twenty-five minutes later, after being shouldered and ankle-kicked away from the only available elevator by a woman who had obviously been in New York before, he was coatless, shoeless, and the storm was evidently keeping the sirens and horns to a minimum down on the street.

All he had to do now was get a good night's sleep and go get the teeth in the morning.

He stretched, yawned, and kept his mouth agape when the bathroom door opened and the knife flew out.

# Eight

Lincoln was already rolling off the bed when the ebony-hilted blade buried itself in the pile of pillows at the carved headboard. He landed reasonably neatly, fell awkwardly backward, cracked his head against the wall, and came up with the gun in his hand. Which wouldn't hold it because his fingers were still numb. Which sent the gun to the floor and him scrambling after it, wondering if he could pull the trigger with his teeth.

He was on his hands and knees, looking anxiously over the top of the mattress, when a woman stepped out of the bathroom, put a black-gloved hand to her mouth, and said in a high, girlish voice, "Gee, I'm really sorry, Mr. Blackthorne. I don't know what happened. It must have slipped."

She was tall, nearly his height, with streaked blonde hair that didn't stop rippling until it reached the middle of her back, large dark-green eyes, a snub nose, a dimpled chin, and lips that were full and naturally red. She wore an elegant lambswool overcoat open wide enough for him to see the tailored wine business suit beneath, complete with matching school tie and ruffled white blouse.

He recognized the coat; it was the woman who'd aced him out of his elevator.

"It slipped?" he said, pushing slowly to his feet.

She shrugged. Beautifully. "I was just cleaning my nails. Tacky, I know, but when one is in a hurry, one tends not to remember the small things, like overnight cases and all that goes with them."

"Slipped?" he said, sitting on the mattress.

She held out her left hand and carefully examined the back as she stripped off the glove. "Of course, with nail polish on, you can't really tell if they're dirty or not anyway, but it's the principle of the thing, don't you agree?"

"Who the hell," he said, "are you?"

After reaching behind her to turn off the bathroom light, the woman strode casually to the armchair and sat, throwing open the coat, crossing her long legs at the knee, reaching to the round table beside her and pulling an ashtray closer to hand. From an inside jacket pocket she retrieved a silver case and took out an unfiltered cigarette, lit it with the matches provided by the hotel, and blew a perfect spiral toward the ceiling.

"I am Tania."

He waited, suddenly feeling rather foolish sitting there with bare feet.

"He used to be an actor."

He stood and began looking for the gun.

"He says you're going to find something for him."

He searched along the baseboard, under the bed, finally found it in the jumbled pile of topcoat, shoes, and socks he had dumped on the floor when first he'd arrived. He picked it up in both hands, just in case, and thumbed back the hammer.

"Very nice." She smiled. "Shall I swoon now, or tell all?"

He padded around the bed and sat on the footboard. He didn't lower the gun. "Tell all," he suggested flatly. "I'm not much for torture, and women who swoon around me tend to get a glass of cold water in the face."

She nodded. "Very well. I'm here to help you."

He smiled, and waited.

She smiled back and blew another spiral at the ceiling.

"That's it?" he said. "That's all?"

"Well, what more do you need?" she asked. "Poppa wants those teeth, you don't want to get them because someone else wants them, and I know why. Ergo, which is Latin, I'm going to help you."

"Do what?"

"Get the teeth."

"I don't need your help. I already know where they are."

"But do you know what they are?"

"Teeth," he said simply, "is teeth."

A small enough lie to get away with, he supposed, since Clarise had already told him that the teeth in question were, to be more specific, a rare set of imitation fangs such as is worn during Halloween evenings and high school lunch hours, which she had admitted was a rather crude way of putting it but sufficient unto the description thereof. Evidently the device fitted snugly over the wearer's existing canines and was extremely effective for those who knew how to use it.

She had also said, before slipping back into her drugged sleep, that these fangs had been carved from a substance known only to the designer. It was that

66

substance, not the design, which was the object of her desire.

A substance, she claimed, which would eventually drive the world into chaos should it fall into the wrong hands.

He had been doubtful. He'd heard similar claims too many times to put much stock in them, except when they were true. What he still failed to understand was how a set of false teeth was going to be a threat to anyone over the age of three.

Someone did, however. Singly and in groups, someone wanted the device so badly they were willing to kill for it, not to mention sending their decidedly better-looking daughter after him to be sure he returned it to the right place.

Tania watched him carefully, her smile languid, her eyes half closed.

Linc took a slow, deep breath. "If," he said, "I do find what you're looking for, I ought to warn you, as I did your father, that I'm doing it for someone else, not him."

Tania sneered. "Vilcroft is an idiot."

"No," he said. "Not George."

"My god," she exclaimed. "Don't tell me the sisters have gotten to you."

"The sisters?" He frowned. "Ah. You mean Irene and Marjorie. I didn't know they were related."

The woman's brief disdain shifted to suspicion. "You mean you're not working for them?"

He shook his head.

"And you're not working for my father?"

He shook his head again, and pulled his legs up to sit cross-legged on the mattress; his toes were getting cold.

With a rather puzzled expression, Tania straightened, shrugged off the coat in such a manner as to warm Lincoln's toes all the way to his ankles, and tapped a thoughtful finger on her knee. "This," she said, as much to herself as to him, "was not what I was led to believe. Not at all."

"Really. And who led you to believe otherwise? Pars?"

Tania leapt to her feet, a hand at her throat. "Pars?" she gasped. "Pars . . . Jannor?"

Linc had the abrupt feeling he'd skipped a page or two. "Yeah," he said. "Isn't he your father?"

"No! My god . . . no!"

"Then who is?"

"Dutch."

"Dutch?"

"Dutch Grange, of course."

"Who the hell is Dutch Grange?"

For an answer, Tania slumped back into the chair and pushed her fingers through her hair. "This is wrong," she muttered. "This is all wrong."

Linc watched her for nearly a full minute, weighing her apparent distress against the possibility of fraud; then, with a silent caution to himself, put the gun down on the bed beside him.

"Listen, Miss Grange—"

"Burgoyne."

He blinked. "What?"

"Tania Burgoyne," she said distractedly.

"But you said your father's name was Grange."

"No," she said, setting her hands palm to palm and resting her fingers against her lips. "Well, yes. Sort of. That's his screen name, you see."

He scratched the side of his neck and pushed backward until he was sitting against the headboard. "Okay," he said. "Okay."

"I mean, really, Mr. Blackthorne. Would you believe in a cowboy whose last name was Burgoyne?"

"Would I believe in a cowboy whose first name was Dutch?"

She stared at but didn't see him, and he used the time to consider the cast he'd been thrown in with. Actors, all of them, and as unknown to the current generation as the steps to the most popular dance of 1904.

Four forgotten thespians, and he had no doubt that the dark man had to be Dutch.

"Miss Burgoyne," he said.

"Tania," she said. "Please. Tania."

He smiled for the first time. "All right. Tania."

"It's my real name."

"Good."

"So is Dutch."

He frowned. "Your middle name is Dutch?"

"No, my father's name is Dutch. That's his real name."

He held up a hand to silence her, gently. "Tania, I'm a bit confused. And perhaps you'd like to tell me why all these people want what I'm supposed to get for someone else."

She fell back suddenly, legs slightly apart, arms dangling at her sides. And just as suddenly, the business suit seemed far out of place.

"My father is an actor." She looked at him. "Does that mean anything to you?"

His shrug was apologetic.

"I'm not asking if you've ever heard of him," she said with a trace of impatience. "Hardly anybody has these days. What I mean is, do you know what it means to be an actor? To work all your life playing characters who don't exist except for a few minutes on the screen?"

"No," he said truthfully.

"It's hell," she said sadly. "If you're good, you lose your identity. Dutch Grange becomes more real than Dutch Burgoyne. And if you're good, you work a lot. And if you work a lot, you want to work more because you want to get better." She sighed and closed her eyes for a moment. "You never retire. You just get too old, and they don't use you anymore."

Her gaze drifted toward the ceiling, and there was silence.

A silence touched only by the tap of snow against the window, the occasional keening of the wind. Someone slammed a door in the corridor. A television was switched on, too loud, and was promptly turned down. He shifted uncomfortably and heard the bedsprings creak.

"Then you die," she whispered, "and nobody cares." A quick tilt of her head. "You know, Mr. Black-thorne—"

"Lincoln," he told her. "Or Linc. Blackthorne is a tailor."

She almost smiled. "A what?"

He waved the question away; there were times when he didn't really believe it himself.

"Your father," he said then. "He's not dead."

She shook her head. "But it was a stunning funeral. I cried a lot."

"Sure." He slid off the bed and fumbled through his coat until he found his socks. As he pulled them on, he looked over his shoulder. "About six years ago, right?"

She gaped. "How did you know?"

"A tailor's intuition." He found his shoes and put them on as well. "The only thing I still don't know is why all these people, who had all these memorable funerals, are still walking around, looking for a set of rare, probably priceless, teeth—"

"Fangs," she corrected absently.

"Fangs," he said, swinging his legs back onto the bed. "So why? To sell in order to finance a comeback?"

"Yes and no," she answered.

"Which is which?"

"Finance, yes; comeback, no."

"With false teeth."

"Fangs."

"Whatever. Just tell me why, so I don't have to ask again. I'm boring myself."

The telephone rang.

Startled, Tania scrambled to her feet and pointed as if she were going to shoot it; Lincoln only stretched out over the bed and held his hand over the receiver. Funny, he thought; no one knows I'm here.

"No one knows I'm here," he said. "Except you, and that's only because you followed me."

"Me?"

Shit, he thought, and picked up the receiver.

"Mr. Blackthorne?"

"Speaking." He beckoned Tania to the bed, indicating with a tilt of his head that she should try to hear the voice. She hurried over and lay beside him; he wished she hadn't done that.

"You ordered two tuna sandwiches on white toast, with chocolate milk on the side?"

"No."

"They'll be right up."

"I didn't order it."

"Sir," the voice said, its inflection Hispanic, its hauteur pure New York, "the Waldorf does not make the mistakes."

"Then cancel the order. I'm not hungry anymore."

"I am sorry, sir. I cannot do that thing."

"All right, then I'll eat it."

"I am sorry, sir. If you do not wish it, the Waldorf does not want you to eat it. It would be against policy."

Linc stared at the mouthpiece, stared at the earpiece, and dropped the receiver onto its cradle. "I don't like tuna fish," he said, turning to look at Tania, who was so suddenly close that a good melodramatic sigh would tear off her eyelashes.

"You think it's a mistake?"

Her lips moved, and he was so busy watching them that she had to repeat the question.

"No," he said.

"Then what?"

Someone knocked on the door.

"Room service," he said, his voice low, his left hand pushing her reluctantly out of the way. "Get your coat."

"But I'm not leaving."

He smiled quickly, rolled off the bed, picked up his own coat and walked to the door.

The knock came again.

He peered through the fisheye-lens peephole, but could not see anything but the door across the hall. "Yes?"

"Tuna fish," came the muffled reply.

"My ass," he muttered, took hold of the knob, and yanked the door open.

"Tuna fish," said the midget waiter, holding up a silver tray with the sandwiches, the chocolate milk, and a rose in a white vase perfectly balanced atop it.

Linc frowned.

The waiter bowed, backed away, and Tania uttered a perfectly convincing scream when a man in a black cape suddenly appeared on the threshold and lunged with his sword and a chilling cry straight at Lincoln's unprotected chest.

# Nine

L incoln sidestepped deftly enough to avoid the blade's piercing his chest, but not quickly enough to keep it from slicing through his shirt and scraping along his ribs. He grabbed the arm that followed, spun about, and used Jannor's momentum to toss him over the bed. The actor hit the opposite wall trying to regain his feet, struck his head, and slumped forward, groaning, his cape thrown up over his back.

The waiter's eye widened, and Linc yanked him into the room and yanked Tania out. He slammed the door and hurried along the silent corridor to the elevators. He would give it fifteen seconds before he made for the fire exit stairwell.

Tania, struggling into her coat, froze when she saw the line of blood staining his shirt. "My god," she said.

"Later," he told her. "He's only stunned, not dead."

"Why didn't you kill him?"

The elevator doors opened; the cage was empty.

"Because," he said as they started down, "I don't know him well enough to hate him."

She stared, bewildered, and he could only smile weakly and accept her help with his coat. His ribs burned, he was feeling slightly lightheaded, but once in the lobby he took her arm and directed her away from the Park Avenue entrance, turning left instead. The first floor was jammed with people trying to find a room for the night, and several times he had to bite down a groan when an elbow or a package inadvertently took him in the side.

Tania said nothing; she was still quite pale. He had no idea what she'd expected when she'd promised to help her father, but personal attacks with weapons obviously weren't part of the package.

They used the back entrance, the cold slapping them, the wind shoving them, and again he took her arm to pull her away from the direction she was taking.

He struggled over a snowbank, ducked around a sanitation truck with a blade in front, and stood for a moment at the entrance to the Doral across the street. He reached down, picked up some snow and, grinning, rubbed it against her cheeks and the tip of her nose.

"We're supposed to be travelers in a storm," he explained as he did the same to himself and led her inside. "If we look warm, they won't have any pity."

"That's the silliest thing I've ever heard of in my life."

"I'm bleeding to death. What do you want, the plans to Fort Knox?"

He shivered uncontrollably as they reached the front desk, smiled as piteously as he could when the clerk informed him there was no room at the inn, and took

74

out some of Old Alice's money, in such sufficient quantity that the clerk was jarred just far enough away from his training to find a key.

"I'm sorry, sir, it's only a single."

"That's all right. We're on our honeymoon."

The clerk smirked.

Linc signed, paid, grabbed the key and Tania, and hauled her across the elegantly silent lobby to the elevators.

"Honeymoon?"

"I'm bleeding to death," he said as the doors opened and they stepped in. "I'm delirious."

They huddled in the corner, shivering less from the cold than from the image of the thrusting blade. He could feel her watching him, trying to figure him out, but he couldn't look away from the illuminated numerals taking them to the seventh floor. By staring at them he took his mind off the fire that raged along his side, off the dampness he could feel gathering at his waist.

And when they arrived, he handed her the key, put an arm around her waist, and was thankful she didn't slap him.

The door closed behind them.

The new room was nearly a mirror image of that in the Waldorf—a full-size bed, night table, armchair, television, prints on the wall, carpets on the floor, draperies drawn over the narrow window, and the heater blowing so hard the place felt like a sauna.

Tania helped him off with his coat, and he staggered into the bathroom, opened his shirt and saw the scratch just under his right breast.

"A scratch?" he said, staring in the mirror over the marble basin. "A scratch?"

Clenching his teeth and swearing at his imagination, he cleaned away the blood with a washcloth, ran the cloth under cold water and pressed it over the wound before going back into the room. Tania was in the chair, smoking, one foot tapping, her hair tangled over her face. When she saw him, she half-rose, dropped back and sighed.

"You're all right."

"I'll live."

She put the cigarette out and lit another. "He'll find us."

"I don't think so. We were running. I doubt he'll expect us just to have ducked across the street and into another hotel."

Her free hand gestured toward the window. "There's a storm out there, remember? Do you think he's stupid enough to believe we'll try to run to the airport?"

With a grunt to tell her the point was taken, he dropped onto the bed and stretched out his legs. At the moment he didn't care. He was cold, he was aching, he was trying to figure out how Pars Jannor hadn't been killed by that truck, and how both the actor and the lady had known where he would be.

It was uncanny; it was, he decided, spooky.

It was also impossible, a consideration he instantly dismissed when he recalled some of the other impossibles he'd run across in his life. Impossibles that were so labeled only because most of the so-called civilized world had concluded that the only way to deal with such things was to pretend they were fairy tales, campfire stories, bad dreams. If they didn't exist, then they didn't exist.

He toed off his shoes, bunched the pillows under his head, and said, "Tell me about the fangs."

Tania looked away. Looked back.

She said, "I don't want my father dying again."

\*     \*     \*

Dutch Burgoyne, she began with a long and melancholy sigh, was a true child of his century, born and raised in a midwestern city and dreaming of growing up to be a cowboy. And when he discovered that cowboys were being replaced by men driving Jeeps and pickups, he took his dream in another direction—if he couldn't be a real cowboy, he would be the next best thing.

So he ran away to California and, being a kid who could talk his way in and out of just about anything, quickly found work in the movies. Menial jobs. Then construction. Stunt work. Writing home about the stars he'd met—Ken Maynard, Bob Steele, Tex Ritter, and all the rest—fading headliners already, but more than willing to help a kid keep on dreaming.

Television killed theater westerns with westerns of its own, and Dutch Grange moved on.

Then westerns died in the United States, and were reborn in Europe, and Dutch Grange moved on.

The trouble was, his daughter said, somewhat bitterly, somewhat wistfully, he never became the star whose name was above the title. But as long as he was in a western, he was happy. So he perfected the small roles to be sure there was always work—the crusading newspaper editor, the smarmy mayor, the unctuous pastor. As he got older he became the town drunk, the prospector, the ancient rancher or mine owner who was killed off before the credits to establish the villains and set up the hero.

He worked in Spain, in Germany, and finally in Italy.

And when the westerns died there, he couldn't bring himself to come home and sit on a porch with nothing to read but his scrapbooks. He knew for a certainty that the form would come back, that the American myth would soon enjoy a revival that would put him, as he put it, back in the saddle again.

"He believed it," she said, "until the day he died, the poor slob."

Linc folded his arms over his chest. "You know, you keep saying that—that he's dead. Then you say he's alive."

"Well . . . yes."

"Yes?"

"Both."

He almost said "impossible," and bit his tongue instead.

She pushed out of the chair and crawled onto the bed, adjusting skirt and jacket so that she could sit in front of him, her legs tucked to one side. "You see, while he was still in Europe, long after he met my mother and they got married and had me and he sent us back to the States to live with his sister who's dead now—"

"Dead?"

She nodded.

"Really dead?"

"It was a lovely funeral," she told her.

"That's what you said about your father's."

"Well, his was too."

His mouth opened, closed, and spread in a smile when she started to laugh.

"He did a lot of traveling, you see, and since he didn't much like cities, being a true cowboy, he met some people ordinary tourists don't even know are alive." Her eyes began to gleam, and she spoke more rapidly. "Part of the thing was, he was looking for someone who could tell him the future. I know it sounds dumb, but he *needed* to know when westerns were coming back. He figured he could hang around long enough to get work again. Dumb. A delusion. Obsession. I don't care what you call it, he spent all his money looking. All of it, the jerk."

He didn't have to ask; he knew the old man had found it.

Then she lowered her head. "The trouble was, when he found out what he wanted to know, he was already dying."

"I'm sorry."

"Don't be. It was a lovely funeral."

"Now cut that out!" he said.

And she laughed again.

But he was past the point of laughing. A shadow was growing in the far corner of the room. A premonition. One he had had many times before. He didn't like it. It was cold.

"Then," said Tania, "he found the Hooded Demon."

Linc pushed an inch or so away from her. "I do not," he said, "want to know what that is."

"It's a cobra."

He glared at her.

"A white cobra."

"No such thing."

"It has fangs."

"They all do. They bite."

"Well, actually, they spit. Then they bite. Or something like that." She scratched her head. "It doesn't matter. You're dead anyway, right? I mean, when all that venom gets into your bloodstream, you're a goner. Poof. All black and swollen and—"

"Jesus!" he said.

"Sorry." She smoothed her lapels. "I get carried away."

"The fangs," he reminded her.

She told him that Dutch was directed by a gypsy to a village in the Carpathians, where he spent months working in the fields. He stayed because he'd heard

79

stories of the Hooded Demon, a preserved white cobra whose fangs supposedly held the secret of rejuvenation. He knew it was ridiculous, he wasn't one to swallow legends, yet he eventually saw the fabled creature itself, kept in a glass case in a crypt beneath the village church; but nothing in any of the tales he'd heard had prepared him for the fangs.

They were in a smaller glass case.

They were carved out of rubies.

"Rubies?" Linc said skeptically. "In the Carpathian Mountains?"

"The Turks," she explained. "Dad guessed the Turks brought it with them during one of their invasions. They figured it would keep them around forever, you see, and they wouldn't have to keep reinforcing their armies."

"It didn't work."

"The Hooded Demon was stolen."

Linc leaned even farther away. "Don't tell me. It was stolen by Vlad Tepes."

She grinned. "How did you know?"

"He was the original Dracula."

She laughed, lunged forward, and hugged him. "God, Linc, I thought you'd never catch on."

His arms, he noted, were not terribly reluctant to return her embrace, though he had to remind himself to keep it all on a brother-sister basis. Then he forgot, and hugged her tighter.

"I don't get it," he said, into the soft perfume of her hair.

"Dutch stole the fangs."

"No kidding."

"He was going to use them to finance his own films. Not to star in, he's too old for that. But to produce, bring back all the big stars and develop new ones. He wants the form back, and he wants to be part it. And

THE FANGS OF THE HOODED DEMON

those fangs, they're so pure, so unique, that even at today's prices he'd be able to make a half-dozen films and still have some left over to buy himself some new clothes." She looked up, and he swallowed. "A great idea."

"Was," he said. "But then he died."

She looked down again. "Yes."

"But you just said—"

"He didn't really die," she admitted.

His eyes widened in mock shock.

"His plan was to sell the fangs, get rich, do his own films, like I said. But the villagers came after him and he had to pretend to die to keep them away. A friend got his body out of the country. I hid him in my place right after the funeral, at home. It was easy. He's an expert at makeup.

"I brought them home too, but a few months ago, while Dad was making inquiries about selling the rubies, they were stolen. Right out from under my nose."

"Ah-hah."

"And then someone else found out about the Hooded Demon—"

"Pars Jannor," he said.

She nodded. "And that sucker really believes in the rejuvenation part. He wants to be young again so he can go back into films."

"Ah."

She was puzzled.

"It begins to make sense," he said, except that he couldn't for the life of him—and he excused himself the expression—figure out why Clarise would want something like that.

"They all believe it, Lincoln," she said. "That's why they're after us."

Gently he pushed her away until she was sitting up again. "And what about you?"

"My father is old," she said. "I want him to be happy."

He would have told her then that she was lying, but he had no chance to get the words out.

The window shattered inward, the draperies puffed, and a row of bullet holes began to march across the wall.

# Ten

Lincoln shoved Tania off the bed and dived after her, holding her down until the firing stopped. Plaster showered over them, a fire alarm began to hoot in the corridor, and as soon as he was positive the attack had ended he grabbed up their coats and hurried out of the room.

Other guests, not panicked but confused, were already heading for the fire exits, and he joined them, cautioning Tania with a look not to say a word other than to exclaim, loudly, that this was a hell of a night for a fire drill. An old man in a homburg agreed, an older woman in pearls threatened to sue, and a young couple wrapped in silk sheets only giggled and hiccoughed.

Lincoln was annoyed.

His side still stung, and he was getting awfully tired of being chased out of his bed. Bad enough that the woman who clung to him so tightly had lied to him, but

now he was going to have to figure out where to go
next so that he could learn the truth, go back to the
Port Authority, and go home where, if all had gone
well, Carmel would have seen the light and not only
recalled the invitations, but also dumped Ellshampton
Yark.

The lobby was jammed.

The manager and several of his harried attendants
were busily trying to make themselves heard over the
complaints, telling everyone that it was only a false
alarm, there was no fire, and they could return to their
rooms with no fear of harm. A few believed and
queued up at the elevators; a few demanded proof; the
man in the homburg and the woman in the pearls demanded to see a lawyer.

Linc pushed himself into a relatively quiet corner
near the entrance where he could see the street, and
the snow falling heavily; but as far as he could tell
there was no one in the Waldorf entrance who appeared to pose a threat. He glanced at the thinning
crowd. He felt in his pocket. He touched Tania on the
arm and nodded toward the outside.

"That's crazy," she protested. "God, I just got warm."

"I just got alive."

She followed his gaze. "You mean . . . go back?"

"They'll never expect it."

"They weren't supposed to expect we'd come here,
either."

He was getting tired of her making points like
that; it tended to undermine his confidence. Nevertheless, he took her hand and, with a wink at the doorman who was trying desperately to ignore the young
couple in the silk sheets cuddled behind a pillar, they
left.

"Cold," he said, puffing over the plowed snow at the
curb.

She grunted.

And grunted again, fifteen minutes later, when they stood in his original room and saw the tuna fish sandwiches neatly laid out with the chocolate milk and the rose on the table by the chair. Otherwise, they were alone.

"Efficiency," he said, and ordered her to pull the shade and draw the draperies. Then he put on the chain, bolted the door, moved the night table against it, along with a standing lamp and the television on its pedestal. When he was satisfied, he stripped off his coat and walked into the bathroom.

"I am going to take a long, hot bath," he announced, walking back out and grabbing one of the sandwiches. "I expect to be thawed out by morning. Until then, do not disturb."

"What about me?" she said, shrugging out of her suit jacket and forcing him to wonder about the organic properties of ruffles.

"You take the bed."

"But you're hurt."

"I am not so much hurt, my dear, as tired of being pushed around. We will sleep. Tomorrow morning, after a decently huge breakfast, we will retrieve those damned teeth—"

"Fangs."

"Whatever. We will get them, I will take them where I am supposed to, and then I will get on with my work."

She turned away from him as she began to unbutton the blouse. "What about my father?"

He leaned against the doorjamb and shook his head. "Tania, that's really not my problem. That's something you and he will have to work out with the others."

"But they tried to kill you!"

He closed the door none too gently and ran his bath water, stripped, sneered at himself in the mirror, and spent the next hour soaking. Thinking. Batting away the steam and listening for sounds of movement in the next room. If the woman meant him harm, this was the perfect time to try something; if she truly wanted to help her father, she'd wait until he had the fangs, then try to take them from him; if she saw the light, and the foolishness of her story, she'd go to bed and give him some peace.

And when at last he grew weary of sitting up and shivering each time he had to add hot water to the tub, he climbed out and dried himself off. There was, on the back of the door, a complimentary robe which, when he put it on, reached almost to his knees. Still, it was warm and he was comfortable, and when he opened the door he was ready to smile.

Tania was under the covers already, only the light on the night table still burning. When she didn't stir, he sat in the armchair and watched her, suddenly thinking of Clarise and wondering if that near-machine of a woman had heard the Hooded Demon stories too. Was there something wrong with her that she hoped the ruby fangs would cure? Did she have someone, as Tania had her father?

It still didn't make sense.

He stared at the telephone on the floor, wriggled his toes, sought an answer from instinct, then slipped off the chair and crawled over. A moment to be sure Tania hadn't awakened, and he punched for an outside line, prayed the storm had not wrecked the communications system, then dialed the Inverness Hospital number.

The night nurse was reluctant to give out information until he told her his name. Then she breathed heavily for a while to relieve the boredom of her shift before letting him know that Clarise had suffered a minor setback once the police had left, the gunman unfound.

"What kind of a setback?" he whispered.

"You know those little green wavy lines on that TV thing?" the nurse said.

"Yes," he said, nodding.

"They weren't wavy for a while."

He rang off and pulled his knees up to his chin.

He looked up at the rise of Tania's back under the blanket.

Sonofabitch, he thought, and crawled back to the chair, pulled it closer to the bed, and propped his legs up on the mattress; sonofabitch.

A painful light opened his eyes, and when sleep finally cleared away he saw Tania dressed and standing at the window. The clouds were gone. The sun was out. And she was nibbling on the lettuce that had come with the sandwiches the night before.

"It's time," she said.

"Right." He dressed, combed his hair as best he could, and put the furniture back in place. His legs were stiff, his side was stiff, and once down in the lobby he ducked into one of the shops and bought himself a new shirt, a muffler, and a new pair of lined leather gloves. He stopped short of getting a new cashmere overcoat with a fur collar because he didn't think Old Alice would understand.

Tania waited patiently as he redressed in the men's room. Then he hooked her arm in his and calmly walked out onto Park Avenue.

"Are you sure we ought to do this?" she asked as he headed downtown, the gilt on the Helmsley Building making her eyes water.

"They won't try anything," he assured her grimly.

The street was crowded, though all the snow hadn't been cleared.

"You're sure?"

"No."

"Then why take a chance?"

"Because I'm the only one who knows where we're going."

She made to laugh, then frowned, then began looking around nervously, hugging his arm close to her side, her heels loud on the pavement despite the thin layer of snow. He didn't look down, and he didn't look around; soon enough he'd see them, and that would be too soon for him.

"Lincoln?"

They were crossing in front of Grand Central Station.

The wind that had blown the storm north funneled down the side streets, almost negating the sun.

"What?"

"I have a gun, you know."

An eyebrow lifted. "So do I."

"No, you don't."

The eyebrow dropped. "I don't?"

They stood at the corner of Forty-second Street and waited for the light to change.

"I didn't have one before."

He stared at her. "You robbed me while I was asleep?"

"You snore."

He glared. "I do not."

"The hell you don't," she said as they crossed over and turned up the hill toward Fifth Avenue. "And you didn't even make a pass at me last night. Do you have any idea how that makes me feel? All night in a hotel room, alone with you, and you don't even make a pass?"

"I was tired."

"So was I, but it's the principle of the thing."

"You have a thing about principles, don't you."

They turned the corner and hurried down to the address he sought, pushed in through the glass door, through an inner glass door, and down a short hall to the elevators. There were five, four with plain doors, one covered with gold paint. He chose the latter and pressed the 'up' button. The door opened immediately, and he ushered her inside, turned, and pressed the only button on the panel.

They rode up in silence.

When the cage jarred to a halt, she said, "You didn't try to get back your gun. You didn't even frisk me!"

The doors hissed open and he took her arm again, smiled as he led her into a grey-carpeted, grey-walled reception area, and whispered, "You're righthanded, my dear. And I've had your right arm since we left the hotel."

"Bastard," she whispered back.

He pursed his lips in a quick sarcastic kiss, strode over to the young, perfectly coiffed receptionist, and asked her where he could find room number twenty-five. She asked who was asking, and he leaned over the low desk, smiled broadly and suggested that a lot of surprises awaited those who asked stupid questions.

Tania gasped.

The receptionist pointed.

Lincoln led the way around a ceiling-high glass partition and along a corridor off of which were several open offices. No one looked up. No one paid them any mind. And at the end he turned left, turned left again, and walked to a door at the end of the short hall.

There was no nameplate, nor were there any sounds behind it.

He tried the knob; it was locked.

He reached into his trouser pocket and took out a key ring, tried several of the attached keys until he heard the lock turn over. Then he pushed in without hesitation, and nodded.

The office, little more than a cubicle, looked as if it had been exposed to the night's storm. Filing cabinets were turned over, the desk and floor were littered with papers and small empty cartons, and there were faded rectangles on the walls where prints or paintings had once hung.

"We're too late," Tania said as she stepped in and quickly closed the door behind her. "Damnit!"

Linc hushed her with a look, took out the paper Clarise had given him, and walked to the window overlooking Fifth Avenue. He glanced at the paper again, looked out, and nodded.

"Yep," he said. "This is the place."

"So what are we going to do now?"

Hushing her with an impatient gesture, he ran his hand over the shallow sill, twice more before curling his fingers under it and pulling.

Tania gasped.

A section of the sill slid open, revealing a space he dipped his fingers into.

"Shit," he said.

"What?" she said anxiously. "Is it a trap? Are you hurt?"

"No," he said, turning. "It's empty. We're too late."

She took out the gun and aimed it at his heart. "You said you were the only one who knew where you were going."

"I know." He sat on the sill and shook his head in disgust at himself. "I was wrong."

"Well . . . wonderful! Just . . . wonderful! So what are we supposed to do now, huh?" The gun swung back and forth, and Linc wished she would put it away. "I mean . . . I mean, what the bloody hell are we going to do now!"

He had no idea, but he pushed off the sill and went over to the desk, shifting papers, not knowing what he was looking for and wishing Tania would stop whimpering, then swearing, then whimpering again. She was getting on his nerves. This whole thing was getting on his nerves. New York always got on his nerves, but this was ridiculous.

Then, at the same time as he realized with a start why the hell some people were willing to kill for a pair of false teeth, he saw it, a message pad partially jammed under the telephone. He pulled it out and held it up to the light.

"What's that?" she asked.

"A pad," he answered, and dialed the number he worked out from the impressions dug into the top sheet.

When an airline answered, he swore; when he read off another number he saw in the bottom corner and the woman on the line told him what their next flight out of New York was, he swore again and, closing his eyes tightly, made reservations for two.

"What?" Tania asked.

He took the gun from her hand and stuck it into his pocket. "We're going on a trip. God, I hate to fly!"

"You think that's where they went? On a plane?"

He put his hands on her shoulders. "Tania, I don't know if there is a 'they.' But the fangs aren't here. Which means whoever beat us to them has already taken them to wherever it is they need to go in order to use them for whatever purpose it is they need them for. Do you understand?"

Her eyes were somewhat glazed.

"Good," he said. "Then let's get going."

"But Lincoln, where?"

"The Hooded Demon," he said grimly as he pushed her out of the office.

"Rumania?"

"No," he said. "Someplace worse."

"Oh my god, Russia."

"No, Oklahoma."

# Eleven

**M**any years ago, after he had ridden in his first airplane and had solemnly, if somewhat hysterically, judged the invention considerably less than successful, Lincoln decided that airports themselves were decidedly unnatural, perhaps even occult. Aside from the fact that voluntarily flying in a zillion-ton machine was unnatural as well, no matter how gaudily it was painted, an airport took up too much space for a purpose no sane man could possibly fathom: there were no trees, no lawns or grass worthy of the name, and no way you could get out once you got in; there were overpriced shops that closed promptly at six even though a hundred flights came in long after, people selling flowers that looked better on graves, and no place he could look that didn't in some way remind him that he was about to leave the ground without a decent set of wings.

People in silly uniforms smiled too much.

He also didn't much like all the high tinted windows, which sadistically enabled him to see not only the rows of airplanes revving on the tarmac, but also the dark clouds that had rolled back in when he wasn't looking, turning the air grey and bringing up the wind.

When, while standing in line to pick up his tickets, he explained all this to Tania, she only giggled, slapped his arm, and told him to move up and stop being paranoid, and when, after the tickets had been duly stamped and paid for, he told her he had a few calls to make, she only shrugged and told him she'd meet him at the gate.

Curious, he thought as he made his way toward the ranks of public telephones; some people just don't mind facing death every day.

A glance at the multi-tiered parking lot across the way, and he dialed the operator and gave his instructions. As he waited for the connection to be made, he let his gaze shift to the terminal's interior, to take in the travelers milling about, lugging baggage, little children, and each other as if they hadn't a care in the world.

Curious, he thought, and decided to ask Macon about possible human-lemming genetic mixtures.

A second look around, and he turned his back on the crowds. He had half-expected to see someone he knew; he was grateful that he hadn't. Apparently Tania hadn't realized that whoever had rented the midtown office wasn't the one who had torn it up, searching for the fangs.

"Dennis, how's Clarise?"

"Lincoln, where the hell are you? It's snowing again, and we're locked in here. It's horrible. You should see it. I'm trapped with all these sick people, and I probably won't get out for days. Maybe weeks. Y'know, the South doesn't have to worry about crap like this."

"Never mind. I'll tell you later. Right now I need to know about Clarise. The night shift nurse said something about those little green wavy lines."

"A minor thing, don't worry about it."

"How can it be minor if those wavy things don't wave?"

"Lincoln, you are the tailor and I am the doctor. I will tell you when to worry."

"Should I worry?"

There was a pause.

"Dennis?"

A muffled cough.

"Dennis, damnit, you told me she was only bruised!"

"I didn't want you to worry."

"Well, I'm sure as hell worried now."

"Don't worry. I'll take care of her."

"I'll call you tonight."

"That's all right with me. It's your dime."

"No, it isn't. I called collect."

"Damnit, you know I don't like collect calls, Blackie. They make me nervous. I'm too old for that. The last time it was from the IRS. Something about outgo and income. I pretended I was senile."

"Alice—"

"They didn't believe me."

"Alice, I don't have the time. Get hold of Macon right away and tell him to check on the possibility of someone like me going to Rumania in a hurry, without bothering with all that official State Department stuff."

"Where?"

"Rumania."

"You mean, as in behind the Iron Curtain? Peasants dancing in the streets? Dracula? That Rumania?"

"Exactly."

"Jesus."

"Just talk to him, okay? I don't care what I go as, as long as I have the proper papers to keep me out of jail. I don't know, visas and stuff like that."

"Rumania."

"Right."

"Is he going with you?"

"No."

"Good. The old fart hasn't stopped talking about that stupid trip to Scotland yet. I couldn't live with him if he had to talk about Rumania too."

"Alice, you don't live with him."

"And a good thing too. Can you imagine living with that fat old man? Jesus. I'd rather move in with Palmer, except that he snores."

"The papers, Alice."

"Hey, Blackie, just because I'm not listening doesn't mean I'm stupid."

"George, I'm going to say this only once, so don't give me any grief. I want you to get on the horn and talk to some of your friends, the ones who know about things I don't want to know about. I want you to ask them if they've ever heard of something called the Fangs of the Hooded Demon. I need to know, if possible, where they came from originally, who made them, where they are now, and how valuable they would be if they were on the open market. I want to know about any stories you've heard about them. I want to know if you or your friends have ever seen them. If there's anything else you can think of that won't upset me, find that out too. I'll call you tonight."

"The Hooded Demon, Lincoln?"

"That's right."

"Oh my god."

"George, that isn't funny."

"It wasn't a joke."

"Swell."

He stood with his back to the telephone and checked the crowds yet again, not moving his head, only his eyes. Then he strode to the wide downward ramp that led to the departure gates. Tania was in a crowded newsstand midway down, opposite a bank of windows that overlooked the airline staging area. She was browsing through a magazine, nibbling on a candy bar, and humming. When she looked up and saw him, she waggled her fingers, signaled that he should wait until she was through, and returned to her reading.

Nerves of steel, he decided, and leaned against the wall to watch the lines of passengers noisily passing through the security check. The chattering hurt his ears, but from the complaints he overheard, he gathered that the storm had backed flights up, and there were far more people traveling than even the holidays could account for.

Surreptitiously he touched the gun under his left arm, pressed his right arm to his side to be sure the knife was still in place, and was pleased to note that the beleaguered guards were doing their usual officious and useless job—gabbing while the bags went through the x-ray machine, impatiently waving others through the arch when the buzzer sounded and the offender either jingled a pocket of change or pointed to either a large metal buckle or a pocket filled with pens.

At no time was anyone asked to go through again.

A hand lingered on his shoulder, gave it a gentle squeeze, and he turned with a smile, which faded instantly to a wince when he saw that the hand was more blubber than bone, and beringed in such a way that a mugger with a cleaver would feel he'd died and gone free.

"A small chat, if you don't mind, Mr. Blackthorne,"

said Marjorie Iddle, resplendent in a fur coat that had seen better days and a few ravening moths.

A glance over his shoulder, but Tania was still reading and nibbling. The large woman tugged insistently on his elbow. He balked. She lifted her chins and insisted again, this time with an expression more imperious than menacing. Though menace was there in the partially closed right eye; the result, he imagined, of a long-ago stroke.

"Sorry," he said.

"Mr. Blackthorne," she said, "this is no time for argument. I'm not a violent person, but—"

"You're not? What about the grenade?"

"Grenade? What grenade?" one of the security guards demanded.

Oh nice, Linc thought wearily; nice.

The potbellied guard stepped around the x-ray machine and came toward them, his left hand cupped over his holstered gun. He was squinting. "You say something about a grenade?"

"Who, me?" Linc said.

"Grenada," the woman said sharply. "We were talking about my trip to Grenada, young man, and I'll thank you very much not to eavesdrop on a person's conversation."

"It's my job," the man said grimly. "And I wasn't eavesdropping. I heard you, lady, because you got a whisper like a foghorn."

"Well, well, well, what's going on, Alf?" a second guard asked mildly, coming up behind the first and hitching his wide leather belt. He was bearded, stout, and too young for the timbre of his incredibly deep voice. "You got a problem here or what?"

Alf, who was clearly new on the job and junior to his friend, nodded, then shook his head. "I don't know, Bert. This guy here says something about a grenade—"

98

"Grenada!" Iddle insisted.

"—and this dame—"

"Sir!"

"—claims they was talking about Grenada. Which I don't know what it is."

"It's a country, you fool," Iddle said with a sneer. "An island off the coast of South America. We invaded it, don't you remember? Or don't you read the newspapers?"

Lincoln leaned back against the wall, checked his watch, and tried to appear as innocent as he could. It was, he figured, as good a way as any to pass the time until takeoff.

"And I am not a dame, as you so crudely put it. Is this the way they train you young people these days?"

Bert sniffed, closed one eye in momentary thought, then stood in front of Lincoln and examined him closely, head to foot. "Grenade?" he asked quietly.

Linc shook his head.

"I demand an apology."

Alf smirked.

"You sure you didn't say grenade, fella?" Bert asked a second time, leaning slightly back and looking at Linc sideways while he stroked his beard with calculated intimidation.

"Nope." He jerked a thumb over his shoulder. "I'm just waiting for my wife to make up her mind what she wants to take on the plane."

The guard tilted his head to look around him into the newsstand.

"Young man, I demand an apology for that insult or I shall take this up with your superiors."

Alf puffed his cheeks as he considered. "Sorry," he muttered. "Sorry."

"Very well, I forgive you."

Bert smiled at her politely. "Your mother?"

"Not likely," Lincoln answered. "I never saw her before in my life."

Alf tugged on what he obviously hoped was a mustache and scowled at the actress. "You sure?"

Linc raised an eyebrow. "I think I ought to know my own mother, don't you?"

"Of course I know my own mother. Don't be a jerk. I mean, are you sure you don't know her?" And he pointed to Iddle, who slapped at the air as if driving the finger away.

"Why, should I?" He took a step away and stared frankly at the woman. "Is she famous or something?"

But it wasn't working. He could see doubt in Bert's half-submerged eyes, and he had the distinct feeling that since Iddle was here, her companion couldn't be very far behind. He scanned the people in line, the people coming down the ramp.

"What are we gonna do, Bert?" Alf asked, shifting his weight from foot to foot.

Bert rubbed his chin thoughtfully. "I don't know. They don't look like terrorists."

"Young man!" Iddle squawked.

"I think maybe we ought to pull a search here." The fat man nodded. "Yeah. A search."

Then Linc stiffened when he caught a glimpse of a triple-chinned, determined chinchilla making its way toward them from the top of the ramp.

"You mean it, Bert?" Alf said in delight. "A real search?"

"I protest!" Iddle exclaimed.

"Look, mister," Bert said reasonably, ignoring the woman's huffing, "I don't want to disturb the other folks here, you can see that would cause some trouble which we don't want, so if you wouldn't mind coming with me to the office for a minute, we can take care of this in no time, and I guarantee you won't miss your flight."

"Absolutely not!" the actress protested, slapping her arms across her chest. "This is an outrage, and I shall be sure to lodge a protest the moment I am brought before your superior. Which right I demand, now!"

Bert was uncowed.

Linc was trying to decide which way to run.

There was no question about it—on the other side of the ramp, standing in front of the windows, was Irene Yoman, looking panicked as she fumbled in a large black pocketbook. Suddenly her expression changed, the three chins settled, and she lifted her head to stare directly into his eyes.

She grinned.

Tania stepped out of the newsstand and said, "Oh my god, Marjorie!"

And Irene Yoman pulled out a gun and fired at Lincoln's head.

# Twelve

The first shot went wild when someone jostled
Yoman's arm; the second one didn't, but the target
was gone. Lincoln grabbed Tania's arm and, in the
midst of the instantly scattering stampede, plunged
with her into those who stormed the security barricade
and charged down the broad corridor to escape the assault.

With an effort that nearly caused his legs to cramp,
he forced himself not to run, counting on the fleeing
mob to give him protection, hoping Bert and Alf
would do their duty and prevent him from dying, hoping at the same time that in the confusion neither
would have the wit to connect him with the two
women.

By the time they reached the far end of the terminal
wing, most of the passengers waiting at the gates had
either gathered excitedly in the pedestrian area to see
what was happening, or had ducked into the restrooms
to ditch whatever contraband they were carrying.

There were no further gunshots.

"Here," he said at last, and guided her to the left, to a small waiting area of black plastic seats behind a deserted ticket-checking counter. A glance over his shoulder showed him no pursuit. He sat with a loud sigh and arranged his overcoat over his legs, pulled Tania down beside him when she didn't seem inclined to move, and suggested that she try to pinch some color back into her cheeks.

The noise level subsided, shouts and screams replaced by agitated conversation.

"She tried to kill you," she whispered hoarsely, leaning close enough to climb into his lap.

He nodded.

"My god, she tried to kill you."

Then she slumped back in her seat and stared blindly at the windows. To the right an airplane was slowly backing off from its jetway; to the left another was being loaded with baggage, and containers for the galley. The sky was darker.

Tania looked over to the corridor.

Linc did his best not to do the same.

Passengers were returning in force now, chattering loudly, nervously, a few trying to joke about the rumors they'd heard. Airline officials were threading through them, smiling stiffly, touching an arm gently, leaning close and listening and nodding and moving away.

There were sirens.

A dark-uniformed man stood over them, asking if they were all right, if they'd been hurt in the crush. Linc shook his head and thanked the man for his kindness, asking if anyone knew what had happened.

No one did.

The official word, the man said, probably wouldn't come until well after they were gone.

Linc smiled.

Tania gripped his hand hard.

And was still holding it when they were finally boarded and had taken their seats. Linc insisted on sitting by the window; he had no intention of looking out once the beast was airborne, but he watched the terminal windows, grateful for the clouds that caused the lights inside to be switched on. There was little reflection now, and he could see no sign that the actresses had managed to escape the guards.

"Lincoln," Tania said.

He looked at her.

"They tried to kill you."

He supposed it was a matter of degree. It was evidently not as terrible to be nearly killed in hotel rooms because, he supposed further, they were relatively private and therefore quite within the bounds of good taste murder; to attempt such a thing in public, on the other hand, was not only gauche, it was a signal that the actresses, and perhaps one or two other players, were so intent on stopping him from getting those fangs that a little bad publicity along the way wasn't going to bother them.

It was little comfort.

But he clung to it with increasing desperation as the engines revved into reverse and the airliner backed away from its mooring.

Nuts, he thought.

"Lincoln," Tania asked, "are you all right?"

He was pleased, though his eyes were tightly closed, that from the sound of her voice she had put the attack behind her and was now looking forward to reaching their destination.

However, he couldn't quite give her credit for leaning over him that way, obviously peering out the window to watch the ground drop out from beneath them; more people like her, he noted glumly, and they'll never go back to riding trains.

There were any number of problems both physical and emotional inherent in flying, not the least of which, he thought grimly, was getting the damned machine off the ground without hitting another damned machine that was on its way down. And once aloft, he was none too pleased to notice that the pilot had chosen to take the high road into the clouds instead of the scenic tour just over the city's rooftops. He would have thought that the man would rather depend on his eyes than on a bunch of silly blinking lights.

Flying through what amounted to prewar London fog was not his idea of fun, no matter how much Tania exclaimed over the glorious shades of black and grey she could see; what he wanted to see was either blue, or green, and preferably from a radically different perspective.

The blue arrived just as he began to fear the pilot was going to test his instruments all the way to Dallas; unfortunately, the cloudbank below too starkly resembled a range of deceptively soft mountains.

An hour later, after discarding his topcoat, he took Tania's hand and pulled her close enough for their heads to touch lightly. He'd already done a check of the cabin and had found no one he'd need worry about; but there was still the sight of Irene Yoman, all chins adrift as she sighted on his forehead.

"Tell me something," he said.

She waited as she traced a disturbingly slow line along the fat of his thigh.

"Why are we going to Oklahoma?"

"I don't know. Because you found that information on that pad in that office, I guess."

"But why Oklahoma?" he insisted gently.

With her coat and suit jacket off, the ruffles clearly knew what to do when she shrugged. And when she looked up at him without raising her head, he knew that she knew how well those ruffles were trained.

"My dear," he said, "this would probably be a good time for me to say that I know you know more than you're telling me."

"Me?" she said, with the saving grace of a smile that was both mocking and playful.

He considered: she had been genuinely distressed that the matrons in dead pelts had nearly done him in; she had been genuinely upset that the fangs hadn't been found in New York, and she hadn't uttered a single word of protest when he dragged her all the way to LaGuardia Airport in order to take her to Oklahoma.

To say that it was suspicious would be to say that the plane was pretty far off the ground.

"Tania?"

She snored in the seat beside him.

"Well," he whispered, and noted her hand lying on his leg. Old Alice would have slapped her awake and threatened her with a grape unless she came clean; Macon would have wined and dined her into submission. And he supposed that if he were truly a man of purposeful action, he could have throttled the answer out of her.

But for what? For her to tell him they were going to Oklahoma because someone near and dear to her was either waiting for them there or was lying in ambush somewhere else? That much he'd already figured out.

She shifted, and her hand did as well.

The plane dropped into a pothole.

Lincoln managed a brief but sincere prayer.

Tania rolled her shoulders and the snore briefly slipped into a comfortable sigh.

No, he decided; there was nothing to gain by torture, not as long as he didn't have much of a choice anyway. There was nothing for it but to go along for the ride, play it by ear, and hope that sooner or later someone would tell him what he needed to know.

If that didn't happen, there was always torture.

He closed his eyes then and tried to emulate the woman beside him, but the plane's constant rocking and shuddering, the unconcerned nattering of the passengers, and the maddeningly efficient ministrations of the crew soured his mood to such an extent that time passed too quickly for him to get up a good head of righteous steam.

In Dallas he fairly marched to their connecting flight.

Tania treated the place as if it were home.

"You've been here before," he muttered.

"Oh, hundreds of times," she said brightly. "You can't hardly get out of this part of the country without coming through Dallas."

"I see."

"Oh," she said.

"That," he said, "is what we in the profession call a slip."

She nodded. "I understand. It's because you're a tailor."

"That too," he told her.

She said nothing more as they continued through the massive terminal, and his mood continued to sour as the distance between gates became directly proportional to the time remaining before missing their flight to Oklahoma City. There was no doubt in his mind that it was a deliberate ploy by the airlines—get the suckers so tired from running from one place to another that they don't have the strength to complain when the fares go up again.

"God, I love it here," she exclaimed.

"Get on the plane," he growled.

And was immediately sorry he'd said it when he realized that the aircraft they were boarding was considerably smaller than the one they'd just taken. To the others crowding into the seats it all seemed perfectly normal; to him, however, it was a sign that the airline wasn't exactly determined to reach Oklahoma in style.

The only good thing he could think of at the moment was the fact that the sky was a crisp and wintry blue, not a hint of cloud anywhere. Now he'd be able to see all the crash sites en route, the better to prepare himself for sending up flares.

He was also relieved that he'd not seen anyone lying in ambush in the terminal or any of the lines waiting at the gates. Nor had he spotted Pars Jannor, and that both puzzled and bothered him. The old actor had virtually kidnapped him from the Inverness Hospital, and it wasn't right that he should have given up now.

Unless, he thought as he buckled himself in, he was wrong, and it was Jannor who had taken the fangs and was now a few hundred miles north of them, doing whatever had to be done with the damned things.

He shook his head.

No. Unlikely. If Jannor had known where the fangs were, he wouldn't have bothered with Lincoln.

Dutch Grange, then? But if he had the fangs, then why was Tania not trying to give him the slip, strand him in Dallas, or somehow contrive to lose him in New York?

Did that mean there was someone else?

Jesus, he thought as the plane bounced along the runway and bounced into the air; Jesus.

"There!" Tania exclaimed suddenly, lunging across him to point out the window.

Swallowing a yelp, he blinked in barely restrained panic. "What?"

"The Red River, Lincoln. Part of the border between Texas and Oklahoma. See?"

With an effort he looked, and saw nothing more than a gap in the dull brown landscape below. It may have been blue to indicate water, but he couldn't really tell. What fascinated him more was the land itself—seemingly flat, clearly divided into fields and pastures, and not a sign of human habitation anywhere save for the occasional streak of what might have been a road.

At least there aren't any mountains to hit, he thought. God, it was flat! Where the hell did all the bad guys hide when all the posses chased them out of town?

Suddenly the plane bucked violently, and Tania was thrown back into her seat with a surprised grunt. Before either had a chance to question the plane's action, the pilot's voice came over the public address system, calm and without emotion: "Attendants, please clear the aisles. Passengers, please return to your seats. We seem to have a bit of unexpected turbulence up ahead, nothing to worry about."

The seatbelt sign pinged on.

Lincoln looked out the window and saw that the horizon curving ahead of them was smeared a dark gray.

"What?" Tania asked.

"Looks like some clouds."

The plane dipped again, sharply, and Linc barely had time to put a trembling hand to his stomach before the blue outside vanished.

Oh, he thought.

The port wing rose as the plane swung to the right and climbed, then pitched forward as if it had run out of sky. The engines surged. Someone behind him gasped, someone else uttered a curse.

"Attendants, please secure the galleys," the pilot asked politely.

Tania squinted at the window. "It's dark out there."

"It happens," Linc told her, "when the sun goes away."

She gripped his hand tightly.

"And when the blood goes away," he said, prying loose her fingers, "the hand turns blue."

The plane dipped yet again, and swayed sickeningly side to side. The engines bellowed, the plane climbed, and when Lincoln checked the window he could see nothing but wing.

Not good, he judged, and perspiration worked its way coldly through his shirt.

The plane shuddered.

When he checked again, there was nothing but grey.

Another prolonged drop sent something crashing to the floor in the rear galley, and the pilot said, "Attendants, sit down!" There was no attempt at courtesy; the order was crisp, clear, and terrifying.

A woman began to cry; a man began to pray; a child began to wail up near the cockpit.

For a few seconds Lincoln watched the heads of the passengers ahead of him bob and jerk, but when his stomach began to fill with bile, he closed his eyes and tried to tell himself he was only on a bumpy road in the middle of nowhere. Sooner or later the bus driver was going to get them back on the highway and all would be smooth again, no question about it.

Right, he thought.

And began to wonder about Old Alice, Macon, Palmer, and Carmel getting along without him, when someone in the cockpit, unaware he was still on the air, said, "Shit, Bill, . . . look . . . ing down . . . damn."

# Thirteen

The muffled strain of the engines was the only sound in the cabin for a disturbingly long time after a loud click indicated the belated severing of communications between passengers and crew.

From behind the security of his closed eyes, Lincoln told himself it was pilot talk, nothing but pilot talk and there's nothing to worry about.

. . . *ing down* could mean anything. Looking down, sweeping down, calling down, sliding down. It doesn't have to mean *going* down. It's pilot talk. Technical stuff. He probably wouldn't understand it even if they tried to explain it to him, which they wouldn't because he didn't want to know.

"Incredible," Tania whispered in something like awe.

The plane shuddered so vigorously he had to stiffen to prevent his temple from slamming into the bulkhead, and in doing so nearly sprained his neck. He would have felt aggrieved if he hadn't been so terrified.

Then a double thump beneath his feet made him squeeze his eyes even more tightly shut—lord, the pilot, in eternally winged optimism, was actually lowering the landing gear. Probably in preparation for an emergency setdown. On a cow, most likely, or in twenty feet of snow. He hoped he'd be able to pry his fingers loose from the armrest when the time came to do . . .

The seat trembled, the cabin vibrated. He began an instant series of deep breaths through his mouth, partly to seek the calm that had deserted him, partly to avoid the distinct stench of fear that filled the cabin.

A finger poked his chest and he grabbed at it, missed, and opened his eyes to glare the obviously hysterical woman into submission. He still wasn't finished saying his goodbyes, was still trying to understand why he was more calm now, relatively speaking, than he had been when Irene tried to give him a third eye. But Tania was too busy peering out the window to look at him, a rapt expression on her face that told him she'd probably already picked out her personal angel.

Then he noticed that the others, though pale and drawn and swaying jerkily, were also craning for a glimpse outside. He turned his head. It had not been his intention to pick out the place of his demise, but since it appeared to be the convention at times like this, curiosity overwhelmed his basic terror.

For a moment he didn't quite grasp what he was looking at.

He saw the clouds—above them and menacingly dark; he saw the ground—below them and still depressingly flat; and he saw the air between, ripped through with a fascinating amount of white stuff that had turned that flat ground from brown to pure white. A white that even from up here he could tell was not simply a thin layer laid down just a few minutes ago for the pleasure of the approaching holidays.

The plane sagged alarmingly.

The pilot told them all to prepare for the landing.

Oh god, Linc thought, and wished the man would scream, just once, just for the hell of it.

Tania wriggled with excitement, and he could stand it no longer—he grabbed her arm and forced her back into her seat, glowered at her, and suggested that she'd be better off saying a prayer or two instead of acting like a kid.

"But I'm home!" she exulted.

"In what sense?" he grumbled.

She gripped his cheek with two fingers and swiveled his head back to the window, through which he noted that the ground was considerably closer than before. There were buildings down there, in fact, and great swatches of black among the white that told him they were about to land at the airport.

If the wind, he thought as he gripped the armrests and fought the plane's swaying, didn't take them back to Texas first.

The wheels touched. The plane bounced. The wheels touched again and held, and spontaneous applause broke out around him, laughter and high-pitched chatter to signal relief. Tania gave him a quick hug. An attendant hurried down the aisle, a clipboard in her hand.

And through the window he could see nothing but snow.

"I am not amused," he said fifteen minutes later, as they hurried through the jetway, shivering against the bitter cold that seeped through the curving walls. "You'd think they'd warn us we were heading for a storm."

Tania, however, was eagerly scanning the reception area, and he didn't care for her expectant look. Since there'd been no time for a call, how could she possibly hope to meet someone? Unless she'd made her call in New York while he was making his and had arranged for a committee of sorts to take them wherever they had to go, which destination he had no knowledge of because he was still playing it all by ear.

As they entered the terminal, he noticed the heavy coats, warm hats, boots—every sign that the storm was no idle flurry. And as he pushed through to a clear spot on the opposite wall, he heard talk of a blizzard, worst in years, and acid complaints that they shouldn't have permitted the flight to leave Dallas.

Damn right, he agreed, and on impulse leaned against the wall, folded his arms over his chest, and waited. The debarking passengers were chattering ten to the dozen, many of them grinning widely enough to split their cheeks to their ears. A few stumbled as if in a daze, and one tiny woman looked as though she would scream as soon as anyone touched her.

Tania broke through the milling crowd a moment later, eyes bright and cheeks flushed, but when she beckoned him to come with her, he shook his head.

"What?" she asked, coming to stand beside him.

"Wait," he told her.

A few minutes later the crew stepped through the door. The pilot, his cap shoved back on his head, was livid, his right hand chopping the air emphatically as he snarled to a shorter, similarly uniformed man trying hard to keep up with him. Lincoln walked behind them for several yards, then dropped away and waited for Tania to catch up.

Her question was a tentative touch on the arm.

He nodded toward the crew ducking through a doorway just ahead. "He says he was given the wrong charts."

"What charts? Doesn't he know how to fly here?"

"Weather charts," he explained. "Someone in Dallas gave him the wrong information. He expected turbulence. He didn't expect to have to land in the middle of a blizzard." He brushed a hand down his chest, amazed that it wasn't palsied. "No one did. We were lucky the runway was still clear. The airport is officially closed to all traffic."

She blanched, and he took her arm, squeezed it gently, and walked along the corridor to the escalators that led down to the baggage area. He tried not to think about how someone could deceive a pilot that way; he tried not to pay attention to his legs, which were still trying to stiffen up enough to let him walk without wobbling; he tried without much success to figure out what he was going to do now. So far, he'd been acting without thinking, first annoyed that Clarise had been attacked, then ticked that he'd nearly been shot to death several times. It was not good planning not to have a plan. In point of actual fact, he reminded himself, it was awfully damned stupid.

He saw a sign. "Will Rogers?" he said, slowing, almost stopping.

"Sure," Tania said. "The airport's named after him."

"By politicians he never met, no doubt," he said, grinning for the first time since leaving New York. "They had their revenge after all."

Then he pulled her to one side, out of the flow of passengers heading for their bags. Now that his brain was working again, he noted that there were still quite a few people here, some of them meandering, some with purpose, and he suspected that the storm had been more severe than predicted, thereby stranding a lot of folks who were hard put to find a way back to Oklahoma City, or any of the motels lining the highway between.

Wonderful, he thought.

"So," he said, "what now?"

She looked at him, bemused. "What now?"

"Sure. This is your home, right?"

"Well . . ."

"So?"

"So?"

He waited.

She waited.

"So?" she said.

He nodded.

She cocked her head, ready to listen.

The public address system let the terminal know that the roads to the city were becoming nigh unto impassable and those who were thinking of driving ought to think twice.

"You see," he said quietly, "I could have done a little snooping around. Talked to cabbies, limo people, things like that. Passed around a description or two to see if our cadaverous friend had been here. I could have talked to rental car clerks, aircaps, people like that. With amazing luck I might even have been able to find out where whoever came out here had gone."

"So?"

He pointed at a window. It was white. "It's snowing, Miss Burgoyne. It's a blizzard out there. Between the time they left and we arrived, do you think anyone was dumb enough to come back here just to meet us?"

Her expression became pensive. "They didn't know we were coming," she ventured.

"Not unless someone told them," he answered pointedly.

"Me?" she said, with a palm against the flat of her chest. "You think I called ahead or something?"

He looked at her.

"Irene could have, you know," she said in a pout.

"Irene is probably in jail for international terrorism and attempted murder," he reminded her.

116

"Irene," she reminded him, "is resourceful. And," she added smugly, "Marjorie may not have been implicated."

"Whose side are you on?" he demanded, and didn't wait for an answer. He grabbed her hand and led her onto the escalator, scanning the faces he saw for recognition of some kind, trying unsuccessfully to ignore a spidery sensation at the back of his neck.

"Swell," he muttered when they reached the bottom.

Hundreds of determined travelers were glaring at the empty, revolving baggage carousels, and there were long and not very patient lines at the rental car agencies. The noise level was high, the crowding and shoving filled with frustration, and Tania hesitated as they stepped into the flow. Linc gave her a reassuring wink and gently pulled her along with him, wandering aimlessly, cursing the storm and flinching whenever a gust slapped snow against the glass exit doors. Every so often, someone would stumble inside, shaking snow from a hat and swearing loudly; every so often, someone else would charge outside and vanish into the white wall that cut off the world.

"Linc, we'll have to do something soon," she protested, "or we'll be stuck here."

"I can see that," he said, wondering if he could cut into one of the lines without being torn to shreds.

"We can't get stuck here."

"I know, I know."

"Dutch—"

He stopped.

She stopped.

He looked at her.

She looked at the ceiling.

"Tania," he said, bracing himself against the tide that wanted to drive him into the nearest wall, "did your father take those teeth?"

She shrugged eloquently.

"Tania," he said, putting his hands on her hips and drawing her close so that she wouldn't be able to avoid the look in his eyes, "is it possible that I am out here in the middle of goddamn nowhere because your father is here?"

Her lips parted in blatant invitation.

A woman screamed.

Lincoln looked over Tania's shoulder. "Well," he said.

"What?" she said.

A man shouted, another one shrieked, and the press of the crowd suddenly became urgent as it moved away from the baggage claim area.

Tania looked over her shoulder. "Wow," she said, in a voice that told him he wasn't watching tradition.

Given the fact that this was Oklahoma, he had not been beyond the expectation of seeing a horse or two during his stay; said expectation, however, was centered on said creature gamboling somewhere in a field or a pasture, or trotting sedately along the roadside. It did not include the possibility that such a beast—three of them, actually—would be high-stepping their way through a crowded airport terminal in the middle of a blizzard.

Nor did it include the fact that the riders, all of them masked and wearing black cowboy outfits under flapping black dusters, would be carrying rifles and, suddenly, firing them at the ceiling.

The panic-stricken crowd screamed as one and surged toward the escalators, the exits, the counters, the carousels, and the restrooms, forcibly separating him from Tania, who cried out his name as she was carried away.

He tried to follow, but the rifles fired again, and pieces of acoustic ceiling showered over the heads of those in the way. A horse protested the noise by rear-ing, instantly redoubling the hysteria and slamming him into the back wall before he could brace himself. He grunted at the pain in his right hip, grunted again when someone tripped over him and sent him sprawling to the floor.

A foot landed on his side.

A heel came down on his wrist.

He tried to regain his feet, using the wall to brace himself, but was thrown down again when a suitcase thudded into his knee.

I'm going to be trampled, he realized, and forced himself to his hands and knees, seeing nothing but legs and shoes and boots and an incongruous pair of bare feet. Something collided with his buttocks, and he pitched forward before he could catch himself, his forehead cracking on the floor, his teeth biting into his tongue. A foot skidded off his right shoulder. Someone stumbled over his legs and fell atop him, scrambled off and was replaced by someone else.

The rifles fired.

He spat blood and bulled his way up again, lifted his head and saw a door not five feet away.

He swung both fists wildly as he lurched to his feet, not caring now who he struck, who he shoved away, damning them all when he was unable to make it higher than a crouch. His vision was blurring rapidly. His limbs were weary from trying to keep himself open. And it was as clear as the elbow ramming into his stomach that the horsemen were herding the people toward him, pressing them in, stealing the air, feeding panic with panic and burying any thoughts of concern for others.

The door.

If he could only reach the door . . .

The rifles.

Screaming.

119

Then the door began to swing outward against the press of bodies. At first he thought it was his imagination. Then he thought it was foolish for anyone inside to try to get outside during a full-fledged riot. But he lurched toward it, praying that it wouldn't close, and grinned in relief when a hand grabbed his arm. It yanked, and he popped through like a cork from a bottle, spilling to his knees and gasping for air.

"God," he said, "thanks."

And looked up just in time to see the swift descent of something that looked just like an iron pipe.

There was no time to react.

There was only a sound like splitting bone, a black fire, and darkness.

# Fourteen

All in all, Lincoln decided, it was better than a plane crash.

Though he hadn't yet opened his eyes, he knew without a moment's doubt that he hadn't been killed by the blow. He didn't question the miracle; tempting fate wasn't good for the soul. He just lay there, on something hard and cool and damp to the touch, and waited until he was sure he could move without setting off explosions somewhere inside his skull. Meanwhile, he noted that the terminal, if that's where he still was, had fallen into silence save for the distant and mournful voice of the wind trying to get in. There were no shots, no sirens, no screams, no sound of running feet.

Water dripped monotonously somewhere ahead of him, the sound oddly hollow, oddly touched with an echo.

Tania. Where the hell was Tania?

His head told him it had more important things to worry about at the moment.

All right, he decided, you can either lie here all day, Blackthorne, or get your ass in gear and get up.

Five minutes later he told himself that he really hadn't been offering a choice. There was a job to be done, and someone was going to pay for giving him a headache.

With teeth clenched and arms rigid, he opened his eyes, bracing himself, blinking, and struggling not to shake his head to clear the fog from his eyes.

"Jesus," he said.

His voice echoed lightly.

Eventually, the fog dissipated and he blinked again, squinting until the light didn't seem quite so bright. He put a hand to the top of his head and began a slow, methodical prodding until, with a shout he only barely contained, he found the place where he'd been struck. It was tender. There was a lump that, if he'd worn hats, would prevent him from wearing them for at least the rest of the year. But when he held the hand in front of his eyes, he could see no blood.

Small favors, he decided as he examined the rest of him and began to feel the bruises and the aches being trampled had provided; small favors, count your blessings, look on the bright side, every cloud and all that.

"God."

He was propped against a white-and-blue tiled wall, facing the glaring white porcelain of a men's room bank of urinals. To his left were the wood-door stalls, to his right a tiled partition on the other side of which he assumed was the exit. The floor was spotted with smears and puddles of dark water. The stench of disinfectant wrinkled his nose.

Carefully, slowly, a painful inch at a time and grateful he wasn't taller, he eased himself to his feet and leaned back against a row of basins, head down until successive waves of dizziness had passed. Then he turned around.

"Oh," he whispered, "my god. What the hell have you done now?"

His hair looked as if his head had been stuck in a wind tunnel, his face was blotched with severe and vivid abrasions, laced with tiny scratches, and there was a thin layer of caked blood over his lower lip and chin. His topcoat was streaked and wrinkled, the collar half folded under, one button hanging by a thread that, the moment he touched it, snapped and sent the button into the sink.

He retrieved it, counting it a victory, and shoved it into a pocket.

Then, with partially held breath, he checked under his arm and on his forearm, smiling grimly when gun and knife were found, wincing when the movement renewed the lease on the fire in his head.

Be brave, he ordered, and slipped the coat off, folded it as best he could under the assault in his skull, and placed it over the sink beside him. Then he turned on the water and looked back at his reflection.

"Well, this is another fine mess, ain't it?"

The reflection sneered.

The quiet squeak of a hinge as the door was opened, and he tensed, cupping his hands under the faucet quickly and lowering his head so he could douse himself and, in virtually the same movement, straightened again to watch a burly, suited man stroll in, glance at him, and make directly for the stalls.

"Goddamn weather," the man grumbled. "Makes you wanna spit, don't it?"

Linc grunted in the common language of strangers conversing in a strange bathroom, and splashed his face again, more vigorously this time.

Another man came in, wearing a battered western hat and a well-used sheepskin coat. He went to the urinals, boots heavy and loud on the floor, and Linc continued his makeshift ablutions, sighing at the touch of cool water on his skin, shoving his hands back through his hair to give it some ridiculous semblance of order.

The man in the stalls continued complaining about the weather, punctuating his disgust with a virtuoso display of masculine flatulence.

The man in the sheepskin coat came over to the sinks and washed his hands without soap. Linc glanced at him and smiled politely, taking in the close-cropped dark beard sans mustache, and the amazingly deep dimple in the center of his chin. The closer look proved he wasn't a young man at all, and Linc rechecked his own reflection, for a second wondering what he'd look like when he was tipping time's scales toward terminally overweight.

Not that it mattered. The first thing he had to do, once he could walk without ricocheting off the walls, was find out what had happened to Tania. Perhaps she was still out there, too modest to knock, too shy to come barging in; perhaps she didn't even know he was in here, in which case she might be frantically searching the building for him; and perhaps she had decided that he'd decided she'd left, and he'd already left on a wild and fruitless search in the middle of a blizzard.

Sure, he thought. Right.

The man in the stalls left, bellowing now about millions lost because pilots weren't what they used to be when they flew by the seats of their pants in all kinds of weather. Soft, he declared, all the goddamn pilots were too goddamned soft.

The man at the sink took off his hat and shook his head. "Big mouth, huh?" he said.

Linc grunted. He didn't want conversation; he wanted to know where Tania was.

"Damned fool'll probably try to bribe someone to take him out of here, bet you dollars to doughnuts. That kind always does. Damned Texan. Don't know shit about civilized people, y'know what I mean?"

Linc stood away from the sink to better examine his reflection. He nodded. Distance was an improvement. He reached for his coat.

The man at the sink put his hand on it and smiled.

"Excuse me," Lincoln said, and yanked the coat from under the palm.

"No problem." He picked up his hat, combed his fingers through hair that, for want of a better description, just might be called sparse, and added, "You ready to go?"

Linc drew himself up. "I beg your pardon?"

The man pointed toward the door. "Go. Out. Leave. You speak English or what?"

Linc put on the coat, stifling the wince when half his muscles protested, and the other half were too numb. Great; I've just been trampled and coshed, and now I've got a men's room pervert.

The man put on his hat, adjusted it in the mirror, and said, "You are Lincoln Blackthorne, right?"

He froze. There were an awful lot of people in this world these days who knew who he was before he knew who they were; it was getting to be a habit, and he didn't like it one bit.

The man faced him, hands thrust into his pockets. "Well ain't ya or ain't ya?"

"I suppose."

"You leavin' or what?"

"I guess."

The man frowned. "You sure you speak English?"

"Only to those with whom I have a nodding acquaintance."

The man blinked a few times, readjusted his hat, then slapped his stomach and laughed. "Well, Jesus and don't that cook a goose!" He stuck out his hand. "Sorry, m'friend, but I forgot my manners."

Warily, Lincoln shook it. "And the name?"

125

"Shit, I thought you knew. I'm Dutch Grange. You ever heard of me?"

As much as Lincoln could tell from shape and design, the vehicle Grange took him to on the terminal's roof parking lot looked like a Jeep; on the inside, however, there was more padding, more cushions, more leather, more glowing dials and gleaming switches than in any cockpit in the history of modern aviation.

But it was warm, which was more than he could say for the outside, where the wind had threatened to crack his skin wide, where the snow had blinded him until he'd protected his eyes with both hands.

As soon as he was seated and buckled in, the snow melted from his hair and coat, pooling on the floor and slipping coldly into his shoes; his face thawed and he worked his mouth to be sure he still had control of his muscles; and when Grange clambered in after swiping at the windshield with his gloved hands, he was astounded at the way the Jeep pulled away and down the ramp without a whisper or a slide.

"My baby," Grange told him, patting the dashboard lovingly. "Takes me just about anywhere I ask her, and a few places I don't."

"You're going to need it now," he answered.

The wind rocked the Jeep, drove the snow, hid most of the lights until it was nearly full dark. There were no other moving vehicles on the road and, when they left the airport for the highway, heading, Grange said, away from Oklahoma City, he could have been in an amusement park ride for all the sensation of movement and time he felt.

"Just for the hell of it," he said as Grange cautiously picked up speed, "where are we going?"

"JO Bar Ranch," Grange answered, leaning over the wheel to stare through the windshield. The wipers were strong; the snow was even stronger.

"Which is?"

"My place. Didn't Tania tell you?"

"Some things she did, some things she didn't."

Grange nodded once. "She's like that. Always has been. Takes her a bit to come out of her shell."

Linc considered that for several minutes, and considered as well how he was going to make it back to civilization when the Jeep, moving far too swiftly now, upended and left him stranded in the middle of the blizzard, miles away from anyplace he didn't want to be in the first place.

"So," he said finally, "are we going to explain to each other what we're doing here, or are we going to play coy and string this conversation out over the next twenty years?"

Grange didn't look at him right away, but when he did, Linc smiled. He was feeling somewhat better, certainly better than being dead, and since he already knew what part Dutch had played in this game, he felt no qualms about going first, although he left out a few things, such as Clarise and the deadly matrons, without any reason to do so save for a caution flag raised at the back of his head.

And he made no comment when he was told between frequent imprecations at the weather that Grange had fully expected to meet his daughter at the airport, thinking she had recovered the fangs, which she was supposed to have gotten from Lincoln once Lincoln had found them for her in New York. How she was going to get them, he insisted quietly, was her business; he had other troubles these days, and his daughter had always been able to take care of herself.

"Really," he said, taken aback at the apparent callousness of the remark. "And where is she now?"

The Jeep bucked against the wind, the snow in the headlamps' glow more like darts than gentle flakes.

"Around, I imagine."

Linc bristled. "She might have been kidnapped by those idiot cowboys, you know."

Grange shrugged the possibility.

"She might even be dead."

"No chance," the man insisted. "No chance." And swore when the Jeep skidded into a slow motion spin that took them across the highway in eerie silence. When it was done, and the vehicle back in the proper lane, he patted the wheel and whistled.

Linc, after finding use of his lungs again, wanted to reach over and throttle him. "What do you mean, no chance? Those guys tried to kill us."

"Nope. Just you."

"Ah."

"Weren't my doing, though, don't think that."

"Who, me?"

And Grange laughed. "Pardner," he said, "right now I'm trying to get us home in one piece, if it's all the same to you. After that, I'll worry about the girl, okay? But believe me, she's not dead, not by a long shot. They wouldn't do that, not until they're sure."

"Sure?"

"Yeah."

"About what?"

"About the fangs."

"What about them?"

"Who's got them."

"Beats me."

"Exactly."

Somewhere in all that, perfect sense had been made, and somehow he'd been told that Tania was safe as long as the fangs were still missing. And from Grange's attitude, if not his curious way of dispensing the English language, Linc was positive neither he nor his daughter truly knew their whereabouts.

"Maybe it's Pars Jannor," he said, regretting it instantly when Grange nearly ran off the road.

"That sonofabitch," the little man spat. "You know what he's up to? Really up to, I mean?"

Linc didn't know, and went on to say that it was no concern of his because all he wanted to do was get to the JO Bar, get warm, and get out of Oklahoma as quickly as he could.

"With the fangs," Grange said flatly.

"That's right."

The wind howled, and the snow sounded like birdshot against the doors, the windshield.

"You know I want them too."

"That," Lincoln said, "is a bridge yet to be crossed."

Grange turned his head and looked at him for so long that Linc had to point at the highway several times before he got the hint.

"So does Jannor."

"So does Jannor what?" Linc said, groaning when he realized that he was going to find out whether he wanted to know or not. Which, as he'd said before, he didn't.

"Want the fangs."

"Watch the road, Dutch."

"He's gonna rule the world."

"Sure. With an army of dentists at his side, drills at the ready. Dutch, just watch the road, okay?"

Grange looked at him again. "You stupid or what, pardner?"

"Alive," he said, pointing. "And meaning to stay that way."

"Then you'd better think about them fangs, Blackthorne, because once Jannor gets hold of them, you and me, we're dead. And everybody else you ever knew in your life."

# Fifteen

A snowplow lumbered toward them, a beast with flashing amber and red eyes, and the spray it cascaded over the Jeep's hood nearly sent the smaller vehicle into a snowbank. By the time the wipers had cleared the windshield, Lincoln realized that he could see his breath, and that the windows were beginning to fog up, the fog turning to frost around the edges.

"Damned heater," Grange said, punching the dashboard. "This thing never works when you want it to."

"I thought you said it was perfect."

The old man shrugged. "Perfect is what I tell it to keep it running; shit is what I think when I'm in twenty-degree weather and the goddamned heater doesn't work."

Swell, Linc thought.

A crossroads sign was speared by the headlamps,

and Grange took the wheel hard, skidding them off the highway to the right, onto a much more narrow road that might have been plowed when the storm first began, but was now inches below the surface, and the wheels began to grind.

The springs, like the heater, weren't up to par.

Linc burrowed his hands into his pockets, tucked his chin close to his chest and scrunched down as best he could, trying to double his body heat back on itself.

There was no sense looking out the window to see where he was—all he could see was white, and once in a while, black.

And the wind, always the wind, with no buildings, no hills, no mountains to temper it as it wailed and keened eastward, the snow bulleting ahead.

"It's like this," Grange began.

"Forget it," Linc said. He didn't want to know. There were lots of secrets in the universe to which he wasn't privy, and he enjoyed the ignorance. It kept him out of trouble. He reminded the former actor that all he cared about was helping a friend who, right at this moment, was lying in a hospital because a handful of old farts were squabbling over gems.

"Old farts?" Grange said in a high, insulted voice.

"I take it back," he said quickly when Grange snapped his gaze from the road. "A slip of the tongue."

"More respect," the man muttered. "Old don't mean decrepit."

Lincoln considered Alice and the Crowleys and accepted the point well taken. What he didn't accept was the belief that these rubies, no matter how they'd been configured, were able to send a man or woman shrieking back to their youth.

On the other hand, people were nearly dying, and belief in this case was nearly as good as fact.

"Jannor," Grange said.

131

"Drive," Lincoln ordered.

"See, all I want out of this, if Tania told you and I guess she did being her father's daughter and all, all I want is a chance to make another picture, you know? Make westerns popular again, back in the saddle, and all that crap."

"Yes, but—"

"Jannor, though, he don't give a damn, see. Acting ain't what he did anywayn, and he sure as hell isn't gonna start now, you know what I mean?"

"Sort of, but—"

Grange hunched over the wheel, almost nose to nose with the windshield. "Back in them days, what got him was the power. You know, the directors, the producers, telling everyone what to do and how to do it. That's why he played monsters and things, because of the power. He loved it, the bastard. He actually loved it."

"I can see that, Dutch, but—"

The old man stabbed a finger at Linc's chest without looking. "He figures, see, that if he can make himself young again, the dumb ass, he can use the money he squirreled away to start building himself a base from which he can radiate lines of pressure on those political and economic groups who can do him the most good—which means, in purely layman's terms, of course, that what he's after is enough money so that he can tell the whole world when to squat and when to shit. It ain't acting he's after, Blackthorne, it's power."

Linc puzzled for a moment over the shift of expressive gears, and shrugged when he decided that as long as the man was driving, he had the right to be Churchill if he wanted.

"Hard job," he said, when Grange fell silent.

"Not so bad," the old man countered. "He gets himself some guys who think the way he does, or who can be made to think the way he does, he promises them practically immortality with the damned fangs except when they die and then that's all she wrote, and he can do whatever he wants."

"With what?"

Grange did look over then, eyes oddly dark in the dashboard light. "Terrorism, young man. He wants to make today's terrorists look like the East Side Kids."

Linc almost laughed. "You're joking."

Grange snorted.

The Jeep turned again, through an open gate and onto an even smaller, more narrow road that switched back and forth, confusing his sense of direction. The wind punched them from behind; the snow was inches deeper.

"You're not joking."

"Jannor knows about extortion, Blackthorne. He knows it'll make him too rich to touch."

"He's nuts," Linc told him. "It'll never work."

"Don't know about that," the old man said, "but it seems to me, pardner, that if you can put an airline out of business, and cripple an oil company, and knock out the resources of a major automobile company with a few well-placed bombs or some clever blackmail, or whatever, you can pretty much do what you damn well please."

"Never work."

"Not even when you have guys who ain't afraid of kicking the bucket?"

"Never."

"Would you take a chance putting a bomb in some oil tank farm if you're getting paid with twenty, maybe thirty years of new life?"

"Impossible."

"You want to walk back to New Jersey? You want to take the train, for god's sake, and not get back in time to see your grandchildren get married?"

133

My god, that's diabolical, Linc thought, and understood with a sudden chill that had nothing to do with the storm that Jannor, assuming the worst and giving him his goals, would not stop with making the United States knuckle under. It was not inconceivable that the man, with an army that didn't mind dying and with power gained at home, could become a contemporary, Hitler-like madman.

"He's crazy."

"I thought you knew that."

"If he's not careful, he'll blow up the world!"

"He's crazy, but he's not stupid."

"Tell that," Lincoln said, "to the Russians."

The road straightened, and Grange leaned back as if relaxing. "Any minute now," he said, wiping his brow with a forearm. "The lights are out but I don't think I'll hit the porch."

Linc barely heard him. He was thinking, and trying to keep warm, and trying not to let the wind buck him out of the Jeep.

"What about you?" he asked at last.

Grange looked at him, frowning.

"For the sake of argument," he said, "I'll go along with this rejuvenation stuff because Jannor will have to be able to prove it to his people or they'll tear him apart. So. What about you?"

The old man smiled. "I can't deny, pardner, it would be something, being young again. But I was already there. And I made all my friends." The smile drifted away. "Most of them are gone now. I don't think I'd want to go through all that again."

"Movies," Linc said.

"That's right."

"Cowboy movies."

"Got it in one."

"Because without them—"

"I'm dead."

Shit, he thought. Why the hell can't the bad guys just be plain bad anymore? In the old days, which in his case weren't all that long ago, the bad guys were so perfectly rotten he never had to worry about motives and psychology and complications like that.

The good guys were over here, the bad guys were over there, and when somebody yelled, "Go!", they beat the hell out of each other because that's what they did.

Shit.

And *shit* again when the Jeep came to a halt in front of a house that suddenly popped out of the storm. A white, three-story home, purely Victorian and purely out of place in the middle of Oklahoma, with a wide, pillared porch smothered in gingerbread, high arched windows, tasseled curtains, and a glowing amber light over the front door.

He looked at Grange, who was grinning.

"This," Linc said in reluctant admiration, "is a crock, you know."

The man laughed and slapped Lincoln's knee. "I know, I know. But I learned a few things when I made them pictures, pardner, and one of them is how to make a homestead look like back home. How can you deny an old man when he lives in a place like this? All alone. In the middle of nowhere. Banks breathing down his scrawny neck, his daughter weeping at his side." His laugh trebled until he started choking. "Jesus, Blackthorne, you should see your damned face."

Long hallways, double parlors, a huge kitchen, a den, a dining room that seated fifteen with ease, four bedrooms upstairs, and a finished attic on top. Bathtubs with lion's-paw feet. Tiffany-style lamps.

135

Monstrously overstuffed furniture. A fireplace with a raised stone hearth and white bear rug. A basement finished off and fixed up as a carpenter's workroom. Closets bigger than some apartments he'd seen. An attached garage that held three cars and was designed to look like a carriage house.

Behind the house, a large corral, several outbuildings, a bunkhouse, fields.

"I'll be damned," he said when the rapid tour was over and he was sitting in a wing chair in the front parlor, a snifter of brandy in his hand.

"You pick up stuff here and there," Grange told him, coat shed and worn flannel shirt darkly gleaming in the firelight. "You get to know the carpenters on the set and they make you something in exchange for something else. Strictly against the rules, but what the hell."

Wine draperies, dark red wallpaper, oriental carpets on polished hardwood floors.

"It's a bitch, ain't it?" Grange said.

Linc nodded and watched the flames in the fireplace, took a deep breath and felt the old man's spell fall away, like spider webs curling away from a match.

"Tania," he said quietly.

"Now look—"

"No," Lincoln said, looking up without lifting his head. "No, Mr. Grange, it's over. A nice place you have here and all that, and I'd love to spend the night on a goose feather mattress listening to the hands singing 'Home on the Range,' but do you realize that except when I ask you, you don't even mention your daughter? If," he added flatly, "she's your daughter at all."

Grange set his glass down on the table between them and pushed himself to his feet. His age showed now, the windlines in his face, the white in his beard, the way he didn't quite shuffle because his legs were giving

out, the way he cocked his head because his hearing
wasn't as perfect as it was.

The cowboy was gone; the old man had come home.

"She helped me when I died, you know," he said,
standing before the hearth, firelight shifting shadows
across his eyes, across his cheeks.

"Don't start."

"We made a deal."

Linc waited.

Liver-spotted hands slipped into loose pockets. "She
didn't want me involved at all, you see, not at the beginning. I damn near got myself killed, as it were, getting out of that fool country, and damn near again
when that fool buddy of mine who played the under-
taker at the funeral forgot the stupid breathing device.
Jesus damn and bite the crows, but it was close there
for a while.

"But when I got out, Tania and I made a kind of
pact—she would help me sell the rubies and start our
own company with whatever we got, and I wouldn't ask
questions about how she got them in the first place."

He swung his head around.

"Those men at the airport, dudes on horseback?"

"How could I forget?"

"They've got her."

He straightened and put down the snifter. "Where?"

"Next ranch over."

"How do you know that?"

"I saw them. She was gonna give me a signal, see,
that you got the rubies, and I was gonna create a diver-
sion so she could get away and meet me here later."

"Oh," he said. "And leave me stranded at the terminal, thinking I'd give up and go home like a good boy."

Grange shrugged. "She said you were a tailor."

"I am."

The old man shrugged again. "Whatever. But them

137

idiots must've followed me and screwed things up and now here we are and she's over there, and I ain't worried because they ain't gonna hurt her, like I said before. All we got to do, less you got ants biting your ass, is wait for the storm to end and then go get her."

Linc tried to remember if the death penalty was in force in this part of the world. "I don't want to sound stupid, but why didn't we go there before?"

"Are you kidding? It's snowing like a bitch out there!"

"You know," Linc said, "it seems to me that in all those movies that you love so much, the father comes to the good guy, tells him what's up, and the good guy straps on his guns and goes get them. He doesn't sit around chewing the fat, waiting for the sun to come out."

"Hey," Grange said, spreading his hands, "you want to suit up, get your guns and go? Then be my guest and go. And I'll take pictures of you trying to draw with nine pairs of gloves on and you looking like a teddy bear with all them coats."

This, Linc decided, is the damnedest mess I've ever been in.

"Who are they? Jannor's boys?"

"Hell no. Jannor has one guy working for him, that's all. Name's Judd Shelger. Looks like a corpse more than Jannor does. Used to be the man's dresser, costumes and stuff. Poke your eye out just for fun, sweet guy."

"Ah." Probably the bastard that ran Clarise down. "Then they belong to the ladies, right? Iddle and Yoman?"

Grange shook his head. "Them is no ladies, but you already know that. Nope, they work on their own. They got a whiff of what Jannor was up to. I think all they want is to give back a half-dozen of their chins."

Linc closed his eyes slowly. "Then the gentlemen on the horses are someone new in this game?"

"Nope."

"Damn," he said, "don't be so negative, huh?"

"You ever hear of a guy called Onbrous? Jesse Onbrous?"

"Nope, and I don't want to, either." With a brief, mirthless smile he stood and went to the first of the two pair of tall windows that overlooked the porch. Pulling aside the heavy drapery, he watched the storm in the porch light, and felt the cold penetrating the glass.

Suddenly, with an expression of pained resignation, he leaned closer to the panes. "Hey, Dutch?"

"It was his so-called production office back in New York," Grange said. "He's the one who took the fangs from me when I got back to the States."

His breath fogged the glass, and he wiped it away with one hand. "Hey, Dutch, didn't you say all the lights were out?"

"Indeed he did," a voice said gravely from the other side of the room. "A careless mistake."

And just as he turned, someone shouted, someone screamed, and someone else tested the resiliency of his skull.

# Sixteen

The guy who said man is a creature of habit ought to be parboiled and flayed by nearsighted nuns, Lincoln complained as he struggled to his hands and knees, waiting for the golden sparks to leave his vision alone. He supposed he ought to be getting used to be being slugged by now, but there was definitely something lacking in the way it was done—no finesse, just a belt across the head and leave him for dead.

He was behind the chair, and though he heard no other sound save the goddamned wind, he took his time crawling away from it, heading for the fire which was disturbingly lower than it had been when he'd arrived, stopping along the way to grab the snifter and the decanter. Then he maneuvered with no little grunting and moaning until he was seated on the hearth's edge. Blinking away the pain. Rolling one shoulder at a time. Noting that the only light in the room came from the flames behind him.

Dutch was gone.

That figured.

He poured himself some brandy and dared the experts to damn him when he took it at a gulp and poured himself another.

There was no sign of a struggle save for an overturned lamp by the couch and a folding of the carpet near the entrance to the front hall. When he stared across the hall into the dining room, he could see nothing but shadow.

In and out? he wondered, the snifter poised at his lips. No, they had already been here, listening. But he couldn't understand why they'd chosen that particular moment to barge in and conk him and take Dutch away.

If he was gone.

If he wasn't lying in another room, injured, if not dead.

"Oh hell," he muttered sourly. Just when he was getting comfortable, the flames all nice and warm on his back, the brandy doing its work in his stomach, now he had to get up and search the damned house. And if that wasn't bad enough, he could see his breath clouding, which meant that someone had turned the heat off, leaving him only the fire.

With a grunt more for the martyred sound of it than an expression of the pain that momentarily dazzled his eyes, he struggled to his feet, found a cradle of logs near the hearth and dumped three more onto the andirons. Then he reached into his tweed jacket and pulled out the gun, looked at it with extreme distaste that extended far beyond a mere curling of his lip, and went into the foyer. A thermostat was on the wall, shattered, bits of metal and plastic scattered on the floor. A house this size would have more than one regulator, but he doubted he'd find any of them working.

A check through the dining room and the rest of the first floor revealed nothing; the basement was almost as cold as the outside; the second floor was eerily deserted, his footsteps echoing when he paused to listen.

In the attic, which had been divided into a three-room guest apartment, he found a chest with Dutch's wardrobe from some of his pictures. An album let him see what Tania's mother looked like: a frail, lovely woman in Central European garb. Another album contained press clippings of reviews that mentioned Grange, all rather complimentary, none indicating a star.

Of Grange himself and the intruders there was no sign, and as he hurried back down the stairs and braced himself for the cold on opening the front door, he didn't think he'd see anything on the porch either.

He was right.

The snow had already reached the top of the steps, and that which had been blown over the railing was banked against the wall, nearly touching the sills. The Jeep was gone. He saw what might have been tracks, vehicles and people, but it was full dark now, and it might only have been shadow.

"So," he said, returning to the parlor to watch his fire blast at the flue, "now what, genius?"

There was a telephone on a sideboard next to the archway that led to the back parlor, and he grunted when he picked up the receiver and heard no dial tone; a second telephone in the kitchen had been yanked from the wall.

It was clear they expected him either to remain inside and nurse his aching head until the storm had blown over, or attempt an escape and freeze to death before he ever reached the road or the neighboring ranch. Neither alternative was terribly attractive, but no matter how many times he paced through the

142

rooms, poked in closets, jumped at shadows, he finally couldn't think of anything else to do but sit, and wait, and curse the day he'd ever gotten involved with such loonies.

It wasn't as if he didn't try to be a good tailor. God knew he worked his fingers to the bone making clothes for those who didn't appreciate his skill, as well as clothes for those who understood from the start that there were few within reach who could speak to cloth the way he could, cajole and persuade and once in a while thrash it into shape. God knew he had tried to make a decent life for himself when all was said and done, and was it his fault that people kept coming up to him and asking him for favors that, had he any brains at all, he'd refuse but couldn't because he was such a soft-hearted chump?

Damn.

And double damn what now, when he heard an engine approaching the house.

Quickly, gun still in hand, he stood to one side of the window and peered out. There was light out there, headlamps aiming at the house, aiming at the sky, as something bumped and jounced across the snow toward him.

He didn't move.

The vehicle skidded to a halt at the foot of the steps: Grange's Jeep, but it wasn't Grange who stepped out and took the stairs at a leap, stamping his feet as he reached the front door and yanked it open without knocking.

Linc hurriedly dropped to the floor in the position where he'd been left, and couldn't imagine anyone who'd be dumb enough to think he hadn't come to by now. On the other hand, there was always a first time, and he held his breath and closed his eyes, gunhand tucked beneath him, while he listened to footsteps tramp from the hall to the parlor.

Then he remembered the renewed fire, and looked up with a bright smile when the barrel of a cold gun pressed against his head.

Palmer's revolver was handed over without a fuss, and he quite properly held his arms over his head while a thin, slightly balding man went through the motions of frisking him before gesturing his return to the wing chair. The man's coat, a heavy monstrosity with a black fur collar, was tossed with a flourish and matching scarf onto the couch, Palmer's weapon beneath; his hat, a wide-brimmed, low-crowned affair was tossed onto the coat; his gloves, black leather with gold straps at the wrists and stripped off one finger at a time, were tossed onto the hat. Then the man positioned himself on the hearth with his back to the fire and his hands clasped behind his waist.

Linc was too bored to make a move. Besides, the man still held the gun and could fire any number of distressing shots before he even got out of the chair.

"You don't know me," the man said, rocking on his heels, holding his head high.

"You do commercials, right?"

The man's eyes widened, and his nostrils actually flared. "You mean, *act*? You mean . . . act?"

Oh Jesus, he thought wearily, and flung one leg over an armrest.

"Okay, you're Jesse Onbrous. You live in the ranch next to this one. You have Dutch and Tania in your possession, and you're here to make a deal for their release. A classic hostage type situation in which you hold all the cards, the upper hand, a full house aces high. Am I right or am I right?"

"The Hooded Demon," the man said, his face darkening as his temper shortened.

"No, you're not."

The man pointed, his head back so far his nose aimed at the ceiling.

"Me neither. I'm a tailor."

"Imbecile!"

He fought to deny it, but the way things were going, he wasn't sure he could without telling an outright lie.

The front door slammed open, and he peered around the chair's wing, mildly intrigued but not terribly worried about someone else entering the game. He had had a feeling, because he knew Onbrous hadn't driven over himself. In fact, he seriously doubted if Onbrous ever did anything himself. He wondered if the man knew Clarise.

When the cowboy walked in, he worried.

It was one of the men he'd seen rampaging at the airport, face hidden but black from hair to boots, but it wasn't until he had taken off the duster and gloves that Linc realized his biology education left something to be desired.

"Jesse," the tall woman said, "it's getting worse."

"It can't get any worse," Linc told her, smiling.

She looked at him blankly, her pallor deepened by the non-color she wore, her height exaggerated by the severe snugness of her clothes and the extent of the spiked heels on her tooled black boots. She was not what he would have called slender, but all that she was was definitely well distributed and well managed by sweater and slacks.

"Blackthorne," Onbrous said by way of introduction.

"Okay," she said, and held her hands out to the fire. "But it's still getting worse. Why isn't he dead?"

"Because it's a clear-cut hostage situation," Linc explained politely from the chair. "You have what I want, and I have what you want."

"Bullshit," she said.

Son, he thought, of a bitch, and swung his leg back down.

"Blackthorne," Onbrous said, arm still out and manicured finger still pointing, "if you wish to lay eyes upon the woman you love again, you will do as you are told, no more and no less."

"Which one?" he asked.

Onbrous wavered. "Which . . one?"

"Which woman?"

"Tania Burgoyne, most certainly," he snapped.

"I don't love her."

The woman in black chuckled.

"But you must! You spent the night together! In New York! The Waldorf Hotel! I know this! You cannot deny it!"

Fascinating, he thought as he recrossed his legs, and thought further that sooner or later all this was going to become suddenly clear and he was going to run shrieking from the house, the hell with the blizzard.

"Listen," he said, ignoring the man and appealing to the woman, "would you translate for me?"

"Sure," she told him, rubbing her palms together, which set up a rippling through her clothes the firelight did nothing but enhance to distraction. "We have the old man and the girl over at our place."

Linc nodded; so far so good.

"The old man has these jewels that Jesse here wants."

Linc almost grinned; this was too good to be true.

"Jesse had them once, but now the old man has them again, and Jesse wants them back." She blew on her nails. "The old man, when we got him back to our place, he said he didn't have them anymore but he said you knew where they were." She buffed her nails across her chest. "So we came back to see if you were dead yet. Since you're not, he, Jesse, wants you to tell

146

him where the jewels are so we can make a few bucks selling them to the highest bidder, which will net us more than trying to fence them around." She buffed a second time and blew softly on her hands. "You get it? Okay?"

"Right," he said, relieved not to hear a single word about rejuvenation.

"Scalia," the thin man warned with a wagging finger, "you tell him too much."

"What difference does it make?" she said. "He's going to die anyway."

"What," Linc asked, "would you have done if I'd been dead when you got here?"

Scalia, examining nails that were long, and black, and unnaturally sharp, shrugged. "Slice the girl up until the old man told the truth, I guess."

"I see."

"Enough!" Onbrous declared, chopping the air with his arm. "Where are the jewels? Tell me now and I shall see that you die swiftly."

Scalia pouted, but didn't protest.

"I don't know."

Scalia smiled.

"You lie!"

"Whatever you say," Linc said, scratching his right forearm. "I came out here to get the . . . jewels for someone you don't know."

"Clarise Mayhew," said the woman.

Great, he thought; just great.

Onbrous waited.

"I don't know where they are. Dutch told me you took them, and he wanted me to help get them back."

"That is a lie!" Onbrous insisted, trembling with indignation. "I do not have them. I did have them, that is true. But I do not have them now. And if you do not have them, then who does have them?"

"Director," Linc exclaimed, getting to his feet. "Jesus Christ, you used to be a director, right?"

"But of course! Do you know me?"

Linc smiled apologetically. "But you don't want to get back into the movies, right?"

"Are you kidding?" Scalia said, chucking the thin man under his pointed chin. "He used to direct Parc Jannor. You ever see those films?"

"Not my fault!"

"He couldn't get a job in the industry if he paid them, no offense, honey. All he wants is the money. It's a lifestyle thing with him, you see."

"The rubies!" Onbrous demanded.

"In a minute," Lincoln said, stepping away from the chair.

"The rubies, you little worm!"

"In a goddamn minute," he snapped back, and gave himself no satisfaction in the way they leaned away from him, exchanging somewhat worried glances. He had his own problems. If these two didn't have the fangs, and the Burgoynes didn't have them, or the two-chinned actresses, or Jannor, or Clarise . . . who did? Where the hell were they? Was there some washed-up producer still to come? Or a second unit director, a sound man, someone in special effects, and while he was at it, what the hell is a best boy?

Jesus!

Suddenly Onbrous began to cough, so violently that Linc turned and watched as the red-faced man doubled over, clamping a vivid blue handkerchief to his mouth. Scalia patted and rubbed his back, frowning in concern before aiming him toward the back parlor, her apparent intent to get him to the kitchen and an abundant supply of water. But when Lincoln made to offer his assistance, she pointed at him, fingernails like black daggers.

148

"The jewels," she hissed.

"I already told you," he answered flatly.

She took a slow, deep breath and narrowed her eyes. Then she walked over and stood before him. He looked up. She looked down and caressed his cheek with one hand. He smiled; seductions for answers were standard procedure, and he prided himself on being able to remain, if not chaste, then at least unashamed.

"You are stubborn, tailor," she whispered huskily.

He nodded his thanks.

She cupped the back of his neck and massaged it while she traced her forefinger along the hollow of his throat.

And pressed.

He stiffened.

"Yes," she said with a slow wink and a one-sided smile. "If you are asking yourself if this nail is strong enough to cut you open, the answer is yes."

He blinked, once.

"The fangs, Blackthorne," she said. "Or I'll slit your throat."

# Seventeen

**H**e could hear Onbrous coughing violently in the kitchen.

He could hear the wind prowling around the house.

He could hear his blood racing, feel his heart pounding, and tried not to swallow as she waited. Patiently. Watching him as she might watch a pinned butterfly dying.

"I—" he began.

"Wrong answer," she whispered sweetly, and the nail pressed deeper.

Seductions, he thought glumly, aren't what they used to be.

Without seeming to move, he tried to lean away from the pressure, but she only held him more securely, one eye half-closed as if daring him to try something that would give her an excuse to have a little fun. He was tempted, but there was nothing he could do.

The moment he readied himself for a kick or a punch, she'd feel the tension, and he'd feel his blood running warm down his chest. What he needed was a believable lie, which was exactly what he didn't have.

Water ran; the coughing stopped.

"I don't have a lot of time," she said.

He glanced toward the front hall, hoping the director would show himself; he glanced the other way, hoping the director would come through the back parlor instead.

"He doesn't like blood," Scalia told him. "He'll wait until I call him."

The coughing fit was a fake then. Onbrous just wanted to be out of the way while his cohort did all the work.

He stared at her for a second, then rearranged his expression into one of obstinate near-defeat. When she said nothing, he allowed his knees to buckle slightly, and her grip immediately tightened, her smile widening as he put a hand on her waist to steady himself.

"Are you ready?" she asked.

He closed his eyes briefly, hesitated, and nodded. And turned and flexed his forearm so that the knife sprang from its sheath before she could move, its edge slicing through her hip the moment he grasped the hilt. At the same time, as her eyes widened in shocked surprise at the burning, his free hand slapped her arm away and shoved while his head ducked and twisted clear, sending her staggering with a curse against Onbrous, who'd just reentered the room.

The collision resulted in a yelp and violent oath, and Lincoln instantly dove over the arm of the couch, scattering hat, gloves, and topcoat to the floor before he was able to snatch up Palmer's revolver. Then he knelt on a cushion and braced his gunhand on the back.

Nuts, he thought.

Onbrous already had his own weapon out and was aiming at the middle of his forehead. Scalia was to one side and just behind him, holding a palm against her hip, trying to scowl through the grimace that had replaced the serpent's smile.

Linc waited, hoping that one of them had a little more sense than to try anything stupid.

Finally, the director said, "Stand-off," haltingly, as if it were a question, or a prayer.

"Oh, just shoot him, for Christ's sake," she snapped, taking her hand away and shaking her head in disgust at the blood smeared across her palm.

"I don't think so," Linc said. "I'm a better shot. I think, Jess, you'll both be dead before I am."

"A bluff," the man ventured.

"You never know," Lincoln told him.

Scalia, meanwhile, pulled down the band of her slacks far enough to expose the shallow wound, then looked with loathing at Linc, who nodded and tossed her the director's silk scarf. She caught it one-handed, wadded it up and pressed it against the cut, pulled it away, and pressed again. "Damn," she said, hissing. "God, it stings, y'know?"

"Are you all right, my dear?" Onbrous asked without looking around.

"A little late for that," she muttered.

"He got the best of you," he said, waving the gun, "not me. I am still in control."

Scalia groaned.

Linc, fearing the idiot might actually go ahead and pull the trigger, suggested as reasonably as he could that they'd all be better off without weapons of any kind. Under the circumstances.

"Do you take me for a fool?" Onbrous declared. "If I surrender, what assurance do I have that you won't put a bullet through my head?"

Scalia came up behind him and slapped his shoulder. "Jesus, Jesse, give me a break, huh? He doesn't have the damned teeth, okay? Put it away."

"But—"

She sighed loudly, took the gun from his unprotesting hand, and slipped it snugly into her waistband, patted the grip, and grinned. Linc grinned back and slipped his own gun into its holster beneath his jacket, patted it, realized what he had done and took it out again.

Scalia sneered.

"I told you!" Onbrous huffed.

"I'm not cheating," he told her. "Just think of it as a security blanket."

"My ass," she said amiably.

"Whatever," he replied, and motioned her to a place on the couch. Onbrous he sent into the kitchen for a first aid kit, with the suggestion that anything else but said kit in his hands when he returned might result in the reduction of the number of players in the game. The director sputtered, yelped when Scalia connected a pointed toe with his shin, and hurried off, declaiming vengeance under his breath.

"Now," Linc said, taking his old chair back and laying the gun lightly on his thigh, his finger still on the trigger, "what next?"

Scalia shrugged. "I don't know."

"Just for the hell of it—do you have a last name?"

"Naidle," she said.

"Nice."

"You're an ass."

"I am not offended," he answered with a smile. "Now how about going back to your place?"

She frowned.

A clatter from the kitchen suggested Onbrous had dropped at least one drawer of silverware.

"Look," he said with not much patience, "this is silly and you know it. Nobody has the goddamned fangs in this farce of a group, and it doesn't make sense killing each other off, now does it? Better we all get in the same place at the same time, and work things out from there."

"You mean, work together?"

He grinned as Onbrous returned. "Not really. I may be dumb, but I ain't stupid."

He waited while the director, with hands as deft as a sledgehammer, attempted to replace his scarf with a gauze bandage of sorts. Scalia tolerated the clumsiness for only a few seconds before grabbing the kit and doing it herself. When she was finished, Linc stood, stretched, and smiled.

"Jesse, I believe it's time we headed back to your ranch."

"Never!" the man said, head high and feet planted firmly apart. "I do not invite the enemy into the castle! It isn't done."

"You didn't, I did, so put on your coat and let's get going."

Onbrous looked helplessly at his partner, who finally shrugged and stood. "I will kill you, Blackthorne," she said as she swept on her fur-lined duster.

"I appreciate the thought. You drive."

"Oh my god," Onbrous muttered.

Lincoln resolutely and, he thought, courageously kept all the clichés about the phantom skills of women drivers to himself as Scalia barreled away from the house without regard to either storm or comfort, safety or those same demeaning clichés; instead, he settled as best he could in the skimpy back seat and concentrated on keeping the gun trained on Onbrous' head, telling himself that it could be worse, he could be dead, or married.

"I think it's getting better," the director ventured almost an hour later.

Linc couldn't disagree. The snowfall was perceptibly lighter, the wind not as constant; but the cold penetrated the vehicle nevertheless, as if neither heater nor heavy clothing were anywhere in evidence.

"Frankly," the man continued, "I prefer Los Angeles. No weather is better than weather like this. It reminds me of the time I was at Cannes at the height of my career. I was trying to convince that slime, Pars, that his next move ought to be toward the English theater. In fact, it was on the beach, as I recall, and we were being catered to by a veritable bevy of—"

Scalia snorted derision.

Onbrous looked pained.

"How far is it to this ranch of yours?" Linc asked before the man could resume his reminiscence. He didn't need to be reminded that somewhere out there, no matter how far back in history, there was heat, there was comfort, there was someplace that wasn't white.

"Not far, tailor, not very far. But a few minutes' drive, that's all."

Linc noted the blizzard and the way Scalia wrestled the wheel as if it were someone's neck. "We've been going a long time."

"You want to drive?" Scalia asked angrily, glaring over her shoulder.

Onbrous squeaked and grabbed in panic for the wheel; she slapped his hand away and swore on both their graves that she'd sooner die than have to be i the same car with either of them again.

"Your office," Linc said when the Jeep steadied ar Onbrous stopped trembling.

The thin man turned slightly in order to see hi only his mouth visible under his yanked-down h "Yes?"

"You had the fangs there, in the sill."

"You snooped!"

Scalia chuckled.

"And someone took them out and brought them here."

Onbrous glared. "Yes."

"But it wasn't you."

"If it was me, tailor, would I permit myself to be humiliated by . . . by . . . someone like you? Darling, you may have him for dinner as soon as we arrive."

Scalia chuckled and buffed her nails.

The wind, though appreciably abated, was still able to rock the Jeep now and again, and Scalia was still able to find every lump of ice on the road.

"Imagine," Onbrous muttered, slumping down in his seat. "The impertinence of the man, Scalia. Imagine!"

Linc ignored him and leaned back without shifting the gun's aim. Whoever had taken the fangs from New York obviously also needed something else, here in Oklahoma, a something that someone had neglected to tell him about. That in itself wasn't surprising. Someone was always neglecting to tell him something, but usually he was able to figure it out long before this. On the other hand, sometimes he wasn't, so he decided that he wasn't any farther behind than he usually was, usually, although it was thinking like that which had gotten him into this in the first place, if not the second place.

The problem was, what the hell was in Oklahoma, of all places, that had anything to do with some probably mythical Turkish-carved rubies out of practically the Middle Ages by way of Rumania? Of all places.

The Jeep veered sharply off the road, plowing through an open gate and under an arch coated with snow.

"The drive," Onbrous told him when he sat forward. "We shall be there soon."

Unless, Linc thought . . .

"Jesse," Scalia said quietly, reaching over the wheel to wipe off the windshield, "where are the guys?"

"They'd better be right where I left them, the oafs." Unless . . .

He saw the house through the snow then, a traditional long and low ranch house with a porch that extended the length of the building. White-coated shrubs framed each of the windows, and the huge front yard itself seemed, by the tire tracks, to be surrounded by the driveway, and separated from it by a low split-rail fence. A quartet of chimneys spouted smoke into the wind. Every light seemed to be on; there was no sign of anyone, on guard or anything else.

I'll be damned, Linc thought, grinning at his own belated brilliance; I'll be damned.

As the vehicle slowed, Scalia muttered darkly to herself, and Onbrous sat up, one hand braced on the dashboard, the other nervously tapping his window while he whistled softly and tunelessly.

Linc shifted his gun to his left hand. "I have a feeling this isn't what you expected to find," he said, keeping his tone light in case he was wrong.

"No shit," Scalia told him.

The Jeep skidded to a halt just shy of the stairs, and they sat there without moving.

"Jesse," Scalia whispered.

Linc saw it—a bundle lying on the porch in front of the door. It was partially buried by blown snow, but enough of it was exposed for species identification. The man's hat lay beneath one of the windows, flattened against the wall by the wind.

Suddenly he slammed the director's seat forward and opened the door, was out and running before either of them could stop him. He took the steps at a leap, skidded, hit the open door with his shoulder, and fell over the threshold. Rolled to his feet. Stepped backward and squinted until his eyes adjusted to the brilliant light that came from several wagon-wheel chandeliers, a half-dozen standing lamps, and candle-shaped bulbs in sconces in the slate-floored center hall he found himself in.

"Son of a bitch," he said. "What the hell happened here?"

# Eighteen

To the right of the entrance hall was an amazingly long room that seemed to take up most of the front of the house, and *shambles* was too tidy a word for the way it had been grievously rearranged: the furniture had been overturned and slashed, prints and oils on the walls had been yanked from their places and trampled upon, several of the standing lamps weren't any longer, and most of the wall-to-wall carpeting had been gouged and ripped to expose equally gouged and scarred floorboards. The stench of liquor was strong from a sideboard whose bottles and decanters had been smashed against the walls. The huge fireplace at the far end had been cleaned out, ashes and partially burned logs scattered far beyond the hearth.

Scalia barged in behind him, gasped, and said, "Damn, tailor, it looks like we're too late."

"Yeah," he said, briefly biting his lower lip.

He stared at the destruction, and motioned her to stay where she was and keep Onbrous with her. Then he made his way swiftly along the narrow hall toward the back. He ignored Jesse's abruptly muffled wail of anger, concentrating instead on whatever sounds the empty house could give him—someone breathing behind a doorway, a running footstep, the grate of a pulled-back hammer on someone's gun.

But there was nothing, not even the wind.

Hefting his own gun nervously, he reached the hall's end and discovered that the house wasn't nearly as traditional as he'd first believed; not by a long shot.

It was, in fact, a large hollow square whose inner wall was glass from floor to ceiling, and in the center of which was close to half an acre of landscaped garden. He paused at the intersection, blinking once in astonishment at several huge and bare pecan trees that reached above the slightly peaked roof, at the pebbled paths that wound through grass and garden islands to come together and separate around an irregularly-shaped pond in the center, in the middle of which was a large boulder topped with white. There wasn't much snow on the ground; from steam rising off the water, he gathered that heating pipes ran under the entire area, and what snow did hit the grass was instantly melted, while the mixture of warm and cold produced condensation on the glass.

There was no one out there.

Onbrous howled again.

Right or left, he wondered, and darted right, pressing against the wall, opening doors with care, peering in, wincing at the destruction he discovered, and moving on. Still listening. Still looking for signs that the Burgoynes were all right. But by the time he reached the first corner he had abandoned caution in favor of speed; whoever had done this had already left.

Little of the light from the front of the house reached him; he was ducking through shadows that reached for him from the courtyard, and they were making the back of his neck prickle with unease.

At the back, in a kitchen large enough to support any number of hotels he couldn't afford, he glanced out the windows and saw nothing but dark and white twisted by the wind, and the near-buried body of a man dressed in black; the last, he thought, of the airport trio.

He wanted to call out. With Onbrous screaming revenge loud enough for a Texan to hear, his presence in the house couldn't be a secret. But he kept silent; just in case.

Twice he was tempted to open one of the heavy glass doors and go into the courtyard, but each time he stopped the wind kicked up, the trees trembled, and he changed his mind. Only an idiot would hide out there, and deserved what he got.

And twice he froze in the act of running, positive there was someone watching him from the shadows. But each time he turned, each time he backtracked, there was no one there.

The feeling persisted.

Finally, at the last room next to the central corridor he leaned against the wall in defeat. Scalia was shouting something at Onbrous, who was bellowing rather loudly for a man of his size. Linc could understand none of it, didn't give a damn, and turned the knob, flung open the door, and gaped.

"Jesus," he said.

It was either a trophy room or a study jammed with trophies. Dozens of gleaming Academy Award statuettes lined the natural pine bookshelves, were tossed onto the heavily carpeted floor, marched along the edge of a massive walnut desk, and served as grotesque candlesticks on a chandelier hanging from the ceiling's center.

It was almost like a shrine.

He stepped in, shook his head in amazement, and was about to call the director when he heard a low, muffled moan, off to his right. Instantly he was in a crouch and gliding across the carpet on his toes, his left arm out for balance. He refused to believe this was a stroke of luck, that the intruder had somehow beaned himself with an Oscar and was just lying around waiting to be picked up and questioned, but stranger things had happened and he prepared himself for anything.

Which was, when he finally rounded the desk, Tania Burgoyne, trussed and gagged and shoved into the well. He grinned in relief and, kneeling beside her and holstering his gun, eased her out and removed the gag.

"You. . . ." She gasped, coughed, cleared her throat, coughed again.

"Yes," he said. He sat her up gently and began working on knots only demented Boy Scouts could understand. "Me."

"It was horrible."

When her wrists were free, he went to work on her ankles. "I know. But you're all right now. You *are* all right, aren't you?"

She nodded somewhat tentatively. "Linc, he was going to kill me."

He paused in surprise, then told her that was rather doubtful. Onbrous wasn't the type; he probably even had Scalia kill all his flies.

"No," she said, sitting up at last and chafing her reddened wrists. "Not him. *Him!*"

He waited, one hand on her ankle, the other tossing the rope aside.

"The skinny guy."

162

He waited, one hand on her ankle.

Tania swiped the hair from her eyes and frowned her annoyance. "You didn't see the skinny guy? Tall? Nose like a chicken? You didn't see him?"

Skinny guy, he thought; the mysterious other player.

He shook his head, took her hands and helped her to her feet. She swayed a bit, and he put an arm around her waist to lead her from the room. When she sighed and leaned trustingly against him, he wondered how much more he would have to take; those ruffles were going to drive him bananas.

"Are you sure you didn't see him?"

"No," he answered gently. "We got back—"

"We?" She froze, refusing to take another step, staring in anxious anticipation toward the front of the house. "We? You mean, my dad is—"

"Sorry," he said regretfully, "not Dutch. Jesse and his pet torturer, and me, that's all."

"Oh my god." She sagged. He held her. She looked into his eyes. "He's got Dutch, Linc."

He looked back into those eyes. "I know."

"You do?"

"I figured it out on the way over."

"You're a little late. I knew that hours ago."

He didn't bother to answer. Late was getting to be a habit these days, but in this case he forgave himself. There was, after all, a blizzard, and several instances of getting hit on the head, and a woman dressed like a black widow who'd just as soon slit his throat as smile at him.

Which bright, nearly pleasant smile Scalia promptly gave him as they stumbled into the front room, where much of the furniture had been righted, and Jesse was slumped on a loveseat, wringing his hands and staring at his feet. Then Linc noted with some puzzlement that the gun was still in her waistband, and he wondered what the two of them had been talking about while he'd been gone.

"I found Tania in the Oscar room," he said, taking her to a high-backed chair by the fireplace. "I didn't realize you'd won several hundred awards, Jesse."

"He hasn't," Scalia explained as she dropped an armful of logs onto the andirons. "It's his room of the future." She smiled again. "He's a good boy, you know, Blackthorne. He's just a little stupid."

"I earned every one of them!" the director insisted loudly. "And I would have won them too, if it hadn't been for that . . . that hideous person!"

Scalia struck a match, lit the fire, kicked ashes off her boots, and grunted.

"Genius!" Jesse declared with a thump to his chest. "They refuse to recognize genius!"

Linc found an unbroken bottle of brandy, half filled a glass, and brought it to Tania. "What happened?" he asked quietly while Onbrous settled back to mumbling to himself.

"They . . ." Tania pointed to Naidle and Onbrous. "They kidnapped me."

"I gathered."

"They tied me up and made me sit all by myself in that . . . that horrible room!"

"Every goddamned one of them!" Jesse insisted.

"Then they went away and came back with Dutch, and they said they'd kill me horribly if he didn't tell them about the fangs. He couldn't."

"Of course not," he said. "Because he didn't know. So he did the next best thing—he told them I knew. So they came to get me. And we came to rescue you. So where is Dutch?"

"I don't know."

"He escaped!" Onbrous exclaimed.

"No, the skinny guy came and took me out," Tania

said. She drank, her eyes watered, she drank again. "When we couldn't tell him anything, he gagged me, shoved me into that place, and took Dutch away."

"Did you hear anything?" Linc asked.

"Just a lot of noise." She glanced around the room. "I guess he was searching."

"You guess?" Onbrous said, standing and pointing. "You guess? Do you realize how long it's going to take me to fix this place up again? My god, forever!"

You should live that long, Linc thought, glancing around at the Danish Modern, the Spanish Pine, the Victorian, the Colonial—a decorator sees this, and he'll choke to death before he screams.

Then: "It must have been Jannor's man," he told them. "Judd Shelger. He must have been the one who took the fangs from your office, Jesse, but Jannor found out that just having them wasn't enough. He had to come to Oklahoma." Thoughtfully, he tugged at an earlobe and looked down at Tania. "He needed someone who knew what to do with them."

"Dutch," she whispered.

He nodded solemnly. Onbrous scowled. Scalia began buffing her nails.

"There's supposedly a ritual of some sort, isn't there?" he asked Tania. "Something Dutch is supposed to have learned in that village before he died. Something that Jannor told me has to be done before dawn on Christmas. Which, I hate to remind you, is only a couple of days away."

Reluctantly, and only after a lot of staring and drinking, she nodded.

Wonderful, he thought; peasants dancing around a fire under the light of a full moon. Jesus.

"So I guess," he continued, rubbing his chin, scratching a cheek, "Jannor wants to take him over to Rumania. To that village, wherever it is, where the

Hooded Demon is. In case the ritual is wrong and some of the people there can help out." He shook his head. "Incredible."

"Well . . ." Tania said.

"I'm hungry," Onbrous announced. "Do you realize it's practically midnight, and I haven't eaten all day?"

"Well what?" Linc said, not at all pleased with the expression on her face. It told him she had something else to say, something about the fangs and her father, and he knew damned well that whatever it was, it wasn't going to make his day any easier.

"The Rumania part."

"What about the Rumania part?"

Her smile was brave and loving; he wanted to smack it up to her forehead.

"I don't think they're taking him to Rumania."

He supposed that was a plus; another plane ride like the last one, and he'd end up in a rubber room.

"I am going to the kitchen to make food," Onbrous announced, slapping his hands on his stomach. "You may come if you are hungry!" And he left, daintily stepping over the carnage with only a single whimper.

Scalia dropped onto the couch and stretched, arching her back off the cushions.

"How do you know that?" Linc asked.

"Because . . ." A tear formed in Tania's right eye. She sniffled. "Because before he took my father away, he came back to that . . . that room."

Several seconds passed before Lincoln kicked himself and said, "And?"

Tania took a deep breath.

Scalia stretched again.

He didn't know which of them to watch, and decided that his professionalism depended on his staring at the logs instead. It wasn't as much fun, but it kept his mind reasonably free of obstruction and side-tracking.

"And," Tania said in a rush, her voice high and frightened, "he told me not to go away because he'd be right back."

Scalia froze.

Lincoln sighed. "By back, I assume you mean here?"

Tania nodded briskly.

"I don't suppose he was bluffing."

"I don't know."

And Onbrous, from somewhere in the house, bleated and shrieked.

# Nineteen

For all that could be said for a bit of thunder and lightning now and then to herald the approach of the bad guys, Lincoln had to give it to the man who stood in the entrance hall just a second or two after Onbrous stumbled in, fell, and crawled to the couch where he buried his head in Scalia's lap—he wasn't one for the dramatic flourish. He simply stepped out of the hallway behind the scurrying director, lifted the machine pistol he carried to prove he was armed and deadly, and waited until the others had spotted him.

Scalia's eyes widened in amazement and she backed into the couch's corner, shoving the director away; Onbrous whimpered, rolled over and sat up, his face gleaming sweat and dark with righteous terror; and Linc took Tania's glass, refilled it, handed it back, and positioned himself behind the chair. He made no move toward the newcomer. Heroics always depended on the arrangement of the odds, and he hadn't yet successfully drawn to an inside straight.

The man—and he was sure it was Judd Shelger, especially after Scalia muttered, "Judd, you bastard"—was dressed in worn denim and wearing a sullied white western hat with the brim snapped up in front. His brow was high and smooth, his eyes were small, and beneath a beak-thin nose his mouth was wide, his nearly black lips never quite closing enough to conceal yellowed, jagged teeth. The rest reminded Lincoln of Pars Jannor—so thin it hurt to look at him, but in this case the man's movements were as fluid as a dancer's.

"You will do nothing," the man ordered, in a high, womanly voice.

"Sure," Linc agreed readily. Then he pointed at the gun. "But would you mind not—"

Suddenly Scalia launched herself with a kick and a roll over the back of the couch and sprinted for a narrow door Linc hadn't seen before, tucked in the far corner behind a low Chinese screen. But she no sooner had her hand on the knob when the pistol fired, and gouges exploded along the doorframe, showering her with splinters and shards of plaster.

She froze, her eyes tightly closed.

Tania screamed.

Linc winced, then noticed that Scalia's gun was no longer tucked in her waistband.

And in the silence that followed, she looked up at the ceiling as if in thanks she hadn't been hit. He couldn't see her face, but by the time she turned around, her expression was a complete blank.

"I don't miss," Shelger warned her. "You don't get another chance."

With what Linc thought was admirable control, she lifted an accepting eyebrow, shrugged, and buffed her nails on her chest, while Tania failed to swallow a sob as she reached blindly for the comfort of Lincoln's hand.

Well, he thought, swell; he patted Tania's wrist and slowly moved away from the chair, arms slightly wide to signal he was no danger, not stopping until he'd reached the hearth and was leaning against the mantel. Silently he cursed Palmer's gun out of practical reach in its holster, and the fact that his knife was absolutely useless now. And though he realized he could probably reach the brass stand that held the fireplace accessories, there was no chance he'd be able to use either poker or shovel without getting himself cut in half, and the others killed with him. He suspected that the thin man used a hammer to kill ants.

The wind rose again, and the lights flickered for a moment before brightening again.

Finally, when it was apparent the man had no pronouncements to make, no threats to offer other than to keep them covered, Lincoln said, "You were the man at the hospital, I suppose."

Shelger turned his attention to him slowly. "Yes."

"And you have Dutch."

A nod.

"You haven't . . . that is, he's still alive I assume, and Pars is not all that far away at this moment?"

The man nodded again.

"Son of a bitch," Jesse muttered.

"So now what?" Linc said.

Shelger tilted his head as if he didn't understand, then looked quickly at the front door when the wind slammed against it so hard the doorknob rattled.

The lights dimmed again, and brightened again, though not at full strength.

"Probably writing his goddamn lines," Onbrous muttered. "The man couldn't say good morning without a script writer beside him."

170

"No kidding," Linc said.

"A ham! A veritable porker! He was—"

"Jesse," Scalia said, voice low and touched with caution. When the director looked puzzledly at her, she nodded toward the gun. Onbrous paled and began stroking his mustache with his thumb.

Shelger watched him blankly, then motioned Scalia back to the couch. When she balked, he raised the weapon slightly and let her see his teeth; when she moved, heels sharp on the floor, he aimed back at Lincoln.

Why me? he wondered; I'm just a stupid tailor.

"So, is it true that Pars wants to be seventeen again?"

Shelger said nothing.

"I'm hungry," Tania whimpered.

To his amazement Lincoln realized he was too. At the mention of food, he realized he hadn't eaten a thing since leaving New York; nor, now that he thought about it, had he slept for any decent length of time since the night before last. A glance at his watch: it was just after midnight.

"Y'know," he said enthusiastically, "that's a good idea, Tania. Hey, Jess, would you mind nipping back to the kitchen and grabbing something for us? It doesn't have to be anything special. Whatever you've got lying around, we're not fussy."

Onbrous stared dumbly at him.

"I don't know—peanut butter, cheese, whatever you've got that's quick, you know what I mean?"

"Lettuce?" Tania asked, smiling apologetically when he stared. "I can't help it, I'm on a diet."

"Red meat," Scalia suggested.

Linc shuddered, but walked briskly over to the couch. "Never mind. Don't bother to get up, Jess. I'll do it, I know where it is. You want anything?"

"Stop," Shelger warned.

Onbrous said nothing, not even when Scalia punched his shoulder.

"Hey, it's all right, I'll think of something," Linc said. "Trust me."

After a long look at the woman in black, and praying they were thinking along the same lines, if not the same railroad, he wound his way through the maze of still-overturned furniture, grinning, bobbing his head, and watching the pistol's muzzle track him across the room.

He felt like an idiot; he hoped Shelger thought he was.

"So how about it, Judd?" he asked, stopping five feet from the man. "Couldn't I get something for us? Hell, where are we going to go? It's snowing out, remember?"

Shelger simply stared.

I don't think, Lincoln decided, this is going to work.

"Hey!" Tania called.

Linc didn't turn.

"Hey, Linc, could you bring something to clean my blouse? I think I spilled some brandy on it. Right here."

He blessed himself for his strength of character, and blessed Shelger in turn for switching his gaze around to whatever the woman was doing.

He held his breath; a sliding step forward.

Tania complained, "These goddamn ruffles aren't worth the money. Look at this, will you?"

A sliding step forward.

Shelger narrowed his eyes.

Linc wondered whatever happened to fairness in the universe.

"See what I mean? Just look, for god's sake."

Oh Jesus, he thought, took a third step forward and, when Tania complained about how even the damned buttons wouldn't work, he threw himself forward, his eyes closed in case Shelger's reflexes recovered too fast.

172

\* \* \*

There was no time to compliment himself on his luck, or Tania's quick thinking.

He struck Shelger just above the knee, at the same time reached up and slammed the gun arm high, so that when the pistol fired a second too late, the only holes were in the ceiling. Under a shower of plaster then, they tumbled grunting into the foyer, twisting, thrashing, and generally doing each other no damage at all until Linc, the forearm still in his grasp, was able to scramble up far enough to butt the man's chin and drive his head hard into the floor. Shelger grunted and went limp, eyelids fluttering, breath whistling through black lips while one heel drummed the floor.

Tania cheered.

Linc wrenched the weapon free and sat astride the man's chest, knees jammed into his armpits, the muzzle tucked into his neck, just below his chin.

Though pale and swallowing and still slightly dazed, Shelger winced; the rim was hot.

Then he glanced over his shoulder, and scowled when he saw the others doing nothing but watch. "Would one of you mind getting some rope?" he asked.

Shelger tensed as if ready to buck him off, and he looked back quickly, shoving the pistol a little harder. "I wouldn't," he said solemnly. "It may accidentally go off. I hate guns, so I don't know much about them."

A moment to check for a bluff, a dare, and Shelger relaxed, though his eyes remained narrow and staring.

"Where's Jannor?"

The man only stared.

"Where are the fangs?"

No response.

"I suppose that means you aren't going to tell me where you've hidden Dutch."

Shelger bared his teeth.

173

Linc shuddered and looked to the others; they were still in their places. "Hey, do you mind?" he said, wondering if they were in shock, or just scared. "What the hell's the matter, are you all deaf? Some rope, okay? If there isn't any, just tear up the drapes."

"Like hell," Onbrous said.

Oh Christ, Lincoln thought. He shook his head, looked back at Shelger. "Amateurs," he muttered, puffed his cheeks and blew a slow breath.

If, he decided glumly, he was going to have many more days like this, maybe being married to Carmel wouldn't be so bad after all.

With a sigh, he leaned forward and kept his voice low and toneless: "Look, pal, I don't give a sweet damn what Jannor told you about me, but if you don't tell me what you're doing here, and tell me soon, I'm going to blow your goddamned head off." He shoved the muzzle sharply against the man's neck, eased back, and parted his lips in a cold smile. "Right off your goddamned shoulders."

"I can't breathe," Shelger rasped.

"Without a head, you won't have to."

The lights dimmed.

A log split, and hissed sparks into the chimney.

"If," Lincoln said, "you're waiting for Pars to come back and save you . . . don't."

"I'm not," Shelger said.

"Fine."

"But if you kill me, the girl's father will die."

Interesting, he thought; another I have and you have situation. And sooner or later he was going to figure out what the hell to do when they came up.

"Linc," Tania said, "what did he say?"

"Nothing. And where the hell is that rope?"

"Coming," Onbrous told him.

"So's Christmas, for god's sake."

He heard movement, some whispering, and Scalia's heels cross the floor. Shelger shifted again, and Linc made sure he remembered which one of them had the weapon.

"I don't want Daddy to die again," Tania said.

He frowned. She was a lot closer than she had been.

"He won't," he assured her. "As soon as—oh damn."

The barrel of a gun touched his nape lightly, Shelger's eyes widened, then narrowed in surprise, and three shadows grew to fill the wall just ahead.

"This is stupid," he said. "I thought we were going to work together on this."

"I need the fangs," Onbrous declared bravely.

"I need my father," Tania said.

And I need my head examined, he thought as the gun at his neck was replaced by the touch of one of Scalia's nails.

"You will move away, tailor," the director ordered, "so that my little one may extract the necessary information from the scum."

Scalia giggled.

For the first time, Shelger looked nervous.

"Linc, please," Tania begged, "don't make this difficult, okay? Just . . . just move, okay? You're not going to get hurt."

Scalia chuckled.

"Tailor, you are wasting valuable time!"

Linc didn't move. It was a stand-off, they all knew it, and the sooner they stopped playing games, the sooner he'd be able to get back to business.

Then something shifted to his left, just beyond the reach of his peripheral vision.

And he wasn't at all happy when Scalia uncharacteristically gasped, and Onbrous suggested at the top of his voice that they all run for their lives, just as the lights finally dimmed to black.

# Twenty

The distraction was all Shelger needed.

In a single, convoluted move that caught Lincoln by surprise, he yanked the machine pistol from Linc's hand and at the same time bucked him over his head. Linc flailed into the wall and hit it with his back, landed with a pained grunt, and immediately scurried along the baseboard on hands and knees as he felt the man scramble to his feet, and heard the pistol's bolt being snapped back. Then he held his breath and dropped, curling into a tight ball when the firing began, his arms wrapped tightly about his head, amazed but not complaining about the fact that, though Jannor's man had the advantage and knew Linc's location, he didn't fire at him but at the others in the room.

The fusillade was deafening, the fall of shattering glass and plaster almost smothered by the din.

Linc curled more tightly.

There were flashes of muzzle-light that produced

stars behind his eyelids, but he didn't bother to check the flashes' location—they'd be too strobic and sudden to do him any good.

A pause.

He waited.

The firing began again, and what he prayed were merely stray bullets slammed and marched into the wall above him, gouged the floor not far from his soles, winged into the ceiling and brought chunks of it down around him; but no one, as far as he could tell, had been hit—or at least no one cried out in wounded anguish or despair. And when, only a few seconds later, there followed another lull too filled with silence to please him, he inched himself along the baseboard toward the front door as noiselessly as he could.

Someone's foot crunched a shard of glass.

Someone else bumped into a piece of furniture.

His nose wrinkled at the acrid stench of gunpowder, and he nearly choked in the effort to restrain a cough when a faint cloud of plaster dust settled over his head.

He paused for a moment, and listened.

No breathing; no movement.

Where the hell were they? he thought, his eyes watering from the strain to see.

The urge to call Tania's name was overwhelming; he swallowed several times to kill it, and tasted bile, tasted acid.

His back began to ache where it had struck the wall, and he straightened as slowly as he could to alleviate it, biting down on the inside of one cheek to offset the throbbing until he was partially stretched out and able to crawl more easily. One hand probed gingerly in front, investigating the darkness for obstructions and pitfalls that might sound an alarm; the other stayed beneath his upper chest, raising him up, dragging him, pulling him, and gripping his revolver tightly.

177

Glass shattered, and he froze, eyes shut, waiting for the firing to begin again.

Nothing happened.

From beneath the door he could feel an intermittent draught that fluttered through his hair and made him shiver.

And still nothing happened.

All right, he told himself sternly, either you're dead, or you're in the middle of a miracle; don't push your luck.

A splinter jammed into the heel of his left hand as he reached out, and he hissed in at the stabbing. He hated pain. It wasn't fun. He pulled the wood shard out with his teeth, missing it only three times in the process, reminding him that he was still alive, though he didn't feel like cheering.

He listened, and heard nothing.

His hand stung, and his back still throbbed.

What he needed to do, he decided, was get across the door and back into the living room where he could move along the outside wall. Going outside, assuming he could make it without a bullet shattering his spine or the back of his skull, was out of the question; he'd freeze to death before he'd taken a dozen steps. But in the living room he figured there was a chance, to find some chair or one of the couches that would offer protection until one of those idiots decided what to do next.

He wasn't going to force anything.

He still didn't know what had made Onbrous sound a warning, but he suspected it had something to do with Pars Jannor.

A foot slid across a fall of plaster.

He frowned, perplexed, when once again the expected firing didn't erupt, and he wondered, somewhat apprehensively, if some of the others were dead; there certainly weren't any wounded or the moans of pain would have begun long ago. But if they were alive, why weren't any of them firing at the noises? A muzzle flash would certainly give someone away, but with all the shields the room offered, no matter how flimsy, surely one of them should have gotten impatient enough to make something happen.

Where the bloody hell were they?

He passed in front of the door, his left hand still out, fingers reading the path ahead as if they knew Braille.

Neither, he knew, was he being all that silent—his trousers scraped on the floorboards, his breathing was ragged, and he was positive that the drag of his shoes was loud enough to be heard in the courtyard.

Yet again, no one fired at him.

It was spooky, and he didn't like it.

Somebody was planning something he couldn't figure out, and in not even being able to make a decent guess, he felt increasingly vulnerable, increasingly helpless, as if he'd tried to whistle past a graveyard and discovered his mouth was too dry.

Nice, he thought when the image of graves and coffins flared by again; nice.

When his hand finally closed gratefully around one of the fallen brass lamps, he measured its cold length and inched toward the heavy, squared base. By the time he was on the other side, almost panting with the exertion, his vision had adjusted somewhat, and though it permitted him no details, he was still able to see faint outlines; more so, he realized suddenly a few seconds later, than he ought to have, until he glanced at the front windows and saw shifting bands of moonlight slowly fill the panes.

The storm was over, snow no longer falling.

And if he didn't get to the wall soon, he was going to be as fully exposed as if the sun were shining.

A cloud momentarily drew back the light, and he moved as quickly as he dared, crawling between an upside-down chair and a sideboard and pressing his back tightly against the wall under the sill of the nearest window just as the cloud passed and the moonlight returned. He lay in a fall of shadow, gunhand across his chest, and felt a drop of perspiration slide in a chill along his brow.

Nothing to it, folks; the man's got guts.

Now if he could only take a full breath, fill his lungs, he could stand, order everyone to their feet, and solve this entire mess in less time than it took for Old Alice to toss a grape at Macon's ass.

But his second wind didn't come, only a slow wave of weariness he found impossible to shake off. And it came to him with a silent, disgusted groan that he was finally exhausted. His arms were filling with cement, his neck could barely hold his head up, and there wasn't much feeling at all in his legs. And why not? Hardly any sleep, hardly any food, tramping through blizzards and sneaking through firefights—who the hell did he think he was anyway, Superman, for god's sake?

He rubbed a hand briskly across his face, hoping to wake himself up, make himself more alert; he pushed along the baseboard, an inch, a foot, a yard, until he was just shy of the center of the wall. But still he saw nothing. Ill-defined shadows on the opposite wall didn't move; the draperies didn't ripple or sway; telltale signs of human movement didn't relieve the silence that had settled over the house now that the wind had apparently gone for good.

He raised himself up on one elbow, the better to look over the top of a toppled end table.

The moonlight brightened for a moment before fading again.

But it was enough to remind him of the door in the far corner, and more than enough to show him that the Chinese screen was down and the door was slightly open.

He sagged, not quite sure that what he felt was all relief. That's where they probably were—Tania and the others. They had ducked out of the room during the fighting, and he had been left, he supposed, to take care of Shelger.

Wonderful; all he needed now was Jannor to come soaring down the chimney with a cannon in his hand. Wonderful.

Then a voice cheerfully whispered, "Tailor," and a thin dark figure slowly rose from the hearth.

The door clicked shut.

Shelger whirled and fired into the wood, snapped back and covered the room again. There was no noise from inside the room, no cries, no running footsteps.

"Tailor."

The moonlight barely touched him, throwing the left side of his face into deep shadow and adding a silver glint to his eye. His lips seemed darker now and thicker, his cheeks more hollow, and as his head swiveled side to side in his searching, it was as if he were pulling an obscene mask from his face, and putting it back on.

"Tailor."

If I don't move, Linc decided hopefully, he won't see me. He'll think I went down the corridor to one of the other rooms. He'll follow. Then I'll run into that room over there and beat the crap out of Onbrous for leaving me out here.

The floor dug into his hip, but he didn't dare shift. Shelger stepped off the hearth and impatiently kicked something away, something that skittered across the room and smashed into the leg of a table.

"Tailor."

Linc scanned the area immediately around him, looking for something he could throw, not at Jannor's man, but in the direction of the hall. Another distraction to draw some of his fire. After all, how many clips could he be carrying? Sooner or later he was going to run out of ammunition.

The cold sifted through the panes above him, settled over his shoulders, settled along his spine.

Then he saw what he needed just a few feet away—a glass candy bowl, empty now and on its side. He could reach it by leaning only a few inches forward, and putting his hand into the light that had turned the floor grey.

He considered the risks.

"Oh . . . tailor."

He considered surrendering and being forced back on an airplane to New Jersey after he'd sworn never, ever, to set foot in this state again.

He wondered why the others in the back room weren't marshaling their meager forces for a charge. After all, it was only one man out here, and Tania and Scalia each had a gun. All they had to do was throw the door open and fire; neither could be so bad that they'd both miss, for crying out loud. This was the West, wasn't it? This was cowboy country. And wasn't Tania raised here? And wasn't Scalia more than just a simple fingernail expert?

Jesus, he thought; you send someone else out to do a tailor's job, and this is what you get.

"Tailor."

Unless, he thought sourly, they were waiting for Shelger to kill him first. *Then* they'd kill him, and figure out what to do about the rubies later. Honor among thieves, he decided, was a stable of Dutch's horseshit.

The man took another cautious step forward, his head jerking about like a radar dish, his eyes squinting to find sense in the shadows, to separate the furniture from the darkness around it. He licked his lips, and Lincoln shuddered. He stepped over a hump of ragged carpeting, nudged something with his boots, sneered and moved on.

Slowly.

Too slowly for Linc's nerves, and he braced himself to make a grab for the bowl. He might as well, what the hell. Sooner, and definitely later, Shelger man was going to spot him crouching under the sill, and the mayor's third cousin was going to have to get married naked.

Something moved in the hallway.

Shelger froze, raising the weapon to his chest.

It wasn't a footstep, and Linc was puzzled. It was as if the wind was pushing something along the floor. Something dry, like crumbled paper being blown slowly across sand.

But the wind wasn't blowing, and the sound came again.

Shelger took a step forward, directly opposite him now and less than ten feet away.

"Mr. Jannor?"

Linc stretched his hand toward the bowl.

The sound; something dragging.

"Mr. Jannor, it's me."

The glass was ice, and Linc closed his eyes briefly as he lifted it off the floor.

The sound stopped.

"Mr. Jannor, I've got the tailor in here."

As he drew his arm back, he realized that Shelger was unaccountably nervous, unsure, leaning forward in an attempt to see through the moonlight to the dark of the hall. And he was gliding, his legs and feet barely moving, shifting like a shadow himself, paying no attention now to anything on either side. Linc was forgotten.

"Mr. Jannor?"

Arm cocked, Linc hesitated. If it was Jannor out there, keeping silent until he was sure it wasn't a trap, then he was a dead man if he let his position be known. If it wasn't, if maybe it was Dutch free of his bonds and the obviously crazy actor, he might be dead anyway if Grange mistook him for the enemy.

What the hell, he thought, and lowered his arm; he might as well let Shelger do his work for him.

And Shelger continued to glide forward, in and out of moonlight, cocking his head, lips pursed in a soundless whistle.

Linc watched, blinking sweat from his eyes, waiting until the man had passed him before moving himself toward the fireplace, gnawing on his lower lip as a talisman against noise.

Shelger reached the hall.

Linc pushed himself to his hands and knees.

And sprinted for the corner door when Shelger, vanished now in darkness, screamed in sudden terror.

# Twenty-one

Lincoln didn't falter at the sound of the man's cry. He reached the door at a dead run, slammed through and threw himself low over the threshold, whirling without releasing the doorknob to close the door behind him and fall against it, ear pressed to the wood, his free arm dangling at his side.

He listened, and heard nothing.

He swallowed several times to get moisture back into his mouth, then blew several times more in relief. He had no idea what had made Shelger shriek like that, and decided that he'd just as soon keep it that way for the time being. He turned then to look for the others. Considering their previous gallant efforts to assist him, he was mildly surprised they hadn't either blown his head off or set up a series of traps that would render him dead.

It was dark; not even the moonlight slipped under the door.

I suppose, he thought, I ought to be pleased.

So why, he thought further, do I feel like a worm waiting for the hook?

"Hello?" he said as calmly as he could.

His voice didn't echo. It fell flat, almost toneless.

It was so dark in fact that he began to wonder if he hadn't trapped himself in a stupid clothes closet. That would be all he needed at the end of a perfect day; hiding among coats and galoshes like a kid afraid of a thunderstorm.

He reached out a hand, and felt nothing but air.

Frowning, he returned his gun to its holster and reached out to either side, and felt nothing but smooth wall apparently papered in fabric.

Interesting; and no closet.

After listening at the door again, and again hearing no pursuit, he took a sliding step forward, and stopped breathing when his foot slipped over the edge of something. He sniffed and rubbed a hand under his nose. He lowered himself into a crouch and let his fingers drift lightly over the floor until they reached the lip of whatever he had found. They curled over it. They followed it down. They discovered flatness again, and he thought, Jesus, it's a staircase.

Carefully, he measured the width by holding his arms out, then let his hands float down until each bumped lightly into a banister. Metal, and smooth, and probably brass.

As he directed his blind gaze downward, he waited for some sign of light from below—a sliver from under a door, a glow from a bulb around a corner he couldn't see. But there was nothing, and he knew now why no one had bothered to help him. They weren't here. They were down there. And he didn't really feel like going down there because it was much too dark for his taste. He could fall and break a leg and not be found until spring; he could fall and break his neck, and then it wouldn't matter when he was found; he could fall and hurt himself and they could find him and . . .

Shelger screamed again.

Lincoln plunged down the stairs, turning himself slightly sideways, sliding his palms over the banisters in case he fell. He didn't bother to maintain silence; if they didn't know he was coming by now, they weren't there to know it.

The bottom was discovered by his trying to take one step too many, and the jarring sent a stinging through his heel to his jaw. He cursed, and with his left hand still gripping the banister, he swiveled slowly and peered upward.

He had rather hoped he could at least hear Shelger running, but even the wind, down here, had no voice at all.

The temptation to return to the landing and find out what had terrified the thin man was only barely suppressed by a desire never to find out. Curiosity and cats, he reminded himself.

Quickly, then, he let his free hand roam over the wall about shoulder height until his fingers skidded over a wall switch. A deep breath. A check to be sure his gun was still snuggled under his tweed jacket, and he dropped into a crouch just as he flipped on the lights.

No one shot at him. No one threw a knife in his chest. No one gasped in astonishment at his discovery of the room.

"I'll be damned," he said, unable to keep it in.

He was standing in a private theater easily fifty feet deep, with twelve rows of four very plush rocker seats set on either side of a downward sloping aisle thickly carpeted in an Oriental design. The ceiling was decorated with miniature Oscars set in starlike patterns.

The walls were masked in deep, red-and-black flocked velvet, broken only by gleaming brass sconces holding bulbs in the shape of candle flames, and by the grilles of eight speakers large enough to service an auditorium ten times this size.

At the foot of the theater was a huge glittering screen, hanging above a stage not quite ten feet deep. The screen was framed by heavy velvet curtains that matched the wallpaper; the left side was tied back by a heavy gold-and-silver rope, the right hung loose.

In the back, to his right, was a standing wet bar with a dozen leather-topped stools at the rail; to his left, a narrow door which, when he straightened and looked up, he assumed led to the projection room.

There were no other exits that he could see.

"Hello?" he said again.

The narrow door was locked.

There was no one hiding behind the bar, which, he noted sourly, was stocked with nothing but bottles of spring water masking as fancy seltzer.

He stood at the head of the aisle and began to make his way down, slowly, cautiously, peering into each row, until he reached the bottom. Where he found Tania bound and gagged and lying on her back.

"You know what I think?" he said as he knelt and untied her and paid no attention to the swearing that didn't improve once he'd removed the gag. "I think that honor among thieves is a crock. I really do. I mean—"

"Oh, shut up, Blackthorne," she muttered, pushing herself into a seat and rubbing her wrists.

He stood over her, hands on his hips. "You will be pleased to know, Miss Burgoyne, that I am not going to ask you why you put a gun to my head out there, because I have a code."

"What code is that?" she asked, clearly not giving a damn because her wrists still hurt.

"The code that says that a lady who lies is going to get slugged if she lies again."

Her mouth opened, closed, opened, then set in an expression of a maiden grievously wronged.

"Thank you," he told her. A look around, and a check of the landing. "So. Where are they?"

She pointed over his shoulder at the screen.

"I know they're in the movies, dope. I—"

"Behind the screen, jerk," she said. She stood, pushed him aside, and hobbled to the far end of the stage. When he joined her, she pointed to a door in the wall. "We weren't down here two seconds, I swear, when that Amazon grabbed me, tied me up, and carried me down to here. Golly, she's strong!"

"No kidding."

She sighed. The ruffles fluttered. Linc hoisted himself up and tried to lift the door's latch. He wasn't surprised when it wouldn't budge, but he counted himself lucky that this time, by the position of the hinges, the door opened outward and would thus be amenable to some judicious battering.

If, that is, he had something to batter with.

He looked at Tania and reluctantly changed his mind; he had a feeling the code probably covered something like this, too.

Then he glanced at the ceiling.

"Excuse me for asking," he said as he jumped down, "but I suppose you didn't happen to see what caused all the excitement."

She shook her head regretfully.

"Nothing?"

"No. I was . . . nervous."

"You were holding a gun to my head."

189

She shrugged. "That's what I mean—I was nervous. I didn't want to hit Judd and get him mad."

One of these days, he promised as he trudged up the aisle, I'm going to be a bad guy for a change. Then I'll get to torture little old ladies and children, and do horrid things to beautiful women whether they deserve it or not, and I won't feel the least bit guilty.

He picked up a bar stool and started down with it again.

Then I'll rob a few banks, off a few G-men, get my picture in all the post offices, and retire to Palm Springs with the rest of the white collar crooks and lizards.

"Why don't we go that way?" she asked, pointing at the stairs.

"Did you see what scared him?"

"No."

"Did you hear him scream?"

She frowned.

"Then don't ask stupid questions."

"But someone will hear, Linc."

"Darlin'," he said, cranking the stool over his shoulder and taking aim on the spot he wanted to hit, just above the latch, "I don't think they really expect us to watch movies down here while they go off and . . ." He paused and looked down. "They didn't happen to say where they were going, did they?"

She shook her head.

"Didn't happened to mention your father, I suppose?"

She shook her head again, which so discouraged him that he swung the stool without bracing himself, and when it struck, splintering the door's center, it also knocked him off his feet.

Tania caught him before he reached the floor.

He smiled brief thanks, grabbed the stool, and glowered at the door.

"Linc?"

He eyed the damage already done and swung, putting legs and shoulder behind the blow.

"Linc?"

A third time produced a small hole just off center.

"Linc?"

"For god's sake, what?"

"Why don't you just shoot the latch?"

He stared at her, stared at the door, and stared at her again. "You're kidding, right? You want me to shoot off the latch and just push the door open?"

She nodded.

"And what if there's a ricochet?"

She shrugged. "They do it in the movies."

Gritting his teeth, he swung the stool a fourth time, just barely managing to hit the door instead of giving way to an inclination to divert it elsewhere. The gap widened, the seat fell off, and he reached through the hole and disengaged the lock. When the door swung open easily, he held out his hand and pulled Tania up to join him.

"Gee, you'd think this was a castle," she said, peering around him to the revealed staircase beyond. "I'll bet there's all kinds of secret doors around here."

He didn't answer. He started up, gun back in hand, toward the door at the top. It wasn't completely closed, which meant Naidle and Onbrous had been running when they reached it, and were running too fast through it to be sure it was caught. A gesture behind him to keep Tania silent, and he put an eye to the crack and saw nothing but darkness.

This, he thought, is getting monotonous; I should've been a damned mole.

"Where are we?" she whispered in his ear then.

"Oklahoma."

She hit his shoulder.

Gently, feet poised to run the woman down if he

found himself facing anything larger than a Yorkshire terrier, he eased the door open and realized that they were at the lefthand corner of the courtyard. Moonlight filled it, and the pond and its tendrils steamed, making the place look like a tropical jungle just after dawn. The sight unnerved him, though why, he didn't know.

"Linc, c'mon."

To his right he could see the darker mouth of the hallway, but despite Tania's urging, he didn't cross the threshold. Shelger, for all his screaming, might still be lurking there, or standing guard by the front door. He guessed their best bet would be to follow the corridor around to the kitchen and leave the house through the back door. Though it was cold, they ought to be able to get around to the Jeep before their toes fell off.

He would worry about starting the vehicle once they got there.

On the other hand, Shelger alive, or at least still functional, was a risk he didn't believe was reasonable to take.

Hell, he thought.

"Stay here," he told Tania, and when she protested, insisting that she was just as capable as he, and probably more so, he asked her if she wanted to search for the thin man on her own.

"That's not nice," she said, pouting.

"Then keep your eye out for the two idiots, okay? Whistle if you hear or see them."

Then he was gone, sliding along the wall, hating the moonlight that revealed so much and changed everything else into things he couldn't pin down. Once, he looked back and saw Tania watching him; when she saw him, she waved and blew him a kiss and made an elaborate show of watching the corridor leading to the back.

I'll kill her, he decided; what the hell, who's gonna know?

At the corner he listened for movement, signs of breathing, anything that would give him a clue about the whereabouts of Jannor's man. And when he heard nothing and was driving himself nuts with tension, he stepped around.

And froze.

"Damn," he whispered, putting his gun back, stepping away.

"It's all right, Tania," he called. "You can come out. Poor Judd is dead."

# Twenty-two

S helger was sprawled in the middle of the hall, one arm thrown up over his head. After picking up the machine pistol, Linc knelt beside him. There was no blood that he could see, no evidence of strangulation. But there was no doubt that Jannor had lost his righthand man to a severely broken neck, and Linc didn't much feel like searching for other possible injuries when whoever had killed the man was probably still in the house.

He looked toward the front and saw nothing.

He got to his feet and returned to the intersection, where Tania was staring through the wall to the courtyard beyond.

"This is incredible," she said.

"C'mon," he said, taking hold of her arm.

"Boy, what a waste of good money, you know? Think of the things he could have done instead of building his own damned swamp."

194

"Tania," he said, tugged, then virtually yanked her behind him as he headed toward the front door. He doubted the Jeep was still there, but there wasn't much else he could do until he made sure.

Tania gasped as they stepped around Shelger's body.

Lincoln gasped at the cold when he opened the door and saw that the Jeep was gone.

"It's a setup, you know," he said, walking her back toward the courtyard. "This whole thing has been a setup."

Tania huddled close to him, gripping his arm with both hands, peering at every shadow and every inch of the floor.

"Once Jannor had Dutch, ol' Judd there was supposed to kill us all and, probably, join him later. Trouble is, Pars had other plans, and they didn't include his faithful dresser."

At the glass wall they paused while Linc tried to decide what the hell to do next.

"How do you know that?" she asked.

"I'm the tailor," he said, starting off to the left. "I'm supposed to know stuff like that."

She followed hesitantly. "Does that mean Jannor killed him?"

"I don't know, but probably. I just don't know how, that's all." He turned the corner. "What I do know is, there's not much we can do now, not without a car or something."

Tania caught up with him and grabbed his arm again. "You mean, spend the night here?"

He stopped and took a slow breath. "Look, it's not all that bad. Jannor has been racing around the country as much as we have, and he's got to be exhausted. Like me. And he's a lot older, remember. Whatever he has in mind, whatever it is that Dutch knows that he needs, will wait until tomorrow."

"Are you sure?"

He opened the nearest door and poked his head in. "I'm sure. He's come too far to blow it now." He closed it and tried the next one. "The jerk really believes in those fangs. He isn't going to screw his plans up just because he can't think straight."

The third door was the charm—a bedroom with a bed large enough to hold a dozen munchkins and a cow. The walls were papered in gold; the ceiling was white and checkered with mirrors; the floor was white shag; the furniture looked like polished steel pipes.

Linc closed his eyes briefly.

When the room was still there when his eyes re-opened, he pulled Tania in, closed the door, and with her help proceeded to barricade it with every stick of furniture they could move. She didn't protest; she was too busy yawning. And when they were done, she fell onto the mattress and cradled her head on her fore-arms.

"Are you going to stand guard?" she asked.

He sat on the opposite side and stared at the tele-phone on the ivory nightstand. "No. He's gone."

"Then why—"

"In case I'm wrong."

He picked up the receiver.

"He could get through the window."

He dialed. "Glass breaks."

She rolled over, hands cupped behind her head.

"Don't do that," he said.

She grinned, stuck out her tongue, and fell asleep.

"You have no idea what time it is, do you," Atwaver grumbled between jaw-cracking yawns Linc could hear quite clearly.

"I could care," he said. "What about Clarise?"

"Stable."

"Stable as in 'critical but stable', or stable as in 'good and stable'?"

"Right."

"Damnit, Dennis!"

"Damnit yourself, Blackthorne. I'm doing the best I can, which won't do her a hell of a lot of good if you keep calling me at three in the morning."

"Jesus, is it that late?"

"You tailors live a high life, Linc."

"Right. I'm going to have someone over there to watch her. Probably Macon Crowley. Do yourself a favor and don't bother him. He gets testy."

"And suppose I tell you that it won't be in the best interest of my patient to have an unauthorized person hanging around all the time?"

"Suppose I tell you it won't be in your best interest to chase him away?"

"Lincoln, we've known each other too long for that kind of talk."

"Then let him stay. He's going to anyway."

"All right. But I don't like it."

"You'll like it less if Clarise doesn't pull through."

"I don't care for threats, Lincoln."

"You should be a tailor."


"What do you mean, you're not going to Rumania?"

"I'm sorry, Macon, but there's been a change of plans."

"Do you . . . my god, do you . . . Jesus, all that beautiful paper gone to waste."

"I'm sorry."

"Just as well, I suppose. I doubt you'd pass as a tractor salesman."

"A what?"

"Well, who the hell else goes to Iron Curtain countries, veterinarians?"

"Macon, calm down. I want you to do something else for me."

"It's almost dawn, you know. An old man needs his sleep."

"Go to the hospital first thing, and camp by Clarise's door. Do not move. Do not let anyone but Dr. Atwaver and his appointed nurses in. Check on her every fifteen minutes. If there's any change, call me immediately."

"Where? Do they have telephones in Oklahoma?"

"I'm not going to be in Oklahoma."

"Well, you're not going to be in Rumania, either."

"I'll worry about—"

"Alice is going to have a fit, you know. You should see her paper—the most beautiful rubles or denares or whatever the hell they use over there. Hell, if you ever move to Bucharest you'll be a millionaire."

"Macon, I'll be in Chattanooga."

"You're joking."

"There'll be a room in my name at the convention center hotel there. Leave messages."

"I take it—Chattanooga?—I take it you won't be there."

"No."

"Then—"

"Just do it, Macon."

"Blackie, do you have any idea who used to live in Chattanooga?"

"Yes."

"He's dead."

"He will be."

"Alice will have a fit."


"Jesus God, Linc, do you have—"

"Yes, I do. And yes, I know you need your sleep. And yes, I'm ready to hear anything you have to say."

"Christ, I wish Clarise was here. She wouldn't let you talk to me that way."

"You love it. Now talk."

"Okay. But it isn't good."

"Tell me something I don't know."

"The Fangs of the Hooded Demon are worth, on the private market—which is far more lucrative than the open market—an estimated twelve million dollars."

"Whoa."

"A friend in London insists that he's seen them, and he says that a clever man could, if he works the private auction right, get maybe fifty percent more, depending on the presentation and the guarantees."

"Jeez."

"The Hooded Demon itself is missing too."

"Oh."

"It disappeared a couple of years ago, right after the fangs. As a curiosity, the Demon is worth a few grand, nothing more. If you're interested, it's an albino king cobra, fifteen feet when extended, and when it was alive, it was one of the deadliest snakes on the planet. My sources tell me that it was a favorite of the Turkish generals because it scared the hell out of the enemy. They loved practical jokes."

"I see."

"So this guy, Tepes or Teppen or something—"

"Dracula."

"Whatever. He got hold of it, and the fangs, and used them to solidify his rather unsavory rule over the peasants of the time. Sweet guy. Did you know that he used to have peasants for dinner now and then?"

"So?"

"I mean, he *had peasants for dinner,* Linc. Hors d'oeuvres, not guests. He used them for torches, too."

"George, I appreciate the history lesson, but—"

"Lincoln, I'm trying to tell you that the snake and

the teeth are bad news. Nobody who has them lives long enough to enjoy them."

"The village—"

"Kept them locked up, in the basement, in a shrine, and chopped off the hands of anyone who tried to take them. Or even touch them."

"Then how did they get taken?"

"How should I know? They were, that's all."

"Are you sure?"

"What? You mean, you haven't seen them?"

"Well, not exactly."

"Lincoln, you are . . . I'm stunned."

"And I'm tired. What else should I know?"

"Look, Lincoln, my advice to you is to let the idiots who want them have them. Come home. It's almost Christmas. Help me find my socks. Clarise hid them and it's too damned cold to go barefoot."

"So buy new ones?"

"With what? Clarise has the checkbook."

Tania had rolled to the far side of the bed by the time he was done, and he stared at her back, the shadowed curve of her legs, before switching off the light and stripping off his jacket, shirt, and trousers.

He tested the barricade.

He made sure the single, huge window was locked and the draperies were drawn.

He listened for sounds in the hallway, and heard little more than the sough of the dying wind.

It was entirely possible that he was making a huge mistake, that Jannor was not, despite assurances to the contrary, going to wait until he'd rested before trying to learn what he believed Dutch knew. Though he was indeed old, based on the evidence of the escape from the limousine, he was spry enough to take on a truck and live. Maybe he was already—

Stow it, tailor, he told himself; there's nothing you can do about it now.

With a weary puff of breath, he lay on the bed and rubbed his eyes, massaged his temples. And with a glance at Tania told himself what a jerk he was, in as many languages and with as many synonyms as he could without making his brain hurt. He should have been able to see from the beginning that Jannor would always be a step ahead of him, not to mention a mile or two, and he should have gone straight to Tennessee the moment he found out the actor was heading for Oklahoma.

Where else, he knew, could Jannor safely attempt whatever that ritual involved? Certainly not behind the Iron Curtain. Certainly not at Dutch's place. The only logical place left had to be the estate somewhere outside the fabled city of Chattanooga, where he could control everything, where he would have no fear of interference.

He grimaced.

Idiot. He was a full-fledged, fat-headed idiot, and why the hell did Clarise want those goddamned fangs? She wasn't old, she wasn't dying—or hadn't been when she'd approached him about the job—and George certainly didn't need rejuvenation. That bothered him almost as much as letting Onbrous and his Amazon get away without answering a few questions.

He grinned mirthlessly at the ceiling.

Work together; right.

Jesus, he ought to be shot for such a bone-headed move. The trouble was, he was watching too much television. Bad guys made deals with good guys for the duration; the good guys won, the bad guys won, and the commercials sold suppositories that were scented with lemon.

Tania moaned in her sleep.

201

Lincoln inched over and put a hand on her shoulder. Immediately, she rolled into him, snuggled her head against his side, and snored gently in his ear. He could smell her hair, feel the silk of her blouse and the bra strap beneath it. He could also hear the wind, and somewhere in the dark the faint sound of someone laughing.

# Twenty-three

"Why is it," Lincoln grumbled, "that every time I get on an airplane with you, something happens?"

Tania, her suit somewhat wrinkled but nevertheless still more than presentable, scoffed without saying a word.

Below them were the hills of southeastern Tennessee, green and misty and too damned close to the fuselage for his comfort. It was bad enough having to return to Dallas, bad enough hopping over to Atlanta because there were no other flights available on such short notice, but to have to get into an aircraft that wasn't large enough for the crew, much less the businessmen who crowded in with them, was adding insult to terror.

That the flight was also something less than thirty minutes long seemed to him to be the height of ridiculousness. By the time the pilot got the plane up, he was getting it down. Sometimes, Linc thought, America makes no sense at all.

"Lookout Mountain below, folks," the pilot said cheerfully.

Linc didn't care for all the meanings of the name.

"You know," Tania said as they marched through the terminal half an hour later, "I don't get you."

"Neither does Carmel," he muttered. And was forced to wait while she bought an overcoat—"It's still December, you know"—forced her to wait while he arranged for an automobile and hoped that it was at least bigger than a breadbox.

It was. Barely.

A haze dulled the blue of the sky, sat like a fog on the winter-dulled hills surrounding the city, but he was grateful that he didn't have to drive through any snow. In fact, as he negotiated the highway into the city proper, he was amazed that there wasn't a sign of the stuff anywhere. It must be heaven, he thought, which was more than he could say for the car, whose heating system refused to shut off, no matter how often he thumped the dashboard with his fist.

Tania wanted to see the famous train station; Linc told her the famous train station was now a shopping mall or something. She didn't believe him until they passed it, its elegant brick facade somehow saddened with the bustle of train riders replaced by last-minute Christmas shoppers. Then she gaped at the convention center in the center of the city, attached by glass and steel to a Holiday Inn whose glass-walled elevators rose up the outside walls.

"I thought Chattanooga was supposed to be quaint."

"There's no such thing as a quaint city."

"There's no such thing as quaint cement, either."

He parked away from the main entrance, on a semi-circle of brick paving. Ahead was a drop into a parking lot, to the right was the center itself, concrete and flashing lights that made it look like an arena. He ordered her to stay put and ran inside to the front desk where he signed and paid for the reservation he'd made by telephone as soon as he'd risen that morning. The clerk was friendly enough, but her beehive trembled a little when he denied having luggage and pocketed the key.

He took the elevator to the ninth floor, stepped into his room and went immediately to the telephone.

He dialed for an outside line.

"I'm here," he said when Old Alice answered.

"Macon's on duty."

"Okay. Now tell me how you get to whatever that place is called."

"Darkriver Plantation."

"Right."

She told him, and he was pleased that she mentioned the actor's funeral only twice.

"All right. I'm on my way."

"Blackie?"

"What."

"If he isn't dead, he oughta be."

"From your lips to God's ears."

She laughed. "What's Tennessee like in the winter?"

"Brown and green."

"Like Macon's meat loaf."

He rang off with a grin, left his key at the desk, and ran out to the car.

"I don't think the clerk believed me," he said, sliding in behind the wheel.

"What did you tell her?"

"That I was here for the tailors' convention."

"There isn't one, is there?"

"How the hell should I know?" He pointed at the

glove compartment. "There's supposed to be a map in there. You be the navigator."

Carefully, then, he followed the signs to the interstate highway that led north and east toward Knoxville, weaving through parts of the downtown area he was positive the Chamber of Commerce would kill to replace. And once on the main road, he began to feel uneasy. It wasn't the ravages of construction that seemed determined to tear the hillsides apart, nor was it the traffic he somehow didn't expect to find in this part of the state.

It was a sense, nothing more, that no matter what he did, it all would be too little too late to help Clarise Mayhew.

It made him angry.

It made him depressed.

And it wasn't until he was climbing above the city, the highway sweeping leisurely around a mountain impossibly choked with pine, that Tania touched his leg, pointed to the outside mirror by her door, and said, "I think someone's following us."

He glanced in the rear view mirror. The traffic was mostly eighteen-wheelers and vans. "How can you tell?"

"That yellow car back there. The one with all the rust. It pulled out behind us when we left the hotel."

A frown made him squint. "Are you sure?"

She nodded, and he was thankful that she at least had the sense not to look back.

He was also fairly sure that she was wrong. As far as everyone was concerned, he and Tania were dead. Shelger had taken care of that. No one else . . .

"Oh shit."

The mountain leveled and they drove past farmland, herds of cattle shivering in the cold, a horse ranch that advertised free rides on unbroken mounts, before they climbed once again. The four-lane highway was less crowded here, most of the traffic heading down into Chattanooga, and he was able to slip past the speed limit gradually, without making it seem as if he were trying to run.

"Who is it?" Tania asked, sitting stiffly, her hands clasped in her lap.

"Five will get you zip it's the director and his lady."

"But . . . how?"

"They obviously didn't feel the need to stay in Oklahoma either. And Onbrous probably knows about Jannor's place. He may be dim but he can add two and two."

"Was he waiting for us?"

He shrugged. "Beats me. Maybe he just got lucky."

She snorted her disbelief, then returned her attention to the map. They were to head toward Knoxville, looking for a sign that warned of the danger of heavy fog for a space of five miles. Midway into that area, Old Alice claimed, there was an unmarked turnoff that looked as if it was heading into a swamp. It was. And Darkriver Plantation was four miles farther on.

"If it's so isolated," Tania said, "won't he hear us coming?"

"Yes. That's why we're going to walk most of the way."

"You're kidding."

"He'll hear us."

"Walk? It's cold out there!"

"Not as cold as Oklahoma."

He kept to the right, wondering how farmers could bring themselves to lease portions of their land for billboards that directed him back the other way, most of them for a place called Rock City. They were intrusive, almost obscene, and he winced when he saw one at the

207

edge of a pine forest, the stumps of fallen trees mark-
ing the line of sight from the road.

The land leveled again, the forest closed in on the
highway, and the traffic in the left lane passed him as if
he were doing no more than thirty. He didn't care for
the way the other drivers seemed to be running; it
made him think that they knew something he didn't,
and ought to.

The yellow car remained half a mile behind.

He slowed.

Tania leaned forward.

The yellow car came up to their bumper, rode there
for a hundred yards, and swept around them. Linc
didn't look over, but Tania did, and she grinned.

"False alarm."

"Great."

And she slapped his shoulder, hard, when he nearly
missed the turn.

Lincoln supposed that Daniel Boone and Davy
Crockett got their starts like this, but he wasn't excited
about the prospect of joining them.

The dirt road narrowed instantly to one lane, pine
boughs slapping at the doors, ruts jouncing the car side
to side like waves butting a rowboat. The late afternoon sun was already low, and though there wasn't
much in the way of underbrush, he couldn't see very
deep into the trees for the shadows that gathered
there, and grew, and grew closer. The wheel fought
him. The engine sputtered and whined. And as soon as
he figured he was halfway in, he pulled off between
two scrub pines and turned off the ignition.

Tania took a loud, deep breath.

When Linc rolled down the window the silence was
too loud; there was no wind, no birds, just the quiet
ticking of the car as it cooled down and the creak of

the springs as he shifted to button his topcoat. He took his gloves from his pocket and pulled them on. He flipped up the coat's collar and put his hand on the door's latch.

"You coming?" he said when Tania didn't move.

"I don't want to," she answered, her voice trembling.

"Neither do I."

"Dutch would be mad."

He smiled and nodded, and waited for her to get out before leaving himself. He made sure not to slam the door, made doubly sure he still had his gun. Then he started up the road, gesturing Tania silent when she joined him.

No wind.

No birds.

Pines giving way to bare branches and lightning-shattered boles that made him think of any number of scenes in any number of Jannor's films—the calm before the midnight storm, the road to the hero's do-or-die confrontation. Even the evergreens seemed dead, trunks scarred, needles browning, split cones littering the forest floor. His footfalls were loud. His breath clouded and drifted away.

The sunlight became grey.

As the haze vanished, the sky darkened, blue shading toward black, and a breeze followed them, every so often taking the flaps of his coat and snapping them against his legs. It wasn't cold enough to be uncomfortable, just cold enough to disturb.

At forest twilight they came to a fork, and Lincoln veered to the right.

"What's that way?" Tania whispered.

"The graveyard."

"Good choice."

Here the road was better maintained. Though there were still ruts that threatened turned ankles, they were

more shallow and filled with gravel to smooth a vehicle's passage. Here and there, on the verge, he spotted
bits of litter—a paper cup, a rusted beer can, a shattered green bottle. The weeds were taller, more brittle,
and when the road swung to the right again, almost a
city corner, he spotted to the left winks and black
streaks of standing water.

Tania took his hand.

He smiled at her, winked, pulled her closer and
moved on.

A bird cried from the swamp, making them both
jump, and laugh nervously, and watch more closely the
way ahead.

The road narrowed.

The water reached the verge, rippling like oil when
the breeze blew, reflecting nothing when the air was
still. Linc tossed a pebble in, and didn't like the sullen
*plop* it made when it landed; it sounded as if it were
striking tar, and it left no bubbles behind.

"Was this really a plantation?" Tania asked skeptically, her right hand gesturing toward the dying
trees.

"I don't know. Old . . . my source claims the name's
an affectation. Unless Jannor harvests mosquitoes in
the summer, I'm inclined to think she's right."

"Maybe it belonged to his family."

He shrugged. He didn't care. Nor did he care to tell
her that someone was pacing them, back in the trees to
the right, and had been for the past fifteen minutes.
He couldn't see who it was, couldn't be positive it
wasn't an animal of some sort. But when he stopped to
pick up another stone to lob into the swamp, the sound
stopped as well.

When they moved on, the sound continued.

"How far?"

He didn't know. But he hoped the darkness would

210

let them see the house and its lights before anyone there knew they were coming. If, that is, it *was* an animal up ahead, and not a guard of some sort.

No, he decided; a place this remote, and with enemies supposedly long dead, Jannor wouldn't post a guard.

Unless either Scalia or Onbrous had returned to the ranch, found Judd dead and Linc and the woman missing. An attempt at ingratiation might have prompted a telephone call. Or there was going to be an attempt at interception.

"Lincoln?"

He unbuttoned his coat.

Tania cried out softly then and leaned against him hard. Her left foot had dropped into a rut and the ankle had turned. "Damn," she said.

"Can you walk on it?"

She sat on the ground and rubbed the ankle gingerly. "Just give me a minute. It stings, that's all."

He nodded, looked away, and saw the woman in the nightgown walking down the road toward them, a machete swinging idly in her left hand.

# Twenty-four

"I'm worried, Lincoln." Tania stood close behind him, nervously breathing over his right shoulder, hands lightly on his back as if ready to shove him away in case retreat was called for. "God, isn't she cold?"

Lincoln had a hand to his chest, scratching idly, waiting to see if it needed to go for the gun. "I don't know. You want to ask her?"

Though the woman was still too far away for him to make out her features in the dimming light, he guessed she was in her mid-twenties, her hair shoulder-length and dark, and the silken nightgown plain and white, long to her ankles, and serving as little protection against the breeze that rippled it, pressed it, billowed it out behind her under a pale pink dressing gown no less diaphanous or still, though she held it closed at her throat with her free hand. On her feet were a pair of simple slippers.

"Can she use that thing?" Tania wanted to know.

The woman stopped before he could respond, and lifted the machete, tilting her head to rest her cheek lovingly against the flat of the broad blade.

Linc smiled at her.

The woman batted her eyelids and tilted her head the other way. "Are you going to my house?" she asked, her voice oddly childlike.

He studied her for a moment, the attitude and the voice, before answering kindly, "I think so. Do you live at Darkriver?"

She giggled.

"Oh my god," Tania exclaimed sotto voce.

Linc turned to scold her, saw the horrified stare, and looked back at the woman. He frowned, squinted, and finally placed what it was that had Tania so frightened.

He refused to believe it. "Tell me," he said, keeping his voice soft, "what's you name, Miss?"

The woman giggled again and touched a finger to the blade's edge.

"Lincoln," Tania whispered. "Lincoln, my god!"

Though the face was considerably less rounded, the eyes not as wide, and the neck still without its picket of fatty wattles, the woman's lashes were incredibly long and dark, her teeth were movie-star white, and there was a prominent mole in the center of her chin. He wished he had asked Old Alice or Macon if Irene Yoman had ever been married. He hoped so. He also hoped fervently that this chid-woman was her grand-daughter.

"Oh!" the woman exclaimed, her lips parting in a sudden, delighted smile. "I know you! You're the tai-lor!"

He took a cautious step forward. "Yes, I am. But you still haven't told me who you are."

With a sly laugh the woman twirled on her toes, the

nightgown following in folds and billows, her hair tangling for a moment over her eyes. The machete stayed at her cheek, and she ran one finger along it now, from tip to hilt.

"I've been waiting for you," she said, covering her mouth and laughing again like a child with a secret.

"Lincoln," Tania said, backing away. "Lincoln, let's find another way, okay?"

He looked at the swamp, at the darkening forest, at the woman who was hopping excitedly from foot to foot. "Can you fly?" he said, and Tania answered with a curse.

"*I* can fly," the woman said gaily, and spread her arms, whirled about again, and hunkered down with a whoosh to drape her wrists over her knees. She grinned. "Did you see me fly?"

Lincoln gamely held his smile though his cheeks threatened to split; they were less than ten feet apart now, and he could see her face more clearly—the flesh not quite taut from abrupt weight loss, the lines and wrinkles about the eyes and mouth not quite shallow enough yet to be called simply laugh lines.

I am not going to enjoy this, he thought.

"Irene," he said, and crossed his fingers.

The woman bobbed her head, then looked up at him from beneath a fall of hair, pouting. "How did you know it was me?"

He shuddered. Damn; and his fingers relaxed. "Because you're so pretty."

Her free hand touched her lips. "Thank you, sir. But I have to admit that Pars helped a little."

Something, an owl, called in the forest.

"The Hooded Demon," Linc guessed, feeling the weight of the night too cold and heavy on his shoulders.

The child-woman nodded immediately. "It isn't nice,

214

though. It's scary. Don't you think it's scary? I do. I think it's really, *really* scary."

"I—"

"But the damn thing sure works," she added, giving him a bright smile. "Damn thing works damn good, you have to give it that. Scary. But it works."

Lincoln held back a sigh.

Irene Yoman was insane.

Her eyes were wide and gleaming, seeing everything, registering very little. And when he looked at them long enough he could see there was nothing behind them.

Granddaughter, he insisted to himself; it's only her granddaughter, and she's a loon.

"I'm an actress, you know," she said, almost crooning.

"Yes, I know. And you're very good too."

"Yes, I am. I always have been." She poked at the ground with the machete's point. "But now Pars says I'm going to be a world-wide star and make lots and lots of money so I can buy whatever I want."

Another step, his hands slipping into his pockets. "I don't doubt that at all."

"But he says he won't help me unless I kill you first."

Well, shit, he thought. "You don't believe him, do you? I mean, he was just kidding, of course."

"Oh no," she said solemnly, shaking her head quickly. "Oh no, he never kids with me." She rose then, and stretched. "I'm going to be a famous actress, and you're going to die." She sighed, loudly. "That's what he said."

He glanced at Tania, who was trying to unearth a half-buried rock. "Forget it," he said sadly, and pulled out the gun.

"Oh dear," Yoman said when he aimed it at her. "Oh, is that fair?"

215

"I think so," he answered. "Why don't you show us the way to the house, okay?"

"Gee, I don't know," she said doubtfully. "I could get in big trouble." She stared at her machete, stared at the gun, stared at the rock Tania finally pried loose. "Pars is going to be awfully mad."

"But not at you," Lincoln told her. "You did what you were supposed to. He'll be mad at me instead."

She started to smile, changed her mind and frowned. "But you're not dead," she declared, rechecking the weapons again and swinging hers slowly. "And you're supposed to be."

"The house," he reminded her, feeling suddenly desperate.

"Are you going to kill her?" Tania asked, standing along side him hefting the rock.

"No, I'm not going to kill her," he snapped.

"I didn't think so," she said, drew back an arm and threw the rock, which struck Yoman just above the right temple, and she crumpled to the ground with a long weary sigh. Then Tania marched over, grabbed the machete, and pointed. "Let's go. It's going to be dark soon."

He watched her walk off, a faint limp to prove that her ankle was still bothersome, then knelt beside the fallen actress. Blood ran slowly from a gash the rock had opened, but his attention was caught by a vicious bruise that spread outward from the base of her throat in a ragged circle, centered by two punctures still clotted with dried blood.

He wished he believed in vampires.

Then he checked her pulse; it was there, barely. He considered leaving his coat behind so she wouldn't freeze before she awakened, then rolled his eyes, and stood.

"Hey, Blackthorne, c'mon!"

It was obvious Jannor had tried the fangs without Dutch's help, and something had gone wrong; or this would be the result with or without Grange—youth truly restored; sanity gone.

Jesus; and he shivered for the loss of the grand-daughter protection. He'd been hoping like mad that the story was untrue and all he was after was a nut who was after some rubies. But it was, after all, the way of his luck. Nothing was ever straightforward these days; people had to make everything so goddamned complex, not caring that it was always the little guy who had to figure things out. Rubies that weren't rubies, a young woman who was an old woman, and now he was trudging down a road toward a plantation that, probably, had slaves in shacks, cotton in the fields, and the theme song from *Gone With The Wind* running on a tape recorder somewhere in the bushes.

"Blackthorne!"

He blew a kiss to the unconscious woman and hurried on, trying not to watch the swamp, not to watch the forest, keeping his gaze instead on Tania Burgoyne who, ruffles and all, was striding purposefully into what looked a long black tunnel.

The oaks, whose boles were a good four feet across, had been thriving and impressive at one time. Now they were dead, long dead, their branches scraping and rasping overhead, so thick and so entwined that very little of what was left of the light managed to reach the road.

Nightthings called out of the dark, sounding like no birds or animals he'd ever heard.

Something splashed in the swamp.

Tania slowed so he could catch up, chopping at the shadows with the machete while she complained about the road, the rapidly chilling air, finally taking his arm and saying, "You know, wealth really isn't all that it's cracked up to be."

"I wouldn't know," he said, watching the way ahead, noting that the trees lining the shoulder were too regularly spaced to be accidental. And the way the road curved in a wide arc to the left made him suspect that they would soon give way to other vegetation—garden shrubs, perhaps, or a lawn, or maybe giant Venus flytraps hunting for something to keep them going through the winter.

"I mean, when you think about it, Dutch and I had it pretty good even though we didn't have a lot of money."

"I guess," he muttered, walking backward a few paces in case Yoman came out of her stupor to follow, and finish what she'd been ordered to do. He wouldn't be surprised. Childlike though her mind might be, there was also something of the zombie about her, following orders unquestioningly and literally. When she woke up, she would be back, and he kicked himself for not taking the time to find something to use to tie her up with, like vines or stringy roots or maybe a miraculous length of ocean liner anchor chain.

"I mean, when you get right down to it, Dutch is too old to be in films anymore. Even as a producer. It's a young man's game these days. The pressure's too great, you know what I mean? Too many people sticking their noses in where they don't belong."

Something splashed.

Something called.

Tania stopped.

Linc kept walking.

"Lincoln?"

If all he had to contend with was Jannor, perhaps Onbrous and the Amazon, there ought not to be more than a few dozen ways that he could be killed. Though that wasn't as cheery a thought as he would have liked, it was better than including Shelger in the equation.

"Lincoln, I'm talking to you."

A little charm, a little bullshit, a lucky shot before anyone decided to shoot him first, and he could be back in Inverness by Christmas, plenty of time to finish that damned stupid suit, straighten Carmel out, and make sure that Atwaver was doing right by Clarise.

Something grabbed his arm. He whirled, gun out, and Tania slapped his arm with the broad side of the machete.

"Don't point that thing at me," she scolded. "It could go off."

The arm stung like hell; the gun vanished into the swamp.

She watched him watch its flight, then looked at the blade and lowered her arm. "Oh," she said.

"You know," he told her as he started walking again, "I suppose I should feel lucky. Most people would have just lopped off my arm, or my hand at the wrist. But not you. No. You had to use the flat, right? You—" He looked at her, and she shrugged. "That knife in the hotel room."

"I practice a lot," she explained.

"Show business?"

"No, I just like knives. A girl needs her defenses, you know. It's a jungle out there." She looked to either side of the road. "Well, maybe not out there, but out there, if you know what I mean."

"How far," he said, feeling recklessly giddy, "can you throw one? Accurately, that is."

"Far enough," she told him. "I usually don't miss, unless I'm distracted."

"You brag."

"I tell the truth."

The road continued its leftward curve, the trees still

in sentinel lines, and by the time it was almost too dark to see more than a few feet in front of him, Linc had a distressing idea.

He stopped. He considered how far they had come, considered the road's direction, and, finally, pointed. Tania sighted along his arm and shook her head.

"Yes," he said glumly.

"But that's a swamp, Lincoln!"

"I noticed."

"And it's dark."

"Tell me."

"We . . . we can't go in there now! We'll die. There might be alligators or something."

"This is Tennessee," he told her. "There are no alligators in Tennessee."

She closed one eye and stared at him. "Are you sure?"

He smiled reassuringly and walked on, ignoring the forest distressingly dark on the right, concentrating on finding the road Irene Yoman had taken out of the swamp. There had to be one. She couldn't have just floated over the water.

Full dark did him no good at all.

Neither did the cigarette lighter that Tania fished out of her pocket. The flame quivered away from the wind, and he was barely able to make out his feet, much less any of the road.

"Lincoln, I think we're going to end up where we started."

"No," he said, ten minutes later.

"Yes."

"No." And he nodded to a narrow bridge that lifted from the verge and disappeared into the dark.

"Lincoln, you can't!"

I wish you were right, he thought, and took the first step over.

# Twenty-five

The bridge was just high enough to clear the surface of the water, and Lincoln wasn't at all heartened by its evident crude construction—slender trunks and branches that still held most of their bark were lashed together by hemp and vine, and unpleasantly damp to the touch. It creaked. It swayed. It ended in a crude winding boardwalk that soon brought them to another bridge over the soggy, unseen ground.

He was, however, pleased; he'd begun to think about things like quicksand and bogs, and though the wooden road wasn't perfect, at least it kept him dry.

"I can't see anything," Tania complained behind him.

"Neither can I."

"Shouldn't there be a moon or something?"

He looked up and saw nothing, not even a star, and

he supposed that a cloud had moved in while they'd been walking.

"What if it rains?" she asked a few minutes later.

"Tania," he said.

"It could snow."

"Do you want to go back?"

"In the dark?"

He grinned and moved on, using the constant, rickety railings to guide him, ordering himself not to listen to the muffled splashings he heard, or the quick beat of wings out there in the dark. He decided that he didn't much care for swamps, even in winter. Though he supposed he ought to be grateful there were no insects to pester and bleed him, he thought he might prefer that to the way things were now. He also wished someone would turn on a goddamn light. Try as he might, he could see no glow of civilization, no betrayal of habitation, no hint that a house was somewhere ahead.

Another bridge, another stretch of planking.

He concentrated on taking one step at a time, testing the bridges' and boardwalks' strength, searching for gaps, thinking that should he ever fall off, one wrong turn and he'd be lost until morning; if, that is, the swamp deigned to let him live that long.

Tania swore when a branch slapped at her face.

A sudden stiff breeze made him adjust his collar more snugly around his neck as he wondered grumpily whatever happened to those lazy Tennessee summers he'd heard so much about, when the sun warmed you and the nights soothed you and there was always music of some sort twanging in the distance.

It was just his luck to get the seasons backward.

Christmas, he thought when the breeze blew again; bah, humbug.

After the third bridge, Tania touched his shoulder. "How far, scout?"

He had no idea. The artificial road wasn't straight, and though it thankfully had no forks to confuse him, its meandering had destroyed his already imperfect sense of direction. For all he knew, the house they were after was in the center and they were approaching it on a diminishing spiral. He refused to consider the possibility that they were, in fact, heading nowhere at all, that he'd been wrong, and their destination wasn't in the swamp in the first place.

"Maybe it's not in here," she whispered.

He scowled. "Of course it is."

"Is that a tailor's intuition?"

"More like a prayer."

"Swell."

He lost count of the number of bridges they crossed, had stopped counting the number of times a twig or small branch had reached over the railing to stab at his hands. And it wasn't much better when the clouds finally gave way, the moon appeared high, and the light it cast gave the swamp some dimension.

"Boy," Tania said when her vision adjusted. "I think I liked it better the other way."

He agreed with a grunt. While the moonlight enabled them to move slightly faster, it also outlined the dead and dying trees, the live ones, the twisted ones, and the hummocks and floating islands that crouched in the black water. It made them all look like things he didn't want to see.

And there was no sign of the house. No sign at all save the wooden road that anyone had ever entered the swamp before them.

The next bridge was the longest thus far, reaching over a huge pool of black completely devoid of vegetation. It was glass, not a ripple to mar it, not a dead leaf on its surface. Despite the chill, Linc felt perspiration matting his shirt to his back, and he took a slow breath before stepping off the planks.

The bridge sagged alarmingly. He shuffled more than walked, keeping his gaze on the far end, his arms slightly spread, his lower lip caught between his teeth. Long sections of the railing were missing, others were obviously held together by threads, and when a plank cracked and threw him forward, he automatically grabbed at the rail without thinking.

It snapped through, and Lincoln yelled.

It all happened in terrifying slow motion:

He toppled, and in flailing, felt himself go sideways, felt his shoulder strike the dangling railing, saw the water rising to take him, then felt something snare his arm and yank him back, twisting him until he was on his hands and knees.

He gulped for air and hung his head, gulped again and pushed himself shakily to his feet.

"Thanks," he said to Tania, who was hugging herself tightly.

Swallowing heavily, she nodded mutely, her face pale, her lips seeming black in the shadow-touched light. Her gaze kept shifting to the water, to the broken railing, then across the swamp as if, he thought, she was thinking of how it would be if he were gone and she was alone.

"Thanks," he said again, and took her in a brief embrace before moving on, this time keeping to the road's center, using the railings only when the support beneath him made him feel as if his balance was going and he had no other choice.

There was sweat now on his face, and it made him feel even colder.

"I just thought of something," she said as they started across yet another bridge, this one poked through with branches of underbrush.

"What?" he asked.

224

"Maybe I should have brought the flashlight."

He stopped. He turned. He pulled her close enough to see her face. "What flashlight?" he said, giving her his best *I think you're gonna die soon* smile.

"The one in the glove compartment."

In lieu of tearing her shoulders off, he patted them instead. "In the glove compartment?"

"Sure. I—"

"Hell."

"Now wait a minute! How was I to know we were going to end up in here, huh? You can't blame me for that, Blackthorne. All I ever wanted was to—hey!"

He grabbed the machete from her hand and forced her to go around him, the railing bending ominously, the bridge swaying as if shaken.

"Damnit, Linc, that's—"

"Shut up," he snapped.

She shut up.

There was someone out there. He had glimpsed flashes of movement along the pathway and between the trees not far behind them, and he knew they weren't caused by anything so prosaic as something dropping into the water. He also knew that unless someone else had arrived at Darkriver and didn't want to be late for the party, it had to be Irene Yoman, mobile again and intent on completing her task.

Okay, he thought, if you're so goddamned smart, what are you going to do about it? You going to stand here and chop her up, her with no weapon and you with a fat sword?

Linc, if you're thinking," Tania said nervously, "you'd better hurry up."

He glanced at the blade, looked down at the bridge, and finally smiled smugly to himself. He may not be able to stop her, but he'd at least put more distance between them.

225

"Tania," he said, "get to the other side."

Then, hearing rather than seeing her obey him, he lowered himself into a crouch and backed away slowly, searching for the weakest connections he could find. He had no idea how old this route was, but if experience was a decent teacher, he ought to be able to locate some area fairly soon where a good smack with the machete would help the decaying process along.

A few long moments later, when it was distressingly clear that all he was going to get was a pain in the back, Tania whistled a warning, and he glanced up just in time to see Irene step onto the bridge.

Nuts, he thought.

In her right hand she carried a large branch that had been stripped of leaves and twigs, a perfect club she held easily, much too easily, on her shoulder. She looked about her at the swamp, at the bridge, at him, and he saw dark streaks on her face that looked like thin cracks in marble, slashes and gleaming smudges on her nightgown, and the childlike expression she'd had earlier had been replaced by a blank mask that lay an ice cube on his nape.

"I want to be a star," she told him, swishing the club in front of her like a practicing musketeer. He could see the branch was heavy; she wielded it like a feather.

Instantly discarding the tactical luxuries of weak spots and vulnerabilities that would have made his job easier and spare him a direct fight with a madwoman, Linc frantically hacked at the lashing that held a trio of broad planks to the underpinning, missing more than he hit and swearing when a wood chip took a bite of his cheek.

"I can't be a star unless you're dead."

The rope wouldn't part.

226

The breeze steadied to a light wind that felt like January cold.

"Pars said so."

He looked back for Tania, but Dutch's daughter was gone, nothing there but jumping shadows and branches that scraped at the ground.

The bridge swayed.

Cursing himself for a soft heart and a softer head, he fell to one knee, slashed again at the rope and watched a part of it begin to fray. When he glanced up, he noticed that Irene was missing one slipper, and she didn't seem to care that the bare foot was bleeding.

She said, "You're not nice."

He hacked again. The rope separated. The planks didn't fall.

He groaned silently and went to work on the other side, had managed two good whacks before he felt the club in the air and threw himself back, out of its way. He landed on his buttocks, arms painfully behind him, and Irene stood there, shaking her head sorrowfully.

"I thought you were nice."

"Irene."

"I thought you were nice."

He pushed himself to his feet and gripped the machete in both hands. He wasn't adverse to fighting women, had done so several times before when it was either them or his fierce commitment to living; but this woman was insane, she didn't know what she was doing, and he felt that this somehow granted him unfair advantage.

She raised the club over her head, and smiled, and he could see that her beautiful teeth were rapidly turning yellow.

"Irene," he said, holding out a placating palm. "Irene, please, don't make me hurt you."

And thought *so much for chivalry* when she lowered the club and laughed. Loudly. Breathlessly. An old woman's cackling brittle and harsh, and a flock of dark birds exploded across the swamp, cawing, complaining, finally vanishing on the other side of the moonlight.

He took a step backward.

Irene stepped toward him, and the planks began to groan as the rope snapped strand by strand. She looked down and hopped quickly forward, landing just as the section he'd been working on fell into the water.

Oh . . . hell, he thought.

"I told you you weren't nice," she said, brushing greying hair from her eyes. "Pars was right. I can't be a star until you're dead first."

Viciously she swung the club, and his immediate instinct was to dodge to one side, and he was barely able to catch himself before he smashed through the railing to the water not all that far below. When he steadied, breathing heavily, the machete jabbed in a warning toward her stomach. She shook her head at it and swung again, this time driving him straight back as she herself was spun around. Giggling. Grinning tightly. Her eyes wide and unblinking.

A cloud touched the moon, and there was only her white gown, spinning as she drove him back, blurring, suddenly flaring when the moon returned and he couldn't move—her face was deeply lined, deeply pocked, a crone's face with blackened teeth, and completely mad eyes.

"Jesus," he said.

And Irene lunged at him, shrieking.

He moved without thinking, ducking under the club and using the flat of the blade to strike her on the ribs.

She whirled with a yell, but too quickly, and she lost her tenuous balance, the momentum of the club's swing taking her through the railing and into the black water.

There was no splashing.

She went under instantly, and the bubbles that reached the surface were viscous, like rising oil.

And he barely had time to wipe the sweat from his face when he heard Tania scream.

# Twenty-six

Lincoln hesitated, torn between charging deeper into the swamp and waiting to be sure Irene Yoman was truly gone, neither of which actually made him glad he was still alive.

Another scream, fainter, less powerful.

One of the bubbles popped with less force than a sigh.

Decisions, he thought, are a pain in the ass; and he raced off as best he could on the wobbly, sagging boardwalk, ducking under grasping branches, at one point dodging what he thought was a bird aiming for his eyes, sidestepping what he knew damned well was a snake taking a nap in his path.

There were no more screams; the only sound was the light tread of his soles on the wood.

When at last he slowed, he was panting, yearning for the good old days when running meant something solid beneath his feet instead of the give and sway of the wooden path that made his thighs ache and threw his sense of balance into near chaos. The topcoat weighed a ton. He could feel his breath turning to fog. And when he adjusted his speed to a slow trot, his lungs strongly suggested he give up and wait for the Mounties.

A minute later he stopped. Despite the moonlight, he realized that the swamp had grown darker ahead, no sign at all of tree trunks or shrubs, and no dim reflection of the nightsky in the swamp's placid surface. He checked for the moon; it was still there. He checked the direction in which he was heading; it was still dark, still formless.

It was unnerving. As if something had decided not to let any light in at all, and he wondered if it would be any better once the sun had finally risen.

He asked Tania to scream again, to give him proof she was still alive; and when he heard nothing but something swimming noisily off to his left, he ran again, taking a corner so sharply he nearly went off the road. Then, a dozen yards later, he realized that the walkway was canting upward, lifting him farther above the surface, soon turning into a sharp incline that had him gasping until he slowed, nearly stopped, and found himself staring at a monstrous wall.

Clever Pars, he thought, and waited for his vision to catch up with his brain.

The wall was a dark-leaved hedge fully twelve to fifteen feet high, easily as thick as a brick wall, and growing around the perimeter of what he assumed was a low hill in the middle of the swamp.

Welcome to Darkriver, he thought, and have a nice day.

The walkway leveled ten yards or so from the barrier, and he took the remaining distance at a slow walk. Watching as the area on the other side slowly came into view, and he saw first the light, then the outline of the house.

Simply going straight ahead was too easy and offended his sense of sneaking up on things, and he wondered if it were possible to go around, and someplace along the way find a convenient gap in the hedge. The answer to the first was no, because the land when he checked was too steep and covered with heavy brush; the answer to the second was the same, because when he put out a hand to test the wall's sturdiness, it was nearly skewered by thorns a good three inches long.

Neither was there was a gate in the gap; there was no need. Anyone who made it this far was either expected, or probably wouldn't get much farther once spotted. And that would be easy, because there were no trees between the hedge-wall and the house, nothing at all but a vast expanse of lawn he supposed took up all the space reclaimed from the swamp.

And the house—a fat and wide three-story affair made of wood and brick as far as he could tell, with a wide veranda running around the ground floor, and matching pillared balconies around the second and third. It was pale beneath the moon, probably white, and the low peaked roofline was broken by at least a dozen chimneys, a few of which were lazily belching smoke the wind took over the trees.

He had no idea which side of the building he was facing, but he could see a shimmering glow in one tall window at the left-hand corner, blurred cracks of light that outlined the edges of draperies and fell in shifting bars on the veranda, not quite reaching the grass.

He waited a few seconds more to see if there were dogs, or guards, or another nut on the loose, then slapped the machete against his leg and began walking.

He had no illusions of bringing surprise with him,

the cavalry charging to the daring rescue; Tania was in there, and Jannor had probably deduced that Linc was not far behind.

And that puzzled him.

For a man intent on such an important, albeit insane, mission, there was a curious, not to mention disturbing, lack of concern for interlopers and invaders. At the very least, Linc would have crammed the grounds with starving Dobermans or ravenous Rotwielers, or imported some alligators, or trained some rattlesnakes, or something. But as it was, there was nothing to stop him, and he made it to the veranda without challenge, passing between a pair of huge clay pots that held drooping palm trees and stopping at a pair of high double doors with a brass knocker in the shape of a roaring lion's head.

He was tempted to use it.

Instead, he moved quietly to the corner and tried to peer through the draperies. The view was dismal. There were curtains as well, and he could see nothing but unmoving dim shapes that could have been people, could have been furniture, could have been wallpaper for all he could tell. He moved back toward the door then, trying each of the eight windows he passed. They were, unsurprisingly, locked. As were those on the far side.

As he puffed against the cold, damp now as the wind blew in from the swamp, he looked around the corner, considered, and carried on, noting that there was no entrance on this side, only more tall windows, another group of potted palms, the stretch of lawn to the hedge. The back of the house was the same, though here there was another set of double doors solidly locked, and a stone path that pointed into the dark. He had no idea where it led, and had no inclination to follow it; Macon would disapprove, but then, Macon was back in New Jersey shoveling snow and singing carols.

By the time he returned to the front, he had decided that he was only wasting effort. The word *stalling* came to mind, but he dismissed it as inaccurate. Close, but inaccurate.

"Nuts," he muttered, and strode back to the door, took hold of the knob, and turned it after taking a deep breath and telling himself what an idiot he was. When it opened, he merely shrugged; when the lights went out, he merely shook his head, hefted the machete, and walked in.

What the hell, he thought; it beats climbing through a window.

The door closed behind him, shrieking on hinges that had been perfectly silent before.

A deep voice said, "Don't move, Mr. Blackthorne, or the girl dies."

Lincoln obliged; there wasn't anything else he could do because he couldn't see a thing.

By shifting his feet, he knew he was standing on a thick carpet of some kind, and he guessed he was in a rather large central hall. If the house followed convention, there would be entrances to rooms on both left and right, and a staircase to the upper floors somewhere straight ahead, flanked by halls that led to the rest of the house.

On the other hand, Jannor could have fitted the place out like Fort Apache, or he could be standing on the lip of a bottomless pit, ready to plunge to a premature death the moment he defied orders and took matters into his own hands, which at the moment were pushing his hair out of his eyes.

Oh Christ, Blackthorne, he thought, put a lid on it, okay?

He listened.

The wind, the distant scrape and whistle of trees and branches, and his own slowly calming breathing; nothing else, not a clue.

"Please, Mr. Blackthorne," the voice said, "place your weapon on the floor behind you and give it a kick."

"What if I don't want to?" he answered, slowly turning his head, trying to get a fix on the voice's origin.

"Don't be foolish. Do as you are told."

He considered telling the voice what it could do with all this melodrama, considered what it could do to Tania, and scowled as he obeyed, grimacing when the machete struck one of the walls; he hadn't meant to kick it quite that hard, or that far away.

"Thank you."

"Don't mention it."

"Please take three steps forward."

He did.

The voice congratulated him for not trying to change that over which he had no control.

And Linc immediately shut his eyes, smiling when the lights sprang on in an obvious attempt to blind him; when he opened them, it took only a second to see where he was and pat himself on the back when he saw the high, closed, sliding doors that evidently led to rooms on either side, the two dark halls that would take him to the back of the house, and the wide, fan-shaped staircase directly in front of him, its steps carpeted in dark red up to a shallow landing where they branched right and left to a gallery above.

It was impressive.

The paneled walls of the central hall were two stories high, painted white and gold, interrupted only by the gallery off of which ran two other corridors, presumably to the rooms on the second floor. There were no pedestals with busts, no portraits, no banners; the

235

carpet, a good twenty by twenty and appearing smaller in the huge room, was royal blue, the hardwood floor around the outside pegged and highly polished, and over his head was a spearlike chandelier whose crystal teardrops multiplied the bulbs alight within.

Pars Jannor stood in the center of the landing, in evening dress, and holding the jackal's head cane.

"Tara," Linc said with an approving smile.

"Darkriver," Jannor snapped, rapping the cane once on the floor. "You are in Darkriver, Mr. Blackthorne, *my* home, and you'd do well not to forget it."

"What about Tania and Dutch?" he asked. He hadn't moved. He had a feeling, nothing more, that a single step in the wrong direction would prove that Jannor wasn't quite so dumb as to greet him without someone lurking in a shadow someplace.

"The Burgoynes are well."

Linc nodded.

Jannor watched him, eyes half closed.

Linc waited, slipping out of his coat and dropping it to the floor. Then he shoved his hands into his pockets, glanced around, and pursed his lips in a silent whistle. It was obvious Jannor was waiting for something, and since he had no idea what to do next, he figured he might as well wait along with him.

Footsteps on a bare floor.

He looked up to the gallery and frowned.

Jannor shifted the cane from right hand to left and cleared his throat. "As I understand it, you were most unpleasant to one of my guests," he said.

"If you mean Irene," Linc said, "she tried to kill me."

"It was her destiny."

"Just like Shelger?"

Jannor dipped his head. "He served his purpose, tailor. He was well aware of the risks."

"But you didn't shoot him."

236

Jannor laughed without a sound. "No. A simple snap of his neck, that's all." He flexed the fingers of his free hand. "It was easy."

Linc turned in a small circle, openly admiring the house, stopping several feet closer to the staircase as he tugged on an earlobe. He had seen no one hiding, the footsteps had stopped, and he was positive the actor wasn't carrying a gun. He scratched his head.

"Irene was . . . I suppose you used the fangs on her, right?"

Jannor grinned toothlessly. "Let us just say, Mr. Blackthorne, that in spite of your reluctance to assist me, I have managed to attain that which I sought, and I have been endeavoring to ascertain the full spectrum of qualities which that object possesses."

"You screwed up," Linc said, shaking his head and moving again, until he was at the base of the staircase and wondering why the man didn't warn him to stop.

Jannor's face darkened and he took a step down. "I do not err, tailor! I test and retest. I do things over and over until they're just right! My films will attest to my devotion. It is the way of it." The grin became a smile. "You will see what I mean in just a few moments."

Linc counted fifteen steps between him and the actor. If he charged now, the man would either turn and run for his life, in which case he'd be easily caught, because of his age; or he'd draw that damned sword out of the cane, in which case Linc would have to figure out a way to dodge the blade, disarm the man, and grab him, all before that blade sliced him to pieces and ruined the carpeting.

Not to mention his own peace of mind.

Jannor drew the blade.

Spoilsport, Linc thought.

"And now, tailor," the actor said, pulling a watch

from his waistcoat and flipping open the lid, "it is time that you and I have a history lesson."

Linc backed away. "I don't think so, Jannor."

Jannor laughed, again without a sound. "You don't understand, tailor. You do not have a choice. You will come with me, or you will die where you stand."

"You can throw that thing that far?"

"No, but my colleague can certainly shoot that far, and rather accurately, I might add."

Lincoln looked up at the gallery, and grabbed for the banister to keep himself from falling.

"You," he said. "Well, Jesus H. Christ."

# Twenty-seven

"Y ou know," Lincoln said, too disheartened to be angry, "I should have known something like this was going to happen." He shook his head in resignation and slouched against the banister, two steps up. "I mean, it was there right in front of me all the time, but I was too dumb to see it. People who knew where I lived, where I worked, people who knew people I knew without me knowing how they knew— so many damned people who didn't belong, that I should have known there was someone in town who was doing most of the talking."

Jannor whipped the sword a few times, slicing the air and humming Wagner right on key.

"Ridiculous," Linc continued. "You made me look like a real fool, you know." He sighed loudly and appealed to Jannor. "He did, didn't he? He made me look like a jackass."

The actor nodded with pleasure.

"That's what I thought." He looked back to the gallery, and the man standing in the doorway, dressed in a dark pullover, dark slacks, and dark running shoes. "What I want to know is, how did you find out about it—the Hooded Demon, I mean—in the first place? I didn't think you were the kind of guy who went in for reading tip sheets and magazines and stuff about antiques and long lost treasures."

Dennis Atwaver stepped to the gallery railing, gripped it, and leaned forward. "I'm George's doctor, remember? Everything he knows, I know. It's no big mystery, Lincoln. You're just a little dim, that's all."

Linc smiled at him briefly. "Thanks. And how's Clarise? She still on those machines?"

The question was asked offhandedly, but Atwaver frowned uncertainly at the tone.

"She's fine. Nothing to worry about. She's in good hands, for the time being."

He didn't miss the threat. "So she knew what you were doing from the start."

"Something like that."

Jannor swished the sword again and moved a bit closer.

"So she tried to get the fangs first so you wouldn't? And she didn't tell George about it because she knew he wouldn't believe her?"

"Something like that."

"She's a good woman."

Atwaver placed a finger alongside his nose. "And she'll continue to be, Lincoln, as long as you don't try anything stupid. As I said—she's in good hands. For the time being."

Christ, he thought glumly, I've got more hostages to worry about than the State Department; and he wished, just once, that Jannor would stop playing with that goddamn sword.

The sword swished.

Linc shifted to look at the actor. "And I suppose he promised you eternal youth, millions of dollars, and a free hand with your conquering the world plan if you'd help him. Have I got that right?"

Jannor's gummy smile widened. "Something like that. Not exactly."

"Actually," Atwaver said, folding his arms on the railing and leaning over again, "*he* came to *me*." Then he sneezed, fumbled a handkerchief out of his hip pocket and blew his nose. "It was almost a coincidence, you might say. Or damned good luck."

"He what?" His neck was getting sore, but he figured it was all in a good cause if he survived this mess.

"I knew of the rumors," Jannor told him, moving down behind the sword's blur, "from my own sources. I also knew Dennis from the old days. His family, you see, tended to my family. Rather well. Right here."

Linc's eyebrow lifted. "For true, Den?"

"The old days are the old days," the doctor said with a hint of warning. "My father was Jannor's personal physician." He made it sound as if the elder Atwaver had been a stable boy in charge of shovels, as well as letting Jannor know that the shoe was now somewhat on the other foot.

"Ah," Lincoln said. "So dear not-so-innocent Clarise, since she does most of George's work anyway, knew about what Dutch had done. But she also figured Grange couldn't be the only one in the picture, so to speak, so she got me to . . ." He exhaled loudly. "Brother."

"True again," Atwaver said. He waved a hand in regret. "And it would have been so much simpler if you hadn't gotten into the act the way you did."

"Hey, no problem," he said, lifting his palms, "I'll leave now if you want me to."

Atwaver glared.

"So, it is not my fault it ended this way," Jannor protested to the man in the gallery.

"Oh really?"

My goodness, Linc thought, dissension blossoms in the ranks of the rich and stupid. He only wished he knew how to exploit it.

The sword stabbed.

Linc took another step up.

Atwaver glowered at the actor and motioned sharply with his hand: *bring the tailor up and let's get on with it.*

Linc wasn't sure what *it* was, or what Dennis hoped to get out of *it* when *it* was finally over, but his instincts told him in no uncertain terms that he didn't want any part of *it*, not now or in the foreseeable future. He also realized that time was running out for somebody pretty damned fast. Christmas dawn was only two days off, and perhaps, assuming the fangs were indeed working properly, he might be able to outrun the old man, lose himself in the swamp until noon of that day, and return to clean up without a single shot being fired. Metaphorically, he sincerely hoped, since a surreptitious check reminded him that he'd lost the damned gun again.

On the other hand, they already had the fangs, not to mention Tania and Dutch, with Clarise in reserve back in the hospital, and all his running would do would get them reasonably dead.

He decided he must be tired; he wouldn't have made that mistake in Oklahoma.

"Pars," Atwaver snapped, and gestured again.

Jannor nodded sharply, stopped just out of Linc's reach and aimed the sword at his heart. It didn't quiver an inch. "Upstairs, tailor," he said.

"Have you ever thought you're a little too old for this kind of stuff?" Linc asked him as he started up.

242

"I have."

"Then?"

"I shall not be old for long," was the answer.

"No kidding," Lincoln said, stumbled, stood, and with an apologetic shrug shifted over to the banister to haul himself up to the landing. Jannor followed closely, the sword whispering while Atwaver slammed an impatient fist on the railing and told them both to get a move on.

Linc lifted a hand—*okay, okay*—and turned to Jannor, just as the posturing actor was at the high point of one of his fancy circumscriptions with his weapon. At that moment Linc jumped, one foot out, one hand back, and his shoe caught the man in the center of his chest. The sword slashed across Linc's knee, slicing through the trouser and a fair cut of skin. But the old man was too surprised to do anything but try to keep his balance, which gyrations and windmilling sent him backward over the banister to the floor below.

Linc, his outstretched hand preventing his skull from striking the step, whirled, scrambled, and began to run—across the landing and up the steps to the gallery, just in time to see Atwaver vanish down the corridor.

Jannor bellowed revenge.

Trying to ignore the burning in his leg, Linc raced across the gallery, took the turn into the corridor, and raced on as the fleeing doctor reached a distant T-intersection and spun to his left. The corridor was long and narrow, dark wainscoting below and white plaster above; once again there were no ornamentations, only a series of tall, carved-panel doors flanked by dimly glowing lights fashioned like flickering candles. Their knobs were brass; there were no keyholes that he could see.

Jannor's bellowing faded.

With little time at hand, Linc had to chose between checking each room along the way, hoping to get lucky, or following Atwaver, instantly deciding on the latter because if the man was heading for the Burgoynes, they'd need Linc's help; and if he wasn't, Linc could always find out where they were once he'd caught up with him.

He slowed at the intersection and looked quickly around the corner. The corridor stretched on, to meet yet another which ran the width of the house in back.

Atwaver was gone.

Linc hurried without running, again ignoring the doors, wishing the lights were brighter, wishing he'd brought a howitzer when he reached the back, looked right, and spotted Atwaver ducking through a doorway midway toward the far end.

The door slammed.

He heard limping footsteps behind him.

He ran to the spot where the doctor disappeared, put an ear to the door, and heard nothing but his own labored breathing.

He tried the knob.

It turned.

He glanced down at his left leg and winced when he saw the bare skin, the oozing blood, the hanging strip of trouser, and suggested strongly to himself that it was no worse than it looked, no worse, in fact, than a badly skinned knee.

Right, he thought, and flung the door open, charged in, and skidded to a halt when he found himself in the middle of a huge empty room. There were no rugs, no furniture, no windows, nothing. Paneling. Bare walls. No dust on the floor to show him a trail.

The man had vanished.

Oh bloody hell, he thought in disgust; the place has goddamn secret passages.

He ran back to the hall just as Jannor limped around the corner. The actor saw him and shook his fists in rage; Linc ran up to him, put a fist into his stomach, caught him before he fell, and dragged him back to the room.

"How?" he demanded, holding the man upright by the collar of his evening jacket.

Jannor tightened his lips and shook his head.

"Admirable," Linc told him, "but if you want to live to see Christmas, old pal, you'll tell me." He didn't give the man a chance to answer; he punched him again and silently asked Macon to forgive him for slugging a fellow geriatric. "Well?"

Jannor was red-faced, thick lips smacking as he gulped for a breath, his hands feebly trying to slap himself free.

"You get one more chance," Linc said. "Then I'm going to throw you down the stairs and burn this place down."

"You . . . can't," Jannor gasped.

"I can," he assured him.

The old man stared, searched his face, and pointed shakily to the far wall.

Linc let him drop, groaning, and walked to the wall, saw immediately that one of the wainscoting panels was slightly lighter and wider than the others. A quick check to be sure the actor was still on the floor, and he ran his hands around the ridged rim; he poked it and tapped it, then he gave up and pushed it; it swiveled open, and beyond was a dank tunnel with steps leading down.

"Christ, you're corny," he said to Jannor, and ducked inside, spun around when the panel slammed shut and left him in the dark. "Christ, you're stupid," he said to himself, and began to descend without bothering to attempt to get out, hands along the wall, going

245

easy on his knee, hunching whenever what he hoped was a spider web brushed lightly across his face. He could hear nothing below, could see no torchlight or candlelight, but that didn't mean a thing, unless, he thought suddenly and ruefully, there was more than one passage, and Jannor knew he wouldn't think of it until it was too late.

He stopped.

He sniffed.

He rubbed his neck, his chest, scrubbed his hands dryly and chewed for a moment on his lower lip.

Then he continued downward until he stumbled onto a landing. There were no exits that he could discover, so he made the turn, and went down again, more cautiously now, estimating that he'd already dropped below the level of the first floor and was somewhere in the vicinity of the basement.

Lower still.

Water dripped in the distance.

The air grew more damp, and was tainted with the stench of rotting vegetation; the walls became stone blocks and felt spongy with what he fervently prayed was only moss, and when he reached the bottom, he swore that if he was in a dungeon, he was going back up to strangle Jannor until his neck was no thicker than a straw.

He kept the staircase at his back and stretched his arms out in front of him. The sensation of being in a large open room persisted, and he lowered them, took several deep breaths, and decided to check the room's size by moving along the walls. He wasn't about to cross over; his eyes were already too strained to see anything but bright spinning lights.

Sideways, then, shuffling and not caring how much noise he made. Atwaver knew he was here; he had to. It was now simply a matter of finding the way out and continuing the pursuit.

246

And when he reached the staircase again, fifteen minutes later, without locating a single exit, a single chain on the walls, he wondered what he'd done wrong.

And when a steel door slammed down and nearly cut him in half, he wondered how he could have asked himself such a stupid question.

Especially when he heard what sounded like a rasping grunt coming from the room's center.

Whatever had made the noise couldn't be human.

And whatever he heard coming toward him most definitely wasn't small.

# Twenty-eight

I will never make cracks about alligators again, Lincoln promised as he pressed his back against the wall and tried to ease right without making undue noise. But that's what it had to be, his imagination insisted; he was in the middle of a swamp in the middle of nowhere and nothing else fit the bill. It certainly wasn't a dog, or a pack of them, and it most assuredly wasn't a snake of some sort; not even a python or boa would sound that large. The unthinkable he refused to think about. Alligator was the only beast that came readily and reluctantly to mind, and it stuck there, tail sweeping the floor, mouth agape, teeth dripping saliva, and its eyes trying as hard as he to see in the dark.

Silence for a moment; the 'gator had stopped moving.

He wiped a hand over his face, then back through his hair.

If only he knew which direction the thing was facing,

where its attention was focused. Beyond doubt, the massive tail was the immediate danger, eminently capable of snapping his legs to splinters should it lash out and hit him, blindly or not; the jaws were no slouch either, for that matter, but they weren't as flexible or quick, and, in a room this size, he ought to be able to dodge them long and safely enough to locate the manner of the beast's entrance.

That alone gave him hope as he reached the first corner, arms spread wide along the walls, fingers out and growing cold in the damp they touched without touching water. The creature hadn't dropped in from above, nor had he heard the slightest sound of a door opening and closing. Which meant there had to be some egress through the floor—a tunnel, a pipe, perhaps another room beneath this one from which it had been thrust.

For not taking the risk of crossing the floor he was now grateful; it was, probably, the first non-dumb thing he'd done since getting up in that morning, and he still wasn't entirely sure he shouldn't have just stayed in bed.

Scraping; something dragged across the stone.

His fingers groped the wall as he maneuvered on, searching for a loose stone, a fragment, anything he might use as a weapon, no matter how feeble. The knife on his forearm was no good to him this time; unless the 'gator conveniently rolled over and exposed its belly for execution, the blade was too thin to penetrate its hide.

Another grunt, softer.

Perspiration rolled into his eyes and he shook his head once and vigorously, wiped his brow, dried his palm on his trousers and did it all again.

He considered dropping to all fours and making his way toward the floor's middle. A tricky maneuver, and most likely the wisest tactic. It would require the keen use of all his senses in order to avoid bumping into the thing, but if it kept heading toward his original position, he just might be able to find the hole and drop through—it didn't make any difference what was below. Anything was better than playing hide-and-seek with an overgrown salamander. Of course, the thing might be tethered, in which case he'd only collide with it, and would then have to either get the hell out of the way before it realized what had happened, or grapple with it if there was no time.

Unless he bumped into the tail. Or the snout.

In which case there was no other case and he might as well hang it up.

At the next corner water landed on the back of his neck, a teardrop of ice that stiffened him and nearly had him shouting at the cold.

The alligator still moved, sluggishly but steadily, as if turning in circles.

How well, he wondered then, does one of those things smell?

It whistled.

Lincoln froze, refusing to believe his ears.

But it was whistling, no question about it—a nearly subvocal tuneless rush of air between lips he knew damned well were not created for puckering.

Unless the thing was simply breathing through its nostrils, and the escaping air only sounded like whistling.

He asked himself how lucky he felt; he answered *don't be stupid* and without delay discarded the notion of speaking, just to be sure he wasn't dealing with something human.

Then he threw his hands in front of his eyes when a sudden explosion of light blinded him, so violent was it that his knees sagged and he nearly dropped to the floor.

"Peekaboo," a voice said. "Is that you?"

Warily, Linc lowered his hands, blinking rapidly to restore his vision, pressing so hard against the wall that his spine finally protested and he ordered himself to relax. Then he squinted, his head turned aside, until the walls came into focus, the darkly damp floor, and the woman standing near the steel plate on the other side, a flaming torch in her left hand, held over her head.

Oh god, he thought wearily, wishing to hell he could deal with that alligator instead.

She wore a hoop-skirted white gown with lace and green ribbons at the bodice, her shoulders bare, her auburn hair done in ringlets and woven through with daisies. She was not slender, her bosom too expansive for its confinement, her hips too broad for the folds and falls of the skirts she wore, but neither was she as large as he'd last seen her, at the airport in New York.

She was also a good thirty years younger.

He shaded his eyes then and spotted the hole in the floor, with just the tip of ladder poking through from below.

"How are you, Marjorie," he said as calmly as he could.

She smiled without humor. "Jes fine, you sweet thang, you. Ah've been lookin' all over the house for you. All that noise you were makin', you think you could hide on me, you li'l devil you?"

He shook his head, held a hand briefly over his stomach where a chill was forming and mixing with bile.

Her arms were bare save for the puffs of material just below the shoulders, and on the left one he could see the repulsive spread of a bruise around two dark punctures. When she saw him staring, she turned aside, lowering the torch and holding it toward him.

251

"It's a risk, tailor," she said, the smile now lop-sided, the accent gone.

"Too much of one, if you ask me," he replied.

Her right eye closed in a slow, obscene wink. "When you have as much to lose as I do, tailor, you can tell me that again."

He eased away from the wall.

"Now," she said, tossing her ringlets and winking again. "Whatever are we going to do with you?"

"Beats me," he said.

"Fine with me," she told him, ducked her hand into the folds of her skirt and pulled out a coiled bullwhip. A snap of her wrist, and the explosion was like a gunshot. "I don't intend to get as close to you as Irene did."

"You know?"

Her lips lost the smile. "I can guess. She wasn't supposed to leave the house, but then she always was one to follow her own mind."

He wanted to tell her that Yoman didn't have a mind left to follow by the time he had encountered her, but he could see the same madness glimmering in her eyes, and kept his silence. He eased forward again, half the length of a shoe, and rubbed his arms as though he were cold.

The whip cracked, and he could have sworn he saw a spark, which he did when she snapped it at the floor by the hole.

"You're thinking," she said smugly, pointing the torch at him, "that you might be able to dive through that bitty little hole before I can wrap this around your neck." Her sharp nod was smug. "You're thinking that whatever you find down there has just got to be better than dueling with poor ol' me, isn't that right, boy?"

"Got it in one," he said truthfully.

She tittered, and the torch trembled. "We could make it a game."

252

"You could let me go."

She laughed, and the laugh echoed.

"You know what's happened to you, don't you," he said. "You know, Marjorie."

"I know what I had."

"Is that better than madness?"

The whip cracked, and he stepped back hastily, blinking because he'd hardly seen her arm move.

"Madness?" She chuckled. "I don't think so."

"You didn't see Irene, at the end."

"Oh, but I saw her before, and she was so . . . so full of youth and vitality . . . oh Lord, it was a sin!"

The whip; he shifted to his left.

"You're going to die," he told her flatly. "Whatever those fangs do, they don't give you what he promised."

The whip; the laugh; she waved the torch and sparks fell.

"Pars is a fool," she said, practically spitting. "He thinks he's going to take over the world. What a fool!" She pointed the torch again, then yanked it back and twitched it at her side like a cat's tail. Shadows swept across the floor, the ceiling, and the walls seemed to contract and drift away, then snap back again, closer and higher.

A sudden step forward, and the whip cracked a breath away from his knee. He flinched and shifted right; the whip split the air just above his left shoe.

"Ah'm pretty good, don't you think, tailor? For a country girl, ah'm pretty good with a man's toy, ain't that right?"

"Marjorie, he's killed you and you don't know it."

She grinned stiffly. "So you say."

"So I know."

She began circling the room, driving him ahead of her, slowly, slowly, the torch swinging, the shadows, the whip chasing him and biting.

"You don't know anything, tailor," she said when his

253

back was to the steel plate again. "There's more to the magic than what you see before you."

"You'd better hope so."

She laughed.

Christ, he thought, doesn't she ever get angry?

"Oh, I know so." A long deep breath that almost spilled her breasts from the gown. "You see, Dennis knows what comes next, and as soon as I'm done, the rest will be taken care of. Pars can perch on a dull tack for all I care."

"Ah." He nodded. "Ah. I see." He flexed his fingers to keep them loose, watched her drift to his left and move him toward the corner. "Dutch. Right, I get it. Dutch is going to finish it, I guess."

"Who?"

He stopped. "Dutch Grange. The man Jannor brought here to teach him about the fangs."

"Oh for heaven's sake, we don't need him anymore," she said. "We know it all now. He's . . ." She glanced at the hole. "Oh, I'd say he'd be in conversation with the Demon just about now."

"I see."

She laughed. "No you don't, Mr. Blackthorne. You think you do, but you don't know shit."

He almost felt compelled to protest her language, decided instead to dodge when the whip arched over the hole and tried to take a piece of his forehead. As it was, a strip of his jacket vanished from his shoulder, and he hurriedly shrugged it off and wrapped it around his left hand.

"My," she said, strutting now, head erect, "I do believe the gentleman is going to attempt to grab the whip when next I strike. He will then attempt to pull me off my feet, do me bodily harm, and escape with both his balls intact." She looked at the walls as if they were an audience. "Tell me, have we seen this before? Have we been subjected to this bit on other occasions?"

Well, hell, Linc thought.

She whirled then and took a long stride toward him, the whip flaring over his head, snapping across his right hip when he tried to dodge. He yelped. She giggled. The whip took his left hip, and a fair gouge from his belt. He yelped. She yelled. And she stopped to take a breather, idly and coyly snaking the whip over the face of the hole in case he had a mind to try something while she waited.

"Screw it," Linc said at last. "This is stupid, Iddle, and you know it."

"Stupid?"

"Okay. Dumb."

"Dumb?"

He put his hands on his hips. "Jesus H., woman, are you going to play cat-and-mouse all goddamn night, or are we going to get on with it?"

"Now you listen here, tailor," she snapped, flipping the torch back and forth so rapidly the whipping shadows made him dizzy, "you just show a little fortitude, you understand me? You just show yourself a man!"

He snorted.

The whip nearly caught his throat.

Marjorie laughed, her head thrown back, her hands on her hips with the torch dangling behind her. It was a pose Linc recalled from whatever horrid film of Jannor's he had seen, and he would have said something about it in order to further enrage her, but instead he said, "Marjorie, for god's sake!" and pointed behind her.

"Quiet!" she ordered.

"Jesus, Iddle, you're—"

She screamed.

With a crackling like crushed paper her skirts ignited as if they'd been soaked in oil, enveloping her in white flame before she even had a chance to appeal for help. Her hair caught, and she screamed again, and raced back and forth across the room before, finally, flinging the whip and torch at him and dropping to her knees.

Linc could do nothing but gape. He'd already unwrapped the jacket from his wrist in faint hope of smothering the fire, but it moved too rapidly, far too rapidly to be natural, and he gagged at the stench of the woman's burning flesh.

She screamed.

He grabbed up the torch and the whip.

She lurched to her feet, and he stared at her in disbelief, could not move when her screams became a bellow of rage and she charged across the room and flung herself at him.

# Twenty-nine

Lincoln froze for a second, gaping, then threw himself to the floor and rolled toward the center, stiffening as Iddle flew over him and landed with a sickening thud against the wall. He scrambled to his knees, saw her arms feebly beating the air as if looking for something to hold onto, and wasted no time climbing down the shaky ladder, not even pausing when he heard her start to moan his name.

Impossible, he thought in near despair; she's dead, it's not possible.

The room below was much smaller, its walls slick with dark water trickling through seams in the blocks, its floor treacherously slippery as inch-deep water sought a series of tiny drains set randomly in the stone. He fell twice, each time managing to keep the torch above his head; the third time he lost his balance, he fell against a thick oak door, its latch rusted when he yanked it, swore loudly, finally loosened it and nearly fell over the threshold.

He could still hear Iddle moaning.

Dear god, I hate Christmas, he thought, and with the torch over his head he found himself at the end of a narrow tunnel that canted upward into darkness. He didn't hesitate; he ran, slapping away spider webs, refusing to look when he heard faint chittering behind him, breathing through his mouth in order not to take in too much of the stench that made the place seem like a long-disused charnel house.

The tunnel turned left, and still moved upward.

The torch began to sputter, its light fading, the shadows it cast darker and larger.

Don't you *dare*, he told it, holding it lower, watching it gutter.

He tripped over something soft and fell, groaned at the impact and slid on his shoulder for several feet before righting himself again. The whip was gone, somewhere back there in the dark. He didn't bother to hunt for it. He ran on instead, around yet another turn where he saw a short flight of chipped wooden steps that ended at an open door.

Though he knew full well the need for caution, he didn't care. The smell of Marjorie Iddle's dying still clung to him, and he couldn't rid himself of the sound of her furious screaming—he took the steps two at a time and exploded through the doorway, not checking for anyone, not stopping until he came up hard against a wall in a room painted to look as though it were a cell in a dungeon.

He dropped the torch and leaned forward, retched dryly, and sagged to his haunches, retched again and sat back on his heels, holding his waist tightly until most of him either stopped aching or went thankfully numb. A look to the ceiling, and he finally allowed himself a full deep breath, and another, forcing himself to take it slowly lest he make himself dizzy. His nose wrinkled at the smell of him, of the dank water that covered him from his falls, but at least he didn't smell like charred and burning flesh.

The torch went out.

"Damn," he muttered, but he didn't even blink when he realized he could still see; it was the least the world could do for him now.

At last, when he was reasonably sure he'd be able to move without falling flat on his face, he regained his feet and stumbled to the tunnel door, closed it, fell against it with a sigh, and looked to his right, to another door with a barred judas window through which he could see a hallway wallpapered in pink roses.

If I ever write my memoirs, he thought, they're going to lock me away.

The question was, now, what the hell to do next?

Obviously, Atwaver the traitor scum and Jannor the pompous bastard (unless it was the other way around, but he brooked no quibbling at a time like this), were at odds with each other for one reason or another. Evidently, Jannor had done something with the fangs without the doctor's permission and without resort to whatever knowledge Dutch supposedly had; unless Dutch had deliberately given him the wrong information, in which case he was probably already dead.

Now, however, Atwaver was here at Darkriver, and it was certain that Jannor wasn't going to try the damned things on himself until he could be assured that the madness that had stricken the actresses wasn't going to take him as well.

Which left only Tania.

God*damn,* he thought.

Not to mention Onbrous and Scalia.

Doing his best to brush himself clean, then, he opened the other door and stepped into the hall. Again he was at the end, and again it led upward, this time to an intersection which, when he reached it, proved level and led both left and right. The wallpaper hadn't changed. There were no doors that he could see. And though he waited a full minute, he couldn't hear a damned thing.

A mental flip of a coin, and he moved to the right, came to the end where another hallway swept past—no doors, a few dim lights, both ends stopping at blank walls. He shrugged, hurried back and checked the other one, and found a doorway at the northern end.

It was locked.

He scowled at it, stood back, and kicked the brass plate of knob and keyhole twice before the frame splintered and he pushed through.

"Well," he said, "I'll be a son of a bitch."

At one time it had obviously been a ballroom. At the far end were two sets of ceiling-high double doors, closed now but probably leading to an antechamber on the other side. The walls were hung with alternating gold and green draperies whose gentle movement suggested some were masking open windows. The ceiling was white and domed, and from it hung five monstrous chandeliers extinguished but for the center one, whose light, though dimmed, was enough to make him narrow his eyes. The floor was bare and highly polished, close to reflecting both walls and chandeliers.

And he found himself on a low stage on which, he guessed, the orchestra sat and played when the stage wasn't covered by the splinters of a shattered door.

A ballroom once; it wasn't one now.

In the center of the floor was a round black carpet ten feet in diameter, and on it was a heavy walnut trestle table long enough to seat a dozen in a pinch. There was nothing on top, but on the far side were two highbacked chairs carved like thrones, and in them were

Dutch and Tania, thoroughly bound and gagged and staring at him as if he were Sergeant Preston without his faithful dog, King.

Though it wasn't the most enthusiastic welcome he'd ever received, he grinned and leapt to the floor, nearly lost his balance when the wax proved too slick and his injured knee stung back to life, and walked carefully to the carpet. "Don't get up," he said cheerfully, moving around the table. "I'll take care of you in a second."

Dutch struggled; Tania's face went red.

He took the knife from its sheath and cut them loose, replaced it, and perched on the table's edge, swinging his legs patiently while the Burgoynes found their breath and chafed the blood back into their wrists and ankles.

"Jesus, you stink," Tania said at last.

"I got here as fast as I could."

She pointed. "You smell like you've been in a sewer, is what I mean."

He shrugged. "You okay, Dutch?"

The old man grunted, massaged the back of his neck, and suddenly leapt to his feet. "Jesus, boy, we got to get outta here! That idiot—"

Linc held up a palm to silence him. "Hold your horses," he said. "Right now they think I'm dead—"

"Again?" Tania said.

"—and I'm not leaving until I get those fangs."

"You," said Dutch, "are an idiot." He took his daughter's hand and pulled her to her feet. "We're getting out. I've had enough of this crap."

"Oh, I don't think so," Linc told him.

"You gonna stop me, pardner?"

He shook his head. "No, but I doubt very seriously that Jannor and Atwaver are walking around this place without some sort of weapons. You going to kill them with your good looks?"

Dutch looked indecisive, but Tania sat down again and crossed her legs. "So what's the plan?"

"I don't know. You tell me." And he told them what he'd learned and what he'd seen—Yoman and Iddle, the doctor and the actor—and suggested that the two remaining bad guys—not counting Onbrous and Scalia who were probably lost in the swamp—weren't going to let Grange leave without explaining what he knew about the fangs and the ritual.

"Goddamnit," Dutch said heatedly, his cheeks turning bright pink, "there you go too, talking funny at me without knowing what you're saying."

"Who, me?"

"Yeah! What the hell is all this crap about a ritual, huh? That old fart Jannor, he keeps on at me about magic words and spells and all that garbage—I don't know what in god's name he's talking about!"

Linc raised an eyebrow. "You mean to tell me . . . you mean, there isn't a ritual?"

"How the hell should I know?"

"But you—"

"Look," Dutch said with enforced calm, taking his daughter's hand and pulling her back to her feet, "all I did was steal the damned things, you already know the why of that. I didn't bring the instruction book too. Jesus damn and feed the cows! Now, if you don't mind, Blackthorne, I'd like to get my little girl out of here and back to Oklahoma so we can spend a quiet Christmas at home."

"But Dutch," Tania protested, pulling back without freeing herself, "what about—"

Dutch spat dryly. "You know what I'd like to do with them damned teeth?"

"Fangs," Linc and Tania corrected without thinking.

"Whatever. I'd like to shove them straight—"

"Daddy!"

"Well, I would, damnit!"

Linc slid off the table then and put a hand on his shoulder. "Dutch, hang on a minute. Let me get this straight. You don't know about any ritual."

"Hell, no."

"And Jannor thinks you're lying."

"Hell, yes."

Linc dropped his hand. "Did you by any chance see how Pars did . . . whatever he did to Irene and Marjorie?"

Dutch stared at the floor and shook his head slowly.

"Lincoln," Tania said then, moving to stand beside him.

"In a minute."

"We don't have a minute." She pointed to the back of the room, and they watched as the left-hand doors swung open, and Scalia Naidle and Jesse Onbrous stepped in. They were each carrying a shotgun, and neither one of them was smiling.

"You're late," Linc told them, shifting until he was standing behind the table.

"You!" Onbrous intoned. "You are not supposed to be living! You are supposed to be dead in Oklahoma! Or the swamp! Or the dungeon!"

Linc smiled, nodded, and said quietly, without moving his lips, "You two going to stand there all night or are you going to join me behind the barricades?"

Dutch and Tania wasted no time hurrying to his side, Tania grabbing his left arm so tightly his hand lost its circulation.

"You are not to move!" Onbrous ordered.

"I'm not," Linc said.

"You were!"

"So shoot me."

Dutch muttered, "Jesus," and Tania released him and stood aside.

"Don't worry," Linc told them without turning his head. "They're not going to kill us. At least not now. They don't dare. If they do," and his smile sweetened as Scalia took a few steps toward him and brought her gun to her shoulder, "Dr. Dennis is going to be awfully mad."

Scalia returned the smile.

Onbrous sputtered and looked over his shoulder, grunted, and stumbled forward as if shoved, stumbled again and fell, the shotgun skittering from his hands across the bare floor toward the carpet.

In the middle of his back was a long thin blade, at the end of which was the silver head of a jackal.

"Oh my god," Tania said.

Scalia didn't move. She merely aimed at Lincoln's chest, winked, and fired.

# Thirty

One of these days those goddamn theories are going to get me killed, Lincoln thought as he dove for the floor.

Scalia ejected the shell and brought the shotgun up a second time. Linc grabbed the edge of the table and, with Dutch's belated help, tipped the table over to form a shield.

It wasn't necessary.

She winked again, and fired at the lighted chandelier, shattering it, raining shards of sparks, crystal and thin chain onto the floor, then whirled as Pars Jannor stepped into the room, his cloak swirling around him.

She chambered another round.

The actor ignored her, looked at Onbrous instead and sighed loudly. "What a fool he was, my dear," he said. "What a fool." Then he brought his right hand out of his cloak and shot Scalia in the chest with a silver-plated revolver.

Tania screamed with both hands clasped to her mouth.

Scalia staggered back, pulled the trigger, and laughed as she fell, and Jannor was punched back into the other room, where he landed, arms thrown over his head, his cloak fluttering down over his bloodied face.

The reverberations of the shots filled the house, echoed, and died away.

And in the silence, Linc peered over the top of the fallen table, touched Dutch's side, and stood. "They were both idiots, you know," he said with regret.

"Lincoln!" Tania said angrily. "How can you say that? They're . . . they're dead!"

"Then they're dead idiots," he told her bluntly. "They should have dropped out of the game a long time ago."

She glared at him, clearly trying to decide whether to stalk away or slap him; but a decision was made for her when Dennis Atwaver strode through the open doorway, a long narrow box tucked under one arm, a machine gun under the other.

"He's right," the doctor said. "Fools don't belong in games where people die."

"Oh shit," Dutch whispered.

Atwaver, without looking away, knelt and placed the box on the floor; then he rose and settled the machine gun more comfortably against his side. As he moved, Linc heard his shoes squeaking, and cursed the man for having the foresight to wear rippled soles. An accidental slip was not going to be the miracle he'd hoped for.

"Mr. Grange," Atwaver said, "Pars tells me you don't know anything about how to work these things."

Linc couldn't help it—he let his jaw drop when Atwaver reached into his pocket and pulled out the Fangs

266

of the Hooded Demon. And he couldn't help walking around the table to stand in front it, amazed by what he saw, and struck by the beauty of them, despite their bizarre configuration.

They were easily as long as his index finger, dark red and smooth and shaped to a needle's point, and they were connected by what appeared to be a bridge of ivory. Clarise was right—they were beyond the mere incredible, and the way they snared the light that spilled over the doctor's shoulder was mesmerizing; it was easy to see why they'd been endowed by legend with mystical power.

Atwaver lifted his eyebrows. "Ah, you're first look, Lincoln?"

He nodded dumbly.

The man tossed them up, caught them in his palm, tossed them again. "I daresay your grizzled friend there could easily finance a dozen pictures or so with the proceeds from their sale. Just," and he tucked them back in his pocket, "as I could either build my own clinic . . . or do a bit of medical magic on my own."

Linc smote his forehead. "God, I don't believe it."

Tania, leaning over the table, tapped his shoulder and whispered. "Why don't you—"

"Hush!" he snapped. His hands slipped into his pockets. "Den, I take it you're going to move to Switzerland or something, right? Set up shop somewhere, Geneva or Lausanne, and miraculously develop *the* sure-fire way to help old, preferably rich, ladies look a few years younger?"

Atwaver applauded him without making a sound. "You are a genius, Linc." And he sneezed.

"I take it you don't care for New Jersey winters."

"Abominations," he said with a sneer. "Since I

267

moved north, I've had more colds than the goddamn Russian army."

"Linc," Tania tried again, "why don't—"

"Dutch, please shut her up," he said pleasantly, smiled at Atwaver and pointed at the box. "And I suppose that's the stuffed cobra?"

Atwaver nodded. "If you will."

Linc leaned back then against the table and folded his arms over his chest. "I don't get it. Tomorrow's Christmas. Wasn't there something you had to do by dawn? Some sort of ritual or something?"

Atwaver nodded a second time. "Indeed there is." He looked at his watch. "And I believe we're running short of time." He shifted the machine gun to remind them he still had it, then nudged the box closer with his foot. "So if you would please set that table back where it belongs and put this on it, I would be most appreciative."

"What ritual?" Linc said without moving. "Dutch says he doesn't know it."

"Damn right," Grange muttered.

Atwaver merely gestured again with the gun, until Lincoln finally gave a *what the hell* shrug and moved cautiously over the slippery floor, skirting Scalia's body with a rueful shake of his head. He lifted the box, and nearly dropped it when its weight surprised him.

"Big sucker, isn't it?" he said as he carried it back. And waited while the Burgoynes righted the table. Then he placed the box on it and stepped away, hands loose at his sides. He decided to be patient; there wasn't anything else short of providing an earthquake that he could do.

Atwaver approved, and directed Tania and her father into the chairs. "Tie them up," he ordered Linc. "Tailors must know all sorts of interesting knots."

At first Linc balked, but the sight of the muzzle describing a rather blatant target across his stomach changed his mind without a twinge of guilt. He gathered up the pieces of cord he'd cut away only a few minutes ago and proceeded to do as he was bidden. Tania glowered at him; Dutch looked sorrowful; Linc assured them apologetically it wouldn't be forever, and sidled away, to the left of the table as Atwaver walked over, soles squeaking above a pair of none-too-decorous sneezes that almost made him drop the gun. Then he motioned Linc to stand between the chairs and, when he was obeyed, he took out the Fangs and held them up.

"See, the thing is," he told them with a slow, feral smile, "Pars was too anxious. He thought all one had to do was stick these in someone and *voila!*, instant youth."

"Wrong?" Linc guessed.

"Correct," Atwaver told him.

"And you weren't about to rectify his error."

"Correct again," was the answer. "The problem Pars had was, he didn't have the Demon. I did. And . . . well, you saw the results of his ignorance."

Linc shuddered obligingly.

"What about that thing?" Dutch asked then, nodding toward the box. "What does that have to do with anything?"

"Oh, everything, my dear trailless cowpoke. Everything under the sun." He leaned over the table, set the fangs down, and put a hand on the box's end, where a stout latch and hook were screwed into the wood. "Pars, you see, knew there was a step missing, but he thought it was some sort of silly spell." He chuckled. "What an ass. He was in too many movies."

"I'll buy that," Linc said.

"What he didn't know was, he had things a bit backward." A finger toyed with the latch, then flipped it over. "The Fangs were needed, but not until . . ." The lid dropped slowly. Atwaver stopped it from opening all the way, leaving just enough room for him to reach inside and pull out quickly a black bar of wood with a leather hoop at one end.

"Oh shit," Linc said, recognizing it immediately.

Atwaver winked at him. "Correct yet again, Lincoln."

Tania sat up. "That's a thing," she said, looking fearfully at her father. "That's . . . you . . . it's . . . a thing!"

"You catch snakes with it," the doctor said with a laugh. "Something like this," and he stood away from the table, slipped the hooped end of the bar into the box and, after a moment's poking and prodding, drew it out slowly.

The hoop was closed behind the head of a cobra. A large cobra, Linc noticed unenthusiastically. Several inches thick, unmarked, and entirely white.

"Excuse me, Den," he said, "but if it's stuffed, why the precaution?"

"Stuffed?" the man said. "Who said it was stuffed?"

"But it is!" Dutch declared. "I saw it. In that glass cage. It's dead!"

The cobra began to stir, a long slow rippling that began at the hoop and trembled a full fifteen feet to the tip of its slow twitching tail.

"It isn't dead," Dutch said, his voice abruptly hushed.

"Oh, absolutely not," Atwaver said. "It wouldn't do us much good if it were dead, would it? A touch of Uncle Dennis's portable anesthesia keeps it quiet. This, you see, is the part Jannor didn't know—*first* the bite, *then* the fangs. I imagine it has something to do with the toxins in the venom and whatever the Turks did to the rubies." He grinned as the cobra began to shift, thumping its side against the box. "I really don't care, as long as it works."

The Hooded Demon opened its eyes.

Tania tried to push herself through the back of her chair, Dutch struggled until he was red-faced to undo his bonds, and Linc could do nothing but stand there as Atwaver stiffened his arm to hold the snake down while his free hand made sure the machine gun was still aimed at the pit of Linc's stomach.

"Don't," Linc said. "Don't do it, Den."

"And why not? A quick test to be sure that I'm right, and then a bit of self-surgery as a Christmas present." The man's smile widened. "I couldn't be happier if I found a set of trains under the tree."

The Demon's struggles intensified, its body lashing wildly now, finally clearing the table top. Atwaver held his ground. The cobra began to hiss.

"What do you say, cowboy?" the doctor asked, his voice tight. "How'd you like to be eighteen again?"

"No!" Tania screamed.

"It makes no difference to me." Atwaver began to move quickly side to side, forcing the cobra to remain on the table while he kept its head down, staying away from the body that coiled, straightened violently, and coiled again, as if it were seeking something solid to push against. "And since neither of you wants to be a martyr for the other . . ."

With a snap of his wrist, he yanked the hoop from around the Demon's neck and jumped back, machine gun trained on it, while Tania closed her eyes tightly and Dutch began to swear.

Lincoln didn't move; he had one hand on the back of both chairs, and it was all he could do to keep from fleeing into the swamp.

The Hooded Demon gathered itself into a loose coil and lifted its head. Slowly. Hissing. Its hood spreading. Its tongue flicking at the air.

It paid no attention to Atwaver.

Tania whimpered.

271

The Demon swung its great head toward her. Hissing. Tongue darting. Leaning back as it rose still farther, until it was looking down at her, the tip of its tail lightly thumping the table.

It bared its fangs.

Its hood widened, the only color visible the gleamless black of its eyes.

Higher still.

Its body in an S-shape that would lend it power and speed when it finally struck.

Hissing.

And swaying.

And Lincoln clapped his hands.

The Demon snapped its head to look at him, the hissing louder and more agitated, the tongue's action more frantic, the few feet of its body still on the table tightening into the spring that would give it the distance it needed.

Lincoln stretched out his arm and moved carefully between the chairs, keeping his gaze on the snake's, sweeping his arm now from side to side in a gentle, continuous, serpentine motion. He began to whistle tunelessly, high-pitched, then low, and high again. The arm always moving, and the Demon soon following it, taking its rhythm, rocking with it, still hissing.

"The knots," he said in a monotone no different from the whistle.

He heard Tania's muffled sobs, heard Dutch grunt and his chair creak softly as he sought to free his hands bound behind him.

The Demon swayed.

Lincoln led it.

And he could see without changing focus that Atwaver was furious, and didn't dare do or say a thing lest the cobra whirl and strike him first.

He didn't feel at all triumphant; he felt, in fact, incredibly stupid for even thinking this would work, and he prayed that Dutch and his daughter would be able to free themselves before his arm fell asleep. Or the cobra got tired and decided it was hungry.

Whistling.

And the hissing.

The Hooded Demon raised above him, back and forth now, closer with each swing, watching his arm while Lincoln watched its eyes.

"When I say," Linc said-whistled.

A whisper from Dutch, another minute too long for his nerves before he heard a whisper from Tania.

Atwaver lifted the machine gun.

The Hooded Demon stopped moving.

Lincoln felt his mouth go dry, and the whistling fell to a labored, helpless breathing.

Then Atwaver yelled, "Don't move, you bastard!" and took a step sideways.

And Lincoln threw himself backward, pulling the chairs over with him.

# Thirty-one

Lincoln didn't wait to see which way the Hooded Demon had struck. The moment he landed there was a scream, and the machine gun began firing. He fell instantly into a back roll, and scrambled for Jesse's shotgun, which he brought to his shoulder as soon as he was on his feet.

"Hurry!" he shouted as the Burgoynes scrambled frantically away from their chairs, pieces of cord dangling from their shoulders and ankles. "For god's sake, move it!"

In the room's dim light he could make out Dennis writhing on his back, still screaming, the cobra off the table now and poised to strike again. The gun was on the floor beside him; his hands were grasping his throat.

Linc sighted with care, and hesitated, blinking the sweat away from his eyes, watching the serpent's dance, and listening to its hymn.

Tania reached him and stood, and when she turned around, she began sobbing.

And Lincoln fired.

And missed.

And there were no more shells in the gun.

The Hooded Demon struck again, and Dennis Atwaver stopped his screaming.

Dutch grabbed his arm. "C'mon, let's get the hell outta here!"

And still Linc wouldn't move, couldn't stop watching the doctor quaking, or the cobra that coiled around him, hissing quieted, tongue still working.

"Oh god, I'm sorry, Linc," Tania said, clinging to his arm. "He . . . you thought he was a friend."

But they didn't understand. He hated himself for it, but he wanted to watch the man die because right now, almost a thousand miles north, that man had probably caused a real friend to lose her life.

Dutch punched his arm, hard. "Goddamnit, tailor!"

"Yeah," he said flatly. "Yeah. Okay."

Tania had already started for the open door, and Linc followed Dutch, pausing only long enough to snatch up Scalia's gun, pleased that she had one more shell left. He had a feeling they were going to need it; when he looked back, the Demon was moving away from Atwaver's body, not rapidly, but fast enough to let him know that the creature was making up its mind where its next victim was waiting.

As soon as he reached the antechamber, he and Grange slammed the doors shut, then bolted across the room and into a hallway that branched off in three directions.

"Which way?" Dutch asked.

"How the hell should I know?" he said testily. "Jannor must have built this damned house out of every goddamned scene he'd ever played in."

Something thumped against the ballroom door.

They ran harder, charging into rooms and charging out again, trying to see out of barred windows that held only their pale reflections; down a staircase wide enough for a marching band; up a short flight of marble steps that brought them into a kitchen only a Pilgrim could love.

"It's going to get out," Tania said when they nearly raced into a closet.

"Not if I get out first," he promised, pulled her away from a butler's pantry, and found another hall at the end of which he could see the central foyer, and the front door.

The door was locked.

Dutch kicked at it several times before Lincoln herded them into the cavernous front room to the right, where he picked up a stool and threw it at a window.

The glass didn't break.

"I don't believe it," Tania said. "I . . ."

"My words exactly," he said, tried it again with a heavy chair, then herded them back into the foyer where he chambered his last round and took aim at the lock.

"Linc?"

"Dutch, if you're going to tell me that the snake is in the hall, I don't want to hear it."

"Okay. But don't miss."

He didn't.

The lock and the wood around it shattered.

And the last thing he saw before he sprinted out of the house was the shadow of the Hooded Demon on the wall of the staircase landing.

Forsaking another trip across the wooden bridge-and-pathway, they took the stone path at a dead run, and as soon as they were through the hedge, they found themselves only a few dozen yards from the fork in the road that connected Darkriver to the highway.

"Don't!" he warned Tania as they ran to the car and jumped in.

"I wasn't going to say anything."

"Right," he said, slapped his pockets and realized he'd lost the keys.

Then Dutch laughed, held up a key ring and said, "I fished this out of Jesse's pocket. I think that's their car back there."

It was.

And it worked.

And though the old man complained about the speed and the dim view of said speed the Tennessee State Police undoubtedly took, Linc didn't slow down until they were winding down the slope, Chattanooga lit and welcome below them. Then he closed his eyes briefly and let out a sigh that fogged the windshield.

No one said a word.

No one looked back.

Forty minutes later they were in the hotel, Dutch lying on one bed while Tania locked herself in the bathroom.

Lincoln stared at the telephone for almost five minutes, then picked up the receiver, and dialed home.

Alice answered on the first ring.

"Well?" she said.

"Done."

"You okay?"

"Clarise."

"Fine. Just fine. I think Macon wants to marry her."

Lincoln looked at the ceiling and laughed.

"About your wedding."

He stopped laughing.

"It was a joke."

He wrapped the cord around his wrist and pretended it was Carmel's throat.

"Mayhew wanted you to do this dumb thing, whatever the hell it was, so she had a talk with that schoolteacher tramp."

"She's not a tramp, Alice."

"Woman wears clothes that tight, she's a tramp. She told the other tramp—"

"Alice."

"—the only way to get you into New York was to make you think you had to run away from getting married."

"Son," he said, "of a bitch."

Dutch opened one eye.

Tania came out of the bathroom, fluffing her ruffles.

"I'll see you tomorrow," he said.

"Merry Christmas," Old Alice said. "You get me a present?"

He dropped onto the other bed. "You'll have to wait."

"Macon got me a Darth Vader watch. Jesus. It'll be like wearing a licorice stick on my arm."

"Tomorrow," he said. "You can tell me all about it tomorrow."

He rang off and laid back on the pillows Tania had thoughtfully thumped and piled behind his head. He stared at the ceiling, then glanced over at Dutch. "I'm sorry about the rubies, Dutch," he said.

Grange shrugged. "It doesn't matter, I guess. I should be thankful I'm still alive."

"Good attitude."

"Besides," Tania said, sitting primly on a chair between them, "when we get back to Oklahoma, we can always loot Jesse's house. What the hell, we deserve it."

Lincoln stared at her.

Dutch blew her a kiss. "My little girl, tailor. You can't beat her nohow."

278

The telephone rang.

It was Old Alice. "I didn't ask you about the old fart."

"You told me he gave you a watch."

"Not that old fart, the other one."

Lincoln opened his mouth to tell her he was dead, this time for good, but for the life of him, which phrase he wasn't exactly thrilled with, he couldn't remember seeing Jannor's body in the ballroom antechamber. Forget it, he told himself, then he remembered the truck.

"Hey, Blackie?"

Lincoln asked Dutch about the body, and Dutch sat up, wide-eyed and trying to frown at the same time.

He asked Tania, who only plucked a ruffle and shrugged.

"Blackie, you got a woman there?"

"Alice, Jannor's dead. So are all the others."

"You sure?"

"Trust me. It's Christmas."

And rang off again, and sat up, and stood, and walked to the window and looked out at Chattanooga.

"Don't think it," Dutch said, laying back again. "Don't even think it. It's bad luck." He sighed and closed his eyes. "Look at the good stuff—them dopes ain't gonna bother no one anymore, ain't nobody gonna find that godawful house before it falls into the swamp, that there snake'll die in the cold, and the rubies . . . the rubies . . . aw shit, god damn."

Tania kissed her father on the forehead and told him to get undressed if he was going to get some sleep. Grange protested, but weakly, and disappeared into the bathroom. Then she stood beside Lincoln and put an arm around his waist.

"Are you worried?" she asked.

He didn't know, but the city was turning off its lights one by one.

"Don't be," she whispered. "Your friend at home is still alive. No matter what you're thinking, Jannor is dead. And," she added, leaning closer, blowing in his ear, "it's Christmas, and you can't believe how horny that makes me."

Lincoln looked at her, then looked back to the bathroom door.

"Don't worry about him. He's asleep in the tub."

"How do you know?"

"Trust me," she said. "It's Christmas."

He smiled. She smiled back, took his hand, and placed it lightly on her ruffles. Sighed. Moved closer still, and froze when she saw the look on his face.

"Oh, Tania," he said, shaking his head in disappointment.

The bathroom door opened.

"I couldn't help it," she said softly, plucking one of the fangs from her bosom. A piece of the ivory bridge was still attached to it. "It was just lying there after that . . . that thing knocked them off the table." She gave him an apologetic shrug. "It was instinct, I guess."

"And you were going to let me go home without it."

"You got it," Dutch said. "God, what a great little gal she is, don't you think, pardner?"

Linc turned, saw the gun, and dropped wearily into a chair. "I hate Christmas, you know," he said while they gathered their things together and went to the door. "I really do."

Dutch slipped the gun into his belt and ushered his daughter into the hall. Then he looked back in and gave Linc a two-fingered salute. "We'll send you your share."

"You do that."

"And if you're ever in Oklahoma—"

"Don't hold your breath."

The door closed.

Linc turned around and looked out the window, sighed, walked over to the telephone and dialed.

"Goddamnit, Blackthorne," Carmel said when she heard his voice, "do you have any idea how mad Poppa is because you left me at the altar?"

He grinned at the wall. "I'll be home tomorrow."

"And a damned good thing! The preacher's getting bored."

He frowned. "Preacher! Alice told me . . . what preacher?"

"The one in the living room, looking at Poppa's shotgun."

Lincoln stared at the receiver.

"Lincoln?"

He stared out the window.

"Lincoln, goddamnit, are you listening to me?"

Christmas, he thought.

"Lincoln Bartholomew Blackthorne—"

Humbug.